AMALGAM

D. Aaron Bramble

To everyone who has helped me realize this dream. Thank you all so much.

Table of Contents

CHAPTER ONE
Arrival

Kelm opened his eyes carefully as he rubbed the back of his head. He knelt on one knee, feeling nauseous and weak. The portal he had just come through was at his back, in the center of a large sandstone chamber. The roof stretched high above, supported by pillars of stacked slabs beneath the eaves, between which daylight poured in as far as it could reach. It was a strange experience, traveling through the portal. He and his companions had stepped in and immediately been surrounded by tendrils of purple...energy? They had writhed and twisted like serpents, struck nearby like lightning, imbuing Kelm with sensations that were almost painful. Suddenly he had lurched forward, as if he had been pushed, and found himself kneeling in the chamber. He looked at his hand as he finished rubbing his head just in time to catch sight of some of that same purple energy dancing down his arm before it disappeared back toward the portal.

He took the time now to notice more of his surroundings. To his left were his companions. Hutta, Daffer, Fuster, Webb, all were there and alive. They had all stood and were studying the chamber. Kelm had been the last one in, so it made sense he should be the last to recover, at least he supposed. To his right was a young man he didn't recognize, down on all fours heaving as though he might retch.

"You alright?" Kelm asked.

The man looked up and muttered something back in a language Kelm could not understand. He shrugged and stood, leaving the man to continue his heaving. Hutta had made it to the edge of the chamber, and now was little more than a silhouette against the intense sunlight.

"Boys!" he called back, "better look at this."

Kelm made his way across the chamber. The large slabs of the floor were all carved with wide lines which formed waves, swirls, and other manner of arcing shapes. The slabs forming the columns were carved in a similar fashion, seemingly without a uniform pattern, but intention all the same. The roof rose from its eaves in an inverse stepped pyramid until it reached an apex so distant that it was shrouded in darkness. The portal stood in a slight depression that was surrounded on all sides by two short steps made up of the same slabs as the floor. Kelm walked slowly toward his companions, his hand raised in order to guard his eyes from the blinding light. He reached one of the support pillars and leaned against it, still not fully recovered from the effects of the portal. In time his eyes adjusted and the view beyond the chamber left his face with the same dumbstruck expression that was already on the faces of his friends.

They stood high on a large pyramid. Every stone in sight was carved in a manner similar to the others Kelm had observed. Despite the solidity of the massive stones, the carvings, coupled with the heat rising all around, gave the structure a fluid-like and impermanent appearance. At their feet was the landing of a great stair, which descended in two runs, each wide enough for ten men to walk abreast. The runs were separated by a smooth ramp in between, upon which was carved a symmetrical pattern consisting of two waves that flowed unbroken from end to end. The base of the pyramid disappeared below them in the dark waters of a lake. At the foot of the stair, a low arch bridge crossed the water until it reached a stone seawall, at which point it flowed seamlessly into a road. All around the lake was a city of low buildings of various styles. Many were stuccoed, some constructed of the same sandstone bricks as the pyramid, and a few were constructed of timber. Rooftop terraces shaded with colorful fabrics and decorated with plantings added some greenery to an otherwise starkly tan vista. Most of the structures were less than three stories tall, and the companions could see none with greater than five stories, leaving all the buildings easily dwarfed by the height of the great pyramid.

Across the water from either corner of the side upon which they stood were statues made seemingly of bronze. Each was some twenty feet high, and stood upon a dais at least as tall as a large man. Both faced the pyramid, gazing toward their respective corners, but with their heads tilted back just enough that they appeared to be looking directly toward the chamber. The one on the companions' left depicted a man of slender but defined build, his torso covered in plate and his shoulders in spaulders, but his arms bare. His left arm rested at his side, a large round shield covering its lower extremity. In his right hand he held high a spear with his outstretched arm, its length perpendicular to the line of his gaze. Upon his head was a corinthian helmet with a large enough gap between cheek projections that both corners of his mouth could be seen, and upon the top was a plume which ran from the front of the scalp to the rear edge at the back of the neck. About his waste was an armored belt which held together a series of long plates draped in skirt-like fashion, reaching nearly to his knees, and his lower legs were covered by solid guards which fastened around his calves and to the tops of his plated shoes.

The statue on the right depicted a figure of greater stature, presumably a man, covered completely in plate armor. A large sugarloaf helmet completely obscured the head and face, and large, boxy pauldrons broadened the shoulders to an ape-like stockiness. The image of a textile drapery extended from the right shoulder to the left hip, and a pair of breechcloths hung from the belt to the knees in the front and back. The figure's legs stood as straight and sturdy as tree trunks, rooted to the dais by massive square sabatons. The upper left arm pointed to the ground, the elbow bent at ninety degrees, while the left hand rested somewhere near the navel. The handle of a double-edged broadsword was tightly wrapped in its fingers, a sharp pommel pointed to the sky above, and the blade, extending downward, was centered between the legs, its tip resting upon the dais. The upper right arm was placed in a similar fashion to the left, but the elbow and forearm bent at an angle such that the clenched right fist rested upon the statue's left breast.

When the companions finished studying the impressive statues, their gaze was drawn farther to the left, where a break in the seawall made way for a river effluent to the lake to cut a meandering swathe through the city. Their eyes followed it, sometimes losing it amidst the buildings, until it breeched the city's walls, turning to the right after some distance, crossing in front of the city, turning left, and snaking away into the distance. A wide road protruded from the city's main gate, the same road, they could see, that began at the foot of the bridge below them, and traveled as straight as an arrow until it crossed the river at another bridge, then mirrored its twists and turns on the left-hand side until both disappeared at the horizon. On either side, this highway and its potamic companion were flanked by large dunes of fine sand. In every direction these dunes defined the horizon and all the landscape up to the city walls. Some appeared to be as big as mountains, and the haze rising and dancing all about created an even more exaggerated effect of fluidity than they had observed about the pyramid.

Presently they became uncomfortably aware of the ambient temperature. Each had a quilted gambeson beneath his armor, and Hutta, Kelm, and Webb all had tufts of fur protruding from different parts of their gear. Fuster and Daffer were each clad in thick leather that offered little ventilation for their now profusely sweating bodies, and both began to tug at their necklines in search of some relief.

As they stood sweltering, Hutta spoke again. "When we entered that…thing…we had to be nearly a thousand feet below ground, and now, here we stand, at least a hundred feet above it. Beyond that, the nearest desert was a thousand leagues away, and across an ocean at that. And not to mention the time. We entered the caves before nightfall, but here the sun is high in the sky, perhaps beyond midday. That much time could not have passed while we were below ground."

"So what are you saying?" asked Fuster, "that we've been catapulted halfway around the known world?"

"I dare not venture to guess," Hutta retorted, "but I can safely say that we are a long, long way from where we entered, and from home."

"And from getting paid," Webb grunted.

"Paid??" interjected Daffer in his usual flustered manner, "We were all nearly done in by the cave-in that bastard caused, and no doubt would have run out of air before we could escape. If not for that portal, we'd be dead right now, and you're worried about getting paid? We didn't even finish the job!"

The young man whom Kelm had spoken to had now recovered from his heaving, and after taking in the view for himself, was now standing by the companions, listening intently, although he could not understand a word.

"And then there's this fellow!" Daffer continued in a blustery tone as he pointed to the man, "Where the fuck did he come from? He certainly wasn't on the other side with us."

Kelm spoke up now, "I tried speaking to him. His tongue isn't familiar to me at all. I would guess he's from somewhere else entirely.

"Great! Now how do we know if we can even get back home?" Daffer threw up his arms in dismay and let them fall limply to his sides as he shook his head.

"Now just calm down, Daffer!" Hutta snapped, "We can figure this out. For now it seems we're safe. Let's just think for a moment."

But the argument continued. Blame was assigned and reassigned. Hutta had organized the job, but Fuster had allowed their quarry to slip behind them and cause the tunnel to collapse. Daffer continued his ranting and exaggerated arm swinging. Kelm attempted to reason with his companions to no avail. The young man continued to listen. Webb just wanted to get paid.

Their bickering was interrupted quite suddenly by a low rumble and the crackle of electricity. They fell silent and turned their attention back to the portal. In its dormant state it had been nearly silent except for a slight drone and the occasional pop from a lashing tendril of energy, but now it flared up with a flash and a roar. It appeared to grow in size as the chamber became illuminated with a purple glow. Tendrils snapped this way and that like whips, violently striking the slabs of the floor or simply disappearing into thin air with a loud crack. The companions had raised their guard and were preparing to flee down the steps of the pyramid when a man stepped gracefully forth from the portal. Almost immediately after his exit it shrank softly back into its peaceful state. For a few seconds energy danced about the man's body before leaping back from whence it had come, disappearing silently into the undulating glow of the now dormant gateway.

Without hesitation the man began walking toward the edge of the chamber, his head held high and his stride long and steady. He was clothed in a full length robe, colored in a regal purple reminiscent of the energy of the portal. The seams and hems were trimmed in a white as pure as snow, and from his shoulder to his hip was hung a sash as black as jet. A headdress of similar style wrapped squarely around his face, covering all the rest of his head. The fabric of it draped down to his breast, curved neatly back over his shoulders, and extended down again to rest on his upper back. A square, white crown piece rose from his brow to about twice the height of his forehead. Upon it were two arced, black lines forming the impression of an eye, with a circle between them defining an iris. The man paid the companions little mind as he approached, but turned up his nose as he passed by, quickly stepping out into the sunlight and beginning his descent toward the bridge below.

"Was that....?" Webb muttered.

"A cultist of Primzahl," Kelm answered.

Fuster began to quietly draw a curved and slender dagger from a sheath at his side. "We should gut that filth while we can."

Hutta reached out a hand and placed it on Fuster's, slowly pushing the weapon back into its resting place. "Let's not be hasty. As much as I'd love to roll his head down those steps, we need to get our bearings. If the Cult has as much influence here as they do back home, we'd be executed before nightfall for his murder."

Kelm had turned his focus to the young man of unknown origin. He had also recognized the cultist, and the same disdain that Kelm and the others felt could be seen in the man's eyes. "I think he knows of the Cult as well," Kelm waved a finger toward the man, "and he doesn't appear to have any love for them either."

Webb grunted again, "Who would?"

The group now moved out from beneath the eave and stood on the edge of the landing, watching the cultist's descent. Up from the bridge there now approached another figure, clothed also in a full robe, but this one colored a subdued golden hue. A gilded helmet shone brightly in the intense sunlight. It came to a point near the figure's breast, rising back in ovular fashion to another point above and behind the crown of the head. This forward plate appeared to be perfectly smooth, and no discernible features were evident from the top of the stairs. All around the neck beneath this headpiece were gilded lames riveted together, layered horizontally until they disappeared beneath the robe. The figure's arms were squared across the abdomen, each forearm slipped into the opposite sleeve such that no skin was visible anywhere on the body.

The two figures met near the halfway point of the stairs and passed by each other without acknowledgment. Soon the gilded figure had mounted the landing, stopping and standing silently before the group. They could now make out two small slits in the helmet that must have allowed some semblance of sight, but otherwise their distant observations had been correct. Without a word the figure stretched out one arm, revealing a ghostly pale hand with which it beckoned them to follow. Returning to its original posture, it turned about without awaiting any consent and began the descent back toward the bridge. After a brief moment of confused and cautious waiting, the companions shrugged to each other and began to follow, thinking it better to move on and gather more information than to continue arguing and baking in the obnoxious heat.

#

The stairs were steeper and rougher than expected, and the newcomers could not mimic the grace with which their robed guide seemed to glide down the pyramid. As they descended the distant dunes disappeared as the buildings rose around the lake. One by one their feet fell upon the landing at the foot of the stair, where their guide patiently awaited them. Once the last of them had reached the bottom, the figure turned about without hesitation and began to cross the bridge, and so the group followed. From each run of the stair a smooth thoroughfare extended out to form the deck of the bridge, and these were separated by a slightly raised cobbled median extending from the ramp. Along each side of the bridge there was a thick parapet of masonry, and every twenty or so feet a large, stone street lamp rose from these. Although their guide strode with an unfaltering purpose, the group wandered with their heads on a swivel, continuing to take in their surroundings. They took turns leaning over the parapet and peering at the water close below. Fish swam quickly by in small schools, and Kelm saw a turtle larger than any he had ever encountered emerge from the depths and disappear beneath an arch of the bridge.

The water was so clear that it seemed as if the fish were flying rather than swimming, and the companions could see now that the darkness of the lake was caused not by the condition of the water, but by its indeterminate depth, for they had yet to be able to see the bottom.

While they walked, Kelm took the time to study their new companion more closely. The young man had a solemn face. His lips were pressed together tightly in neither a smile nor a frown, and a sharp nose rested between pale brown eyes that Kelm could tell had seen their share of sorrow. His jaw and cheeks were smooth, and his skin of light complexion. His auburn hair was so short it was almost shaven, and if not for the brightness of the sun overhead its color would have been indeterminable. A loose cotton shirt and wool breeches covered his body, and his feet were tightly encased in leather moccasins. He was of average height and of lean build, with sinewy muscles and vascular arms, but his posture and demeanor still gave the impression of lankiness and even somewhat of frailty. As they walked he often wrung his hands tightly together as he looked about, and his feet landed lightly and uneasily, as if at the slightest provocation he would take off at a sprint.

In truth, although he was uneasy, he was not so flighty as he seemed, and was doing some studying of his own. He particularly reciprocated the curiosity of Kelm, whom he could tell was looking at the surrounding world with quiet intelligence. At first glance Kelm appeared nearly as brutish as his compatriots. He was armored in full plate of a gray and heavy steel, and the fur of some animal protruded from beneath his pauldrons and from the crease between his cuirass and his waistcoat. Wrapped around his neck and flowing down his back was a heavy brown cloak, marked here and there with the stains of travel and combat. At his waist hung his various armaments. A broadsword with a simple grip and pommel hung snuggly in a leather sheath at his left, and on his right a squarely bladed dagger was slipped through a loop in his belt, from which was hanging a small iron buckler. He was over six feet tall, but not by a huge margin, and his shoulders were broad and his back straight, but his musculature could not be seen beneath the bulky gear, though the young man guessed he must be quite strong if only from moving about in such a burdensome outfit. But his eyes were what separated him from the others. They were dark, but were opened wide and shown brightly. In them could be seen the conflict between unchecked wonder and tightly bridled skepticism. And they were the ornaments of a kindly face. Between them sat a thick but proportionate nose, and beneath that his lips were slightly upturned in the beginnings of a welcoming smile. His complexion had once been light, but a life outdoors had given him an olive tan that was still spared the wrinkles and damage of overexposure to a harsh sun. The shadow of whiskers that had rarely been properly shaved had begun to wrap his cheeks and upper neck, and dark hair fell like a mop upon his head, reaching to his brow and covering the tops of his ears.

They had just enough time to familiarize themselves with each other's features when the group reached the end of the bridge. Here they had to pass beneath a decorative archway. It rose in smooth columns on either side of the bridge, and a third, thicker than the others, in the center. At its base the center column prevented the median from running any farther, and the other two formed the ends of the parapets. A simply carven cap sat atop the columns, and upon it, directly above the center support, was perched a sculpture. Made of metal, it consisted of an outer circle about six feet in diameter, and inside a series of arcs and crooked shapes, surrounding and emanating from a central ovular plate. Had the newcomers arrived via the street they would have found this sculpture odd, but given the fresh experience of their deliverance to this new land they knew exactly what it represented. From each end column a slightly lower parapet capped the seawall encircling the lake. In some places this formed the border of a wide promenade, as around the great statues facing the pyramid, while in others the walls of a building plunged directly into the water. Along the wall they could now make out patches of lake bottom, a fine sand that served as media for vibrant vegetation, but these fell quickly away into the darkness below.

Through the archway they walked into the wide street, and after only a block or so they were engulfed in a throng of people. Far ahead they could see the top of the city gate, and around them the upper stories of the buildings were ever present, although they were too separated to provide any shade from the still harsh sun. But at eye level they could see no more than a few feet through the thick crowd. Each had to check his wonder and focus intently on following their guide, who snaked through the crowd with the same ease with which it had descended the pyramid. The companions huddled together in order to keep from becoming separated. Even the young man kept himself within arms length, but he was particularly careful to stay close to Kelm. Hutta placed Webb at the front of the group, for his imposing figure could most easily part the crowd, and with a hand on the large man's back kept his eyes glued to the robed figure gliding between passersby. The others followed more or less double file, keeping their eyes forward despite the temptation to study the surrounding crowd. It was not long before their guide stopped in front of a building on the right hand side of the street and turned about to face them.

The edifice was large and stuccoed, and was positioned on the corner of the main thoroughfare and a much smaller side street. Small, colored windows set into decorative arches ran the length of building, and the main door was positioned near the corner close to where the guide had stopped. Above the door hung a wooden sign engraved with writing that was unrecognizable to the newcomers, but beneath the lettering was depicted a mug and a bed, and so they rightly guessed that their escort had led them to an inn. Once again the figure stretched forth one of its ghoulish hands and beckoned them to enter. The companions exchanged hesitant glances, but Hutta led them through the door, out of the sun and into a cool and welcoming darkness. Their guide waited patiently until the last newcomer had entered before moving quickly back the way they had come, disappearing into the bustle of the street.

Inside, the group stood in a small entryway and allowed their eyes to adjust before moving cautiously around a corner into a large room. Close at hand was the end of a bar constructed of small sandstone bricks and capped with a top of dark, polished wood. From there it ran nearly the length of the room before ending in symmetrical fashion. Opposite this was a row of booths, centered at each of the windows and separated by ornately carved wooden screens and colorful draperies. The room was smoky and dimly lit, with only a few lanterns and sconces hanging here and there, and the colorfully diffused daylight streaming in through the windows. Behind the bar a man stood shuffling bottles and glasses. He was short and thickly built, with a wide face and a large belly. Thick, dark hair covered his arms and head, and unkempt whiskers jutted sharply from his face. He wore a stained cotton shirt that likely at one time had been white, and a dirty apron rested on the front of his baggy pantaloons. Looking up from his shuffling and noticing his new guests, his face now beamed with a welcoming smile. He did not speak, but excitedly beckoned them over with his hand. When they had gathered around the bar, he reached beneath it and produced a squat wooden box. Opening it revealed neatly stacked rows of bottles containing a pink, almost luminous liquid. Waving his index finger he counted the newcomers before removing six bottles and returning the box to its resting place. Sensing their hesitation, he uncorked a bottle and took a sip of it himself, and then beckoned them all to drink.

"It's a trap. It's gotta be a trap." A flustered Daffer was the first to break the silence.

"Oh come off it, why do you think he drank some himself? To show it's safe, you idiot," Webb snarled.

"He's probably immune to…whatever it is," Daffer retorted matter-of-factly.

"You two shut up and let me think." Hutta rubbed his cheeks and placed his hands on the bar, studying the bottles.

After a pause, it was the young man who sprung to action. Throwing caution aside, he grabbed the nearest bottle, uncorked it, and downed its contents in a few gulps. The liquid was not pleasant but not offensive, and after finishing he paused and waited a moment, but felt nothing. Then the barkeep began to speak. The others glanced at each other confused, for the language was unlike anything they had heard before, but the young man's eyes widened and he turned excitedly to the others and beckoned for them to drink. Kelm quickly grabbed a bottle and drained it, and the others soon followed. When they had all finished the barkeep smiled at them wryly.

"Welcome," he said, "to Amalgam."

CHAPTER TWO
The Voidwalker's Respite

"Where?" The entire group seemed to speak at once, but Hutta's commanding voice came through the clearest.

The barkeep spread his arms, palms up. "The world of Amalgam. More specifically the city of Artesia. And this is the Voidwalker's Respite, offering the finest lodgings and libations in town. I am Byron Sur, proprietor."

"Did he say world?" Daffer whispered to Kelm.

"Yes," Kelm replied, "yes he did."

"I've never heard of Amalgam, or Artesia. Is this the Reitan Desert? Which princedoms are nearby?" Hutta could have gone on with more questions, but the barkeep raised a hand to halt his inquiry.

"Over the years I've heard every variant of question I can think of, and most aren't worth asking, so let me offer a simple but powerful piece of information." The barkeep lowered his hand and spoke slowly and seriously. "You have passed out of your plane of existence and into another one entirely: this one." He then added in a lighter tone, "or so the scholars tell me."

"So…we're dead?" Daffer asked in a nervous tone.

Byron chuckled. "No, no, you are quite alive, and no worse for wear from what I can tell. You're also free to return to your world at any time, just walk back through the portal and you will find yourselves in the exact spot you left."

The young man was the next to speak up, and with surprising confidence asked "And this concoction you had us drink, what is it exactly?"

"Ah yes! Babel Brew! A gift from the alchemists of the Empyrean Magehold. It's sole effect, as I'm sure you've realized, is to make us understand each other. You'll find all manner of folk here, from many different worlds, so until this potion came along language was quite a problem. As long as you remain in Amalgam you will be able to communicate with anyone you encounter, but if you leave the effect will not carry to another world. And unfortunately it doesn't help with reading. For that you would actually have to learn our common tongue, Leerwandlish."

Hutta, returning his hands to the bar, let out a forceful, exasperated sigh. "There's nothing simple about this. Many would think your 'simple' explanation impossible. At any rate, we, with the exclusion of this fellow" he waved a hand toward the young man, "can not yet simply return. A cave-in cut off the chamber we were in. The portal was the only way out."

"Hmm, well that is a predicament," Byron gave his chin a scratch, "but for now you are safe, and have time to think. I assume you were led here by a man in gold?"

"Yes."

"One of the portal priests. Strange fellows, but I was able to cut a deal with them years back. In exchange for a stipend, I offer all newcomers a night here at the inn. You may bathe, eat, and rest. Your cave-in problem can certainly wait until morning. Or, you could always stay and explore. There is much more to see beyond Artesia and the desert. Come, let me show you your accommodations."

"One more thing," Hutta now spoke with as innocent a tone as possible, "there was another that came through the portal just after us. A man in a purple robe with an eye upon his headdress. Is he one of these...priests?"

Byron's eyes narrowed and a faint shiver of disgust ran through his body. "That's one of those Cultists. Best steer clear of them, especially if you're a magic user. They are allowed to pass freely through Artesia, as is everyone, but they're a bad bunch. Almost universally hated by sensible folk."

The simultaneous relief felt by the entire group was almost tangible. Things were not as they had feared. Their minds now more at ease, they allowed the barkeep to conduct them on a tour of the inn. He first led them down a hall behind the bar and showed them a room with latrines, and beyond that the bathhouse. At the end of the hall they proceeded up a stairway to the upper floors. They passed right by the second, which Byron explained consisted of private rooms for paying customers, and up to the third, which consisted of one long room with bunks throughout. Each newcomer was free to choose a bed for the night, and an unlocked chest at the foot of each was provided for their belongings. The north side of the room opened onto a rooftop terrace that capped half of the second story. From here was a clear view of the lake and the pyramid, and the rears of the statues looming on either side. Byron explained to them that dinner would be served in the common area just before dusk, and he would be there for the remainder of the day should they have any questions or be in need of anything. With that he took his leave and allowed his guests to settle in.

The five compatriots quickly claimed a row of five bunks in the far corner of the room, while the young man chose one against the opposite wall, near one of the doors to the terrace.

Hutta now turned his attention to the young man. "So, what's your story?"

The young man looked up at him. He was a tall and imposing figure, second in height only to the much larger man who had been used to part the crowd. He appeared to be well-muscled, but not large of frame; despite his height he was not as broad as his curious companion whom the young man had studied on the bridge, but he made the two others look quite small. His hair was a mix of red and brown, neither fiery nor dark, and reached well below his shoulders. A matching beard hung over his chest to his upper abdomen. The skin of his face was light and freckled, and despite the presence of a few pockmarks that could have been scarring or the legacy of some illness, his complexion was fair. His greenish eyes were locked on the young man, harsh but inquisitive.

After a moment the young man answered hesitantly, "My name is Eshwar Strand."

"And?"

"And what? There are many places one could begin in situations like this."

"Let's start with where you come from, and how you ended up here. You arrived at the same time as us, but you definitely didn't depart from the same place."

"No, I didn't. But judging by your reactions to the Cultist, I believe I can speak freely with you." Despite this assurance, Eshwar spoke nervously, and often tugged at the neckline of his shirt. "Where I come from I was an academy student. I'm a mage, you see, in training. The Cult of Primzahl has spread its influence over some of my world, and they recently turned their attention on our school. They arrived a few days ago in force and rounded up most of the instructors and then the students. Many were executed, burned at the stake, some were taken prisoner, a few escaped, and the non-magic users were pardoned and free to go. 'For Primzahl is a merciful master' (he spoke this last part sarcastically and with particular disdain. The others nodded knowingly, they had all heard the phrase before.) I escaped with one of our instructors. He had been to Amalgam before to study in the Empyrean Magehold, the place the barkeep mentioned. The Cult controls the portal on my world, but my instructor had a contact who secured me passage, and here I am."

"Why didn't your instructor come with you?" Kelm asked.

"He wanted to stay and help with resistance to the Cult. But he said I needed to be someplace safe to continue my studies, so he sent me here alone."

Fuster broke in, "We get transported beyond everything we've ever known, but we still can't escape those bastards. And from what this kid is saying, they're doing the same thing on other worlds as they're doing on ours, persecuting magic users."

"And this might explain why they seemed to appear out of nowhere with such numbers and fanatical force," Kelm replied, "They're probably not from our world at all."

"Likely not," Eshwar interjected, "and they're certainly not from mine. It's no secret that they came from beyond the portal, an army of zealots bent on domination and extermination. Now may I ask how you came to be here?"

"Fair enough. But I suppose introductions are in order first. I am Hutta Rike." Hutta then introduced each of his companions in turn. Kelm Hekssen, cousins Fuster and Daffer Norgaard, and Webb. Just Webb.

"We come from the Kingdom of Lovik, and our world is called Riisgard. The Cult appeared there roughly a decade ago. At first they operated insidiously, winning over Lord Lovik with promises and sweet words, and gold I'm sure. After a few years they overthrew the king with an army no one knew existed, and have been executing their foul Inquisition ever since. But their influence has not spread beyond Lovik, and outside its borders their men are hunted just as ruthlessly as they hunt mages.

"As to how we ended up here, we were contracted by some townsfolk out in an area of no-mans-land, about a week's journey from the edge of Lovik. They said a rogue conjurer was unleashing all manner of unnatural beasts from his holdout in an abandoned fort. Figured he was doing it in defiance of the Cult, but mostly he was just causing trouble for innocent locals, so they asked us to take care of it. We got to the fort and chased him down into an old cave system. When we discovered the portal chamber he gave us the slip and set off some booby-trap cave-in. Using the portal was the only way out, so here we are."

As the conversation continued, the five Riisgardians began to remove their armor and sweat-soaked clothing. The armor was placed in the chests by their bunks, but their gambesons had to be laid out on the terrace to dry. Soon the group collectively decided it was time to bathe. There had been three basins in the bathhouse, so they split into two groups of three. Kelm, Eshwar, and Fuster went down first, and to their relief there were no other patrons utilizing the baths. The bathhouse was built like a crypt, with pillars throughout the room supporting a series of arched ceiling sections. In the center of each a dimly lit lantern hung from a chain, illuminating the space with a low but comfortable light. Three deep depressions in the floor served as washbasins, with steps around their entire perimeters descending into the waters. In truth, up to four persons could have bathed in each simultaneously, but good fortune allowed each companion to choose their own.

They stripped from their underclothes and lowered themselves into the water, which was cool relative to the air, but comfortable nonetheless. The trouble of their minds washed away with the filth of their bodies as they relaxed, and they spoke jovially with each other as they bathed. Eshwar was slightly disquieted when he saw Fuster's body, which was riddled with scars, but he held his tongue and did not inquire their origin, and soon guesses at their dinner options and the quality of Byron's ale put him at ease. This setting was a far removal from where he had been just hours before, passing through a camp of Cultists to the portal, praying not to be caught. Once they felt sufficiently refreshed they returned to the bunk room, knowing the others would be eager to partake in the luxury of the baths. Hutta, Daffer, and Webb now made their way downstairs, eager to wash away the sweat and grime. There was still an hour or two to wait until supper, and Fuster and Kelm were able to fall into peaceful naps, but Eshwar remained awake, pondering the next step of his journey.

\#

In time the others returned and roused their sleeping companions. The group made its way back downstairs to the common room, which had now become a lively venue full of patrons. Byron greeted them as they passed by the bar, and directed them to an available booth near the far corner. They filed in and filled the space, taking their places on various cushions positioned around a low table. Outside the sun was now low in the western sky, but enough light remained to trickle through the tiny window and cast a pinkish glow inside the booth. Smoke drifted this way and that from pipes and hookahs, diffusing the lantern lights hanging from the ceiling, and creating a swirling coalescence of color from the windows. Chatter and laughter filled the room, but the screens and draperies provided enough acoustic obstruction that the din was little more than a garbled mess of sounds, and it seemed to the companions that they could speak freely should they choose.

Byron soon arrived with bowls of thick broth for each of them, followed by a loaf of fresh bread and a slab of roasted meat to share. He then asked each what they would have to drink. All decided on ale, and he produced tankards full of a deeply colored brew before excusing himself to tend to his other patrons. The group attacked the meal without ceremony. None had eaten for what felt like a day, and while the heat had stolen their appetites for a time, the aroma and sight of the food before them filled each with an insatiable hunger. It was not long before their bowls and tankards were drained, and the table was covered in crumbs and gristle. Byron returned to fill their mugs and make a quip about their voracity before flitting quickly off again throughout the room.

They sipped this round more conservatively, and lounged back on their cushions reveling in the fullness of their bellies, except for Webb, who emptied his tankard without a breath and held it out impatiently for the barkeeper's next pass. Conversation did not seem necessary, and they fell instead into a few welcome moments of post-meal lethargy. They stayed until they were asked to make room for other patrons. The spending kind they assumed. Begrudgingly but politely they vacated the space, thanked their host, and returned to the bunk room.

#

Upon their return they discovered that a few more of the beds had been claimed by such clientele as didn't desire to pay full price for a private room. Twilight was now engulfing the desert, and as the companions moved out onto the terrace they saw that groups of people gathered beneath lantern light were enjoying the coolness of evening out on other rooftops across the city.

Below, the streets still bustled with passersby, and lamps and torches provided ample light even on the side streets. The bridge to the pyramid was fully illuminated by its tall, stone lamps, and high in the chamber the purple glow of the portal could just be made out. Brightly burning braziers danced their light upon the brazen statues, creating a shifting reflection that made them look molten and fresh, as if they had just been removed from the mold of some great forge. Pleasant scents came and went, emanating from incense, fireplaces, and kitchens. Laughter and other sounds of conviviality drifted on the evening air, unspoiled by any clamor of contention or strife. Artesia was a comfortable and welcoming place, far more so than the places from which they had traveled.

Beyond the city's walls, the gathering darkness in the east was slowly transforming the khaki dunes into the waves of a tumultuous, dark blue sea, creeping ever closer to the orange glow retreating into the west. Fuster looked up and pointed to the sky.

"Look, there are no stars. Not a one," he said.

Daffer pointed to a large white orb slowly climbing in the eastern sky. "At least there's a moon rising."

Eshwar smiled. "That, to me, is troubling, for on my world there are two."

Daffer eyed the young man and frowned.

"I'm interested in these statues," Kelm said. "I wonder who they are and how they came to deserve such monuments."

"I can answer that." The voice came from a man lounging on a chaise nearby. A smoldering pipe and tankard of wine rested on a table beside him, but neither had been much used. Dark brown hair flowed from the top of his head into a tight ponytail, except for the occasional wiry strand that denied its imprisonment and reached out into the void of the night air. He wore a pale yellow linen shirt, its thongs untied nearly to his navel, and leather pants. His feet were uncovered, and propped up casually on a cushion at the end of his long chair.

Kelm looked at the man and cocked his head. "Do tell."

The stranger's voice was smooth and his accent refined. He spoke with confidence juxtaposed with a softness that suggested that every word that passed his lips could be either the most sacred truth or the most intricate of lies. "The gentleman to the right," he gestured toward the statue with the spear, "is Praxis Elias, first Consul of the Foskaran Republic, a great nation that used to lie to the east, where the Shattered Republic now lies. The heavily armored fellow on the left is Kirjath Reutlinger, who led the first settlers of

Amalgam as a great general of the Kingdom of Leerwandler. In the distance there, you can see Devonna Willet, founder of the fortress of Bastion."

He pointed across the lake, to a statue directly across from that of Kirjath, facing one of the rear corners of the pyramid. This one depicted a woman saluting the pyramid with an outstretched sword. Her feet and lower legs were covered by heavy boots and greaves, and a mail skirt wrapped about her waist and covered her thighs. Her form-fitting plate cuirass featured the device of a shield embossed beneath the breast. Her right shoulder and raised sword arm were uncovered, but her left was protected by a pauldron and plate, down to a heavy gauntlet around her clenched fist. Upon her back they could make out the top of a quiver filled with arrows, and with it a longbow extended from near her knee to well above her head. Braided hair fell from her uncovered head down over her shoulder to rest upon her breast.

"And finally, what you cannot see," the stranger continued, "is a statue of a robed elf across from the far corner of the pyramid. That one is Gath Lenel, the first Chancellor of the Empyrean Magehold. Each is a pivotal figure in Amalgam's history."

"You must be a local," Hutta said.

"Far from it," replied the stranger, "I have only been to Amalgam a handful of times, but I make it a point to learn all I can of the places I travel. My name is Enoch Banes, of the world of Magna."

The group made its way through another round of introductions, and after establishing that their new acquaintance was not a supporter of the Cult, recounted the tale of the cave-in and that of Eshwar's deliverance. They then inquired the purpose of Enoch's travels.

"A comrade of mine has been here for some time assisting the war effort at Bastion. He sent word to me in order to retrieve one of his personal effects, and so I am making the journey there before returning home," Enoch replied.

"War effort?" Kelm asked.

"Yes. Bastion is currently engaged in a cold war with the Cult. The conflict could escalate at any time."

"We are all familiar with the Cult's usual activities, but what's this war about? Does Bastion house mages?" Eshwar asked.

"This is not one of their extermination attempts if that's what you're asking," Enoch said, "My friend tells me that they're after something called the Heart of the World, for what purpose one can only guess."

"Heart of the World..." Kelm whispered to himself as he turned his attention back to the horizon.

"And you think your friend's item can help?" Webb asked.

Enoch's eyes narrowed as he studied the gorilla of a man leaning against the parapet. He stood at least two heads taller than Hutta, and could have been at least as broad as two men, with tree-like limbs and a huge, round head. "It is of...personal importance only," he said.

"This is troubling news," Hutta said. "It's bad enough that they're here, but to be staging a war, and who knows what they think they can gain from this 'Heart'. If I were the Artesians I would be executing every purple-robed bastard that stepped through that portal."

"The Artesians have always striven to be a tolerant bunch," Enoch said, "but you are no doubt correct in thinking that that policy can be dangerous."

Hutta nodded. "And now we must decide our next course of action. Eshwar's path is somewhat clear, but the rest of us are stranded in an unfamiliar world. I doubt the five of us could clear the cave-in, if we could even still breath in there, and if the conjurer were working alone he certainly won't have it cleared anytime soon. We cannot go home, and we don't have enough coin to stay here for long. If our coin is even accepted."

"It won't translate exactly, but as long as it is made of precious metal it will be accepted in some form," Enoch explained. "I leave tomorrow for Deltaville, to the south. You are welcome to accompany me. From there the whole of Amalgam shall be open to you. I will provision at the markets in the morning, and you should do the same. Byron is a lenient host, but he will want us packed and gone by early afternoon."

"A generous offer," Hutta said, "And one we would be fools not to accept given our situation. We will accompany you."

Night had now fully fallen, and most of the group retired immediately to the bunk room. Kelm and Eshwar leaned against the parapet in silence, lost in their thoughts as they stared out into the starless sky. Only barely now could the dunes be made out, for the light of the moon could not overcome the glow of the city's many lights. It seemed to the two men that they now sat on an island floating alone in a great void, and that they looked upon a nothingness that must extend on forever. Enoch continued to lounge about for a time, smoking his pipe and sipping his wine, until he too bid them goodnight and retired to one of the private rooms on the second floor. The remaining pair continued their contemplation well into the night, until fatigue finally conquered them and they returned to their beds to fall into a deep sleep.

CHAPTER THREE
The Bazaar

Morning light had already filled the bunk room when Enoch roused Kelm and Eshwar. The others were already fully awake and were breakfasting on an assortment of breads that had been provided by Byron. Webb opened the chest at the foot of his bed and began to don his armor.

"No no," Enoch said. "We shall return for your armaments later. For now we should make our way to the markets and provision ourselves for the journey to Deltaville. There's no need to cook yourself yet."

Webb grunted and returned his belongings to their resting place.

Kelm remained in his underclothes and wrapped his cloak about himself. Hutta had braided his long reddish hair and beard, letting them fall down the center of his chest and back, and adopted the same outfit as

Kelm. The other Riisgardians put on their gambesons as loosely as possible. Enoch led them downstairs and explained their errand to Byron before moving out into the street. The crowd was not yet as bustling as it had been the previous afternoon, but it thickened as they moved in the direction of the walls and approached the market. They were about halfway to the walls when the buildings on their right side gave way to a large, open square.

At its center was a round basin filled with water, and breaking through the surface were five obelisks, four in a square pattern and one, larger and taller than the others, in the center. From each of their peaks water flowed out and down, covering their faces in a glistening cascade. A circular courtyard surrounded this fountain, walled by benches and beds of greenery and flowers. The boundary of the courtyard was broken by wide thoroughfares leading to each side of the square. The remaining space was filled with market stalls arranged in a series of concentric arcs, with aisles sweeping in between from thoroughfare to thoroughfare. The companions now stood at the foot of the path on the street side of the square. The far side was dominated by the facade of a massive bazaar with a domed roof.

"I recommend we split up here," said Enoch. "Our journey is not long, less than forty leagues. It should take us no more than a week at a leisurely pace. Fill your packs with just enough rations for the trip. There will be ample opportunity to resupply in Deltaville. Except for Eshwar, you will all need new clothes. I recommend linen. It will make the journey through the desert much more bearable, and nowhere on the mainland should you need any more warmth than your armor and cloaks can provide. You will find higher quality garments and foodstuffs inside the bazaar. As for currency and trades, it is up to individual shopkeepers what they will accept. Meet at the fountain when your shopping is concluded."

From here the group dispersed. Enoch headed straight toward the fountain and entrance to the bazaar, while the others began to meander among the stalls. Eshwar remained close to Kelm, and the pair slowly perused their way toward the bazaar. The stalls seemed to be organized in no particular order; they passed a weapons vendor stationed next to a man selling fruit, followed immediately by a stall full of dusty rugs. Most of the shopkeepers simply watched them pass, or were busy with other customers, but some of the more aggressive ones earnestly solicited their business. Eventually they came between the last few stalls before reaching the bazaar, when Kelm saw something that made him stop in his tracks.

He turned to Eshwar and whispered, "Is that...a bird?" He pointed to a figure examining the wares of a vendor a few stalls away.

It was tall and slender, and clothed in a white, short-sleeved thawb decorated with elegant brown stitching. Most of the exposed portions of its body were covered in fine white feathers, but from the wrist down its hands had a flaxen, saurian appearance. Sharp black nails tipped its thumb and three fingers, which it passed carefully over the various pieces of jewelry on the stall counter. Its face was elongated, and around the jaw the feathers gave way to a bone-like protrusion that could only be described as a beak. Above this were sharp eyes that leaped quickly and purposefully between the items placed before them. They were colored a deep red, with abyssal pupils and no discernible iris. A masculine but shrill voice reached their ears when it spoke to the shopkeeper, and its speech was accentuated by the occasional click-clack of its maw.

"My world has its fair share of other races, but I've never seen one so...avian," Eshwar replied.

"Other races? What do you mean by other races?"

"Well, like him. Non-humans. You don't have non-humans where you come from?"

"Riisgard has giants, dwarves, and elves, but aside from height and some pointy ears we all pretty much look the same. I've never seen something so bestial."

"Then it seems I won't be the only one getting an education on Amalgam. Now let's head inside. I'm sure this won't be the only marvel we see today."

They continued on to the bazaar entrance, with Kelm moving uneasily past the avian man, who seemed to be completely unconcerned and unaware of the disquiet which he had caused in his fellow shopper. They now passed through the massive archway that led into the bazaar proper, and once they had journeyed far enough they were relieved to meet the coolness of the shade. Shop counters and storefronts lined the walls all around them, and stacks of crates, barrels, chests, and surplus goods flowed over into the hall itself, where patrons and vendors alike squeezed past each other as they traveled to and fro. Additional hallways branched off every once in a while, some ending shortly after, others leading to more turns and junctions, creating a veritable maze of shopping options. It was all more than slightly overwhelming. The shops inside did, however, seem to be more categorically organized, and they judged by the rolled rugs, tapestries, and selection of furniture that they were now in a section dedicated to decor. They continued snaking through the crowd on their search for clothing and food.

High overhead skylights allowed the light of day to fall into the building's upper rafters, but the sun was still too low in the east to allow any rays to reach the floor. Instead, massive ornate lanterns suspended from heavy chains illuminated the halls. They were shaded with rough panes of colored glass, complementing the myriad of bright mosaic tiles that broke the monotony of the sandstone walls and floor. The sweet scents of confectioneries drew them down a side hall where they were happy to find many purveyors of foodstuffs. Among them they were relieved to discover Enoch filling his pack with a wholesome selection of rations.

"Well Kelm, I see you've found your way here before finding any clothing," he said. "No doubt thanks to the smell of those pies." He pointed across the hall to a counter where freshly baked pies sat steaming.

"I wish I could deny that," Kelm replied.

Enoch smiled. "When you're finished here, go back to the main hall and continue up to the next left, down that way you should find all the outfitting you require." He closed his pack and tossed a vendor some chunks of gold. "Oh, and feel free to sniff to your heart's content, but I'm sure you know pie doesn't keep well on the road. I'll see you at the fountain." With that he made his way toward the main hallway and disappeared into the crowd.

Kelm and Eshwar explored the area thoroughly before settling on their rations. All the essentials were here; cured meats, hardtack, dried vegetables, but also fresh fruit, soft breads, and all manner of cakes, cookies, and pies. Another side hallway offered the promise of fine wines, and yet another was lined with barrels of beers, ales, and meads. Given the brevity of the journey ahead, they opted to forgo the longer term necessities in favor of more palatable options, such as fruit and fresh bread. Their initial interaction with a shopkeeper was a baker, who wore a leather cap and a flour covered apron. In exchange for his loaves, Eshwar produced a pouch of gemstones and laid them on the counter, and Kelm set forth a bag of gold coins. The baker frowned and raised an eyebrow.

"New here?" he said.

"Second day," Eshwar said.

"I'm no jeweler, so I'm afraid I won't accept these," the baker gestured to the gemstones, "but these I can work with." He picked up a few of Kelm's coins and put them on one side of a scale. On the other he added a few small weights. For a few moments he allowed the scales to shift and tilt, then he removed one of the coins, and grabbing a large knife clove it in two upon the counter. Returning one half to the scales brought them to balance, and the other half he slid back to Kelm. "This is enough to cover both of your purchases."

"Very well," said Kelm. He turned to Eshwar, "this one's on me. Maybe someone in the clothing section will accept your gems."

This process was repeated in similar fashion with a butcher and a produce vendor, and when their packs were sufficiently stocked for the journey, they returned to the main hall and moved deeper into the bazaar. Following Enoch's instructions led them to a side hall lined with outfitters and tailors. Options ranged from rugged wear to finery, light linens to, surprisingly, fur-lined winter garments. A hall filled with jewelers was around a corner, and Eshwar was able to exchange his pouch of gemstones for gold chunks similar to those Enoch had used to pay for his food. He was then able to purchase some quality linens for Kelm and still have a heavy pouch of gold left over. With their packs provisioned and Kelm no longer walking around in his undergarments they headed for the rendezvous at the fountain.

They arrived to find Hutta and Webb already present, and Enoch sitting on the edge of the fountain's basin, running his hand lazily through the water. Hutta was also now clothed in linen, which he explained he had found at a stall in the square. Webb still wore his gambeson, and sweat beaded on his bald head like dew on morning grass, but a bundle at his feet indicated that he had acquired something more appropriate to the climate. He leaned against one of the border walls, attempting with little success to catch the shade of a shrub planted above, when he snapped his head toward one of the thoroughfares.

"Oh what the fuck, Daffer?" he said.

Daffer approached carrying a large basket of fruit, cookies, and bread. His gambeson had been replaced by a blue silk shirt and striped pantaloons. A yellow, patterned shawl shaded his neck and shoulders, and conveniently covered the worn leather pack that would have otherwise marred the appearance of his new outfit. A large ripe apple was clenched between his teeth. He bit down, removing a hearty chunk and catching the bulk in his basket.

"What?" he said, still chewing the chunk of apple. "Some of us like to be comfortable, you brute. And enjoy the finer things." He set his basket down on a bench and retrieved his apple.

"May I ask what you have in your pack that requires you to be carrying your rations in a basket?" Enoch asked.

"My old gambeson. It actually takes up a lot of space. And maybe...a few other garments I liked," Daffer replied.

"How much gold did you spend?" Hutta asked.

"None of your business, boss. Rest assured I have enough for our resupply," Daffer retorted.

Fuster appeared now from the opposite way Daffer had come. He was clothed now in a white cotton shirt and loose pants. He tossed his pack down lightly next to the fountain and took a long draw from a canteen.

"Well, I see I'm the last to arrive," he said as he wiped his mouth. "I also see that Webb was the only one of us too ashamed to change in public." The big man growled but to Fuster's disappointment made no retort. "And cousin, you've spared no expense."

Daffer tugged at his new clothes, "There's some wonderful stuff in this market, I figured I'd enjoy some."

"Wonderful indeed," Fuster said, "the man who sold me my clothes was, well, he was a lizard."

Kelm perked up. "A lizard? Eshwar and I saw a man that looked like a bird."

"Yes," Fuster said, "He was covered in scales, and had sharp teeth and strange eyes, but otherwise he was a pleasant fellow."

Daffer frowned, let go of his shirt and crossed his arms. "Birdmen and lizardmen? Never mind, I don t like it here. I'm glad I was spared such sights."

"Daffer, you haven't liked a place since you left Aunt Helga's womb." Fuster's comment earned a hearty laugh from the rest of the group.

"Say what you will," said Daffer, "but there were no surprises in there. I would've been just fine if that midwife had never pulled me out."

Enoch leaned close to Hutta and whispered, "I'm not entirely sure why you keep that one around."

"Quirks aside, he's an excellent tracker," Hutta replied. "I'd choose him over a hound any day. And besides, every group needs a clown, wouldn't you agree?"

"True. Even my company has one, and I was fool enough to leave him in charge while I'm away." Enoch raised his voice now and addressed the whole group, "It seems you've had your first encounters with beast races."

"Not Eshwar here," Kelm interrupted, "his world is apparently full of them."

"Some worlds are," Enoch said, "Mine has none, and my first encounter was quite off-putting. But they are people, just like us. While not as ubiquitous as humans, or even dwarves and elves for that matter, you will find many here on Amalgam. Discerning eyes would have found much more than two in this very market." He eyed Daffer, "you would do well to get used to them."

"Get used to them?" Daffer huffed. "If it wasn't for that fucking cave-in I would've left for home already. For now I'll go deeper into this strange new land, but I don't have to like it."

"Fair enough," said Enoch. "Now we should be returning to the inn. I'd like to begin our journey before the hour grows too late."

#

With the sun now high overhead they returned to the Voidwalker's Respite. Enoch returned to his room on the second floor, and the others stepped out onto the terrace for one final look at the city and its great pyramid before preparing themselves for the journey ahead. Hutta, Kelm, and Webb removed the fur linings and tufts from their armor, and resolved to leave the pieces with Byron should he desire them. Webb left his arms uncovered up to the shoulders, easily fitting the unworn pieces of his armor into his modestly provisioned pack. Hutta and Kelm opted for a more cautious approach, hanging their gauntlets from their packs but otherwise fully armoring themselves. Fuster and Daffer donned their leather as loosely as they could, and the blue silk of Daffer's new shirt could be seen trying to escape at his neckline. Foregoing his leather cap, he fashioned his shawl into a shemagh covering his head and lower face.

Enoch was already awaiting them when they entered the common room. His arms were bent by his sides, his hands resting upon the pommels of two sabers strapped to his waist. He was dressed now in tight leather armor, decorated with ornate inlaid patterns of darker material. The lames of his riveted spaulders reached nearly to his elbows, which, along with his knees, were reinforced with plates that featured engravings of similar patterns to that of his leather inlays. The others were fixated upon him, for his armor was as much a piece of art as it was protection. He stooped down and lifted his pack from the floor, strapping it tightly across his back. He then reached beneath one of the overlaps in his left vambrace and produced a folded piece of paper. This he gave to Byron, along with a few small chunks of gold.

"For the next bird to Bastion," he said to the barkeep. "My friend will want to know I'm on my way. As always, thank you for your hospitality. Now, let us be off before the day is old."

Byron bid them farewell, and reluctantly accepted the furs from his guests, as well as Daffer's gambeson, which could not be squeezed into his overflowing pack. The street was once again packed with people, but with clear purpose they managed to weave their way quickly toward the main gate. The crowd thinned once more after they passed the market square, until it receded almost completely near the city's walls.

They looked now upon the gate that stood between them and the new world beyond. It was flanked by two squat turrets, with shingled roofs and tall flag poles from which streamers limply danced in what little breeze managed to fly above the dunes. Between them a crenelated arch housed the upper reaches of a raised portcullis. Beneath this two great wooden doors stood ajar. They were carved with the same patterns as the pyramid, and seemed to the companions to be more decorative than defensive.

The road beyond was sparsely populated. A few wagons approached from the distance, accompanied by small pedestrian groups, but otherwise the outside world looked quite desolate and uninviting. The dunes rose high around, and if not for the river the sun would have cast its light on little more than a monochrome landscape. Yet Enoch assured the others that this was only the gateway to a world with sights they would not soon forget, and with a few uncertain steps they left Artesia behind and moved into Amalgam proper, to what end they did not yet see.

CHAPTER FOUR
The Road to Deltaville

After the initial plunge they moved more assuredly down the road. It was paved and well kept, and surprisingly, fairly clear of sand. Enoch informed them he wanted to strive to cover five leagues before they rested for the night, but promised they could move more leisurely in the full days ahead. Their brisk pace brought them soon to the bridge. The river was clear and colorless, as if the water was not there at all. Within it were thriving grasses, and fish darted in and out of sight in abundance. It drew their gaze often for the rest of the day, offering a much needed escape from the monotonous and hazy landscape about them. They easily met Enoch's goal before darkness overtook them, and made camp on the bank of the river with the lights of Artesia still glowing in the distance.

They rose and continued early the next morning, and were able to move quickly before the heat of the day began to stifle them. Not far along the road they came to a junction. A much smaller road led off due south through the valley between two dunes. A cautionary sign marked with a skull and crossed bones stood just off the main road.

"What's that way?" Fuster asked.

"A trader's road," Enoch replied. "It is wild and very dangerous, and it is recommended that none but the most seasoned travelers use it. It cuts significant distance off the trip, but it is not worth the risk."

"What's so dangerous about it?" asked Webb.

"Well, the desert itself is danger enough. The main road follows the river for a reason. Something about it keeps the surrounding area in order, but out there the sands are in a constant flux, and I'm told the heat is nearly unbearable, though I can't imagine how it can be any worse than it is here. And beyond that are the beasts that call the desert home. Creatures that somehow survive the harsh climate, and will make anything and everything their prey."

"Sounds fun," the big man said.

The group moved on, uninterested in getting into any trouble this early in their journey, but Webb remained, looking past the warning and down the path into the sands. After a few moments he called after the group.

"Hutta! What say we make a little wager, for old time's sake?"

"What did you have in mind?" Hutta called back.

"You and I take this path, while the rest of them follow Enoch. Whoever gets across the desert first gets treated to the finest drink available at the next tavern we come to."

Hutta laughed. "Leave it to you to want to risk life and limb for the promise of a free drink. Still, I've always been a sucker for a bet. Daffer, come with Webb and I, we may have need of your tracking skills."

"I want to advise you that this is a terrible and foolish idea," Enoch said. "This land is not to be taken lightly."

"I'm inclined to agree with our new friend here,' said Daffer, crossing his arms.

"Why Daffer, if I didn't know better, I'd say you look as yellow as that ridiculous headdress," Webb called.

"Come, come," said Hutta. "We may not be familiar with Amalgam, but we've blazed trails before. We'll be enjoying a well-earned drink in no time."

"Fine," Daffer huffed, and begrudgingly walked toward Webb.

"There is a camp of desert dwellers about halfway across," said Enoch. "They will be able to resupply you with water should you need it. But I once again advise that you should follow my course."

Hutta smiled and turned about. "We'll see you in Deltaville!"

The remaining group watched as their three companions stepped off onto the trader's road, and shortly disappeared between the dunes.

Enoch tightened the straps of his pack and walked off. "They've likely made a huge mistake," he said. "Hutta is your leader, is he not? Why would he make such a foolish wager?"

"He is a good leader," Kelm said, "but he's also a gambler. Webb knows that, and this isn't the first time they've made some reckless bet, usually without asking the rest of us if we even want to entertain their wager."

"I'm also surprised Daffer was convinced so easily. He comes off as very risk averse," Enoch continued."

"He is," said Fuster, "but he trusts Hutta, more than anyone, besides his mother."

By midday they reached the great bend where the river itself turned to the south. Here, nestled in the crook of the bend, was a small but well-populated trading post. A caravansary and several small buildings lined the road, while a large warehouse stood by the riverbank. Wagons sat in wait nearby, some half loaded with various goods, and beasts of burden grazed on what little vegetation was available in a shaded pen. Two wide quays pierced the river near the warehouse, and a barge filled with crates and barrels was being unloaded by several dockworkers. Another barge, this one empty, was making its way downriver, propelled by two men with long poles.

"This is where supplies from Deltaville are brought up the river. Most of the general goods you saw at the markets pass through here. Of course, some items come up the road your friends took, but those are usually smaller, more precious things."

"Can't we ride down on one of those barges?" asked Fuster.

"They are slow, and we would have to pay for our passage. We will do better to walk," Enoch's words were final and did not leave room for debate, and so they moved on on foot.

From here on the river deepened, and the dunes seemed to be pushed farther back, leaving a wide swath of flat land on either shore. Farmers had packed the sand as much as they could, and created makeshift fields in which they were growing some sort of cane-like crop. The added greenery made the scenery much more welcoming, but the sun was still unrelenting, and thick tendrils of heat constantly rose from the bricks of the road. Despite this, they had no trouble out-pacing the barge, just as Enoch had predicted, and they continued to cover ground at a good clip. Mid afternoon, however, brought a storm from the west, with heavy rain and a gusty wind. Misery forced them to seek shelter early, and a kind farmer agreed to host them in his storehouse for the evening.

"I hope the others make out alright through this," Kelm said as he hung his cloak up to dry and began to remove his armor. What the rain had not reached his sweat had drenched, and his linen clothes had already lost their newness.

"Hope is all we can do at this point," said Enoch.

#

The next morning they were slow to start, for the sacks in the storehouse had made for comfortable makeshift beds. After breakfasting they re-donned their gear and thanked the farmer for his trouble. The weather had cleared, but the deluge had left the desert with a humidity that up until now they had been spared.

It was nearly unbearable. Fuster was forced to remove much of his leather, and Kelm unstrapped several pieces of his plate, letting them hang loosely but awkwardly about his body. Even Enoch, who had been stoic the entire journey, appeared visibly uncomfortable. Eshwar trudged along with his head down, finding no comfort in being the least covered of any of them. The going was slow, and they were scarcely able to cover five leagues before being forced to stop by fatigue and dehydration.

Once again they made camp on the riverbank. They bathed and washed their clothing in the waters, and at Enoch's encouragement drank a more than gracious amount from the river. "On my first trip to Amalgam I was told that the waters flowing from Artesia are pure and rejuvenating. We can have our fill and replenish our canteens," he had said. After laying their clothes out to dry they strung their cloaks among some palms in a semi-successful attempt to create some shade. For the remainder of the day they rested here, and the sun had long dipped behind the dunes before they could muster an appetite.

They gathered together, digging through their packs to get to their food. There was no dry kindling or fuel with which to make a fire, and they resigned to eat and talk in darkness, until Eshwar cupped his hands and raised them to his mouth. He wrung them together softly and released a few breaths into the space in between. After a few seconds the others could see an intensifying glow coming from between his fingers. It illuminated his face, and with a smile he raised his arms up above his head and unfolded his hands. A ball of light no bigger than a fist rose up from his outstretched hands until it stopped and began to float a few feet above their heads. It was not overly bright, but it was more than enough for them to eat and talk in comfort.

"Nice trick, Eshwar," Fuster said. "You should join our little band. If nothing else that skill would be invaluable on all the delves we seem to end up undertaking."

"Definitely better than carrying torches," Kelm added.

"Unfortunately, I'm not yet good for much else," Eshwar said. "I came late to the academy, and haven't studied magic for very long. This, a few wards, and some elemental tricks. Nothing really suited to mercenary work."

"I'm sure you will learn much in the Magehold," Enoch said. "Spells beyond anything you've yet seen. And knowledge. To me the most important commodity. I have learned but little of Amalgam, but someday I wish to visit there and learn all I can, of this world and others."

"I'd like to see it myself," Kelm said.

"You can," Enoch assured him. "This world is open to you. It's your choice where you roam."

"At the risk of sounding like Webb, I think I'll stick to the simpler things in life," Fuster added. "And Hutta has yet to decide where we go from Deltaville."

"Let's hope he's around to make a decision when we get there," Eshwar said.

For a while they continued with light conversation, but their minds went often to the other Riisgardians and what circumstances they might have found out in the wild of the desert. When their fatigue returned they crawled beneath their cloaks, finding little comfort in the wet sand beneath them, but falling asleep nonetheless. The ball of light slowly faded until it disappeared with a tiny flash, leaving them with the starless sky and the dull light of the rising moon.

#

The morning brought with it a relatively more bearable climate, and they were able to fully equip themselves and resume their previous pacing. As they walked, vegetation began to become more common. Tufts of sharp grass sprung from the ground, and soon even shrubs became intermingled with the palms. Another five leagues or so and the desert gave way to a savanna, though the soil was still quite sandy. Shortly thereafter they approached another junction, and just off the road sat Hutta and Webb. A man stood over them, wearing a dark thawb and shemagh. He pointed to the group coming down the main road. Hutta nodded, and the man walked swiftly off due north from the junction.

As the group drew near, they saw that Webb's left arm was mounted in a sling, its lower portion wrapped in a bandage that featured two large bloodstains side by side. Hutta had a bruised and swollen cheek, and sat with his chin resting upon his fist, his eyes solemn and brooding. Fuster looked about frantically, his heart sinking in his chest.

"Where's Daffer?" he asked.

Webb said nothing, and continued to stare at the ground. Hutta just shook his head.

"What happened?" Fuster pleaded.

After a moment Hutta spoke, "A naga, the desert folk called it." And after another pause he began to recount the tale of their journey since the parting two days prior.

The going had not been easy. The road was not well kept, and some stretches had been swallowed by the sand. Tall way-markers topped with red flags provided some semblance of direction, but these were dwarfed by the height of the dunes, and in some places the road was utterly lost until rounding a bend and being greeted with the relief of a flag. Their boots sunk deep into the fine sand, and their footsteps were slow and heavy. They had no way of knowing how far they traveled that day, but it could not have been far, and Daffer often said that they should go back. That night, the storm rolled in with more fury than it had had at the river. The wind carried with it a volley of sand from the crests of the dunes that stung their skin and clouded their vision. Water poured into the roadbed, creating treacherous streams and pits of quicksand. They could not stay there, and had no choice but to climb up and over the dunes to the east, and were left to the mercy of the elements that carried them down the opposite side.

They awoke the next morning, half buried in thick, wet sand. Their surroundings were unrecognizable. Everything had shifted, and there was no telling how far they had crawled before passing out. Hutta and Daffer were almost side by side, but Webb was found some distance away, dumping sand out of his boots. Together they climbed to the top of the nearest dune, but no way-markers could be seen. They resolved to walk west as straight as they could, and hope to find obvious signs of the roadbed or one of the flags. That's when they found the naga. Or rather, it found them.

Like a snake it had been, but larger even than Webb. It rose up out of the sand as they approached, like a whale breaking the surface of the sea. From the waist down it was no different than a serpent, but above this sat a torso reminiscent of a man's, but covered in scales and thick, leathery skin. Powerful arms hung from its shoulders, one of which clutched a large spear. A necklace with a ruby pendant encircled its neck and rested upon its breast. Its head was once again that of a serpent, with a long snout and flared nostrils, and a forked tongue darting in and out of its mouth. A hood like that of a cobra flared out from the top of its head, extending beyond the width of its shoulders before tapering down to reattach at the small of its back. It stared at them momentarily with slit-like pupils, but did not waste the opportunity of its surprise appearance before beginning its attack.

It raised its spear and hurled it like a javelin toward Webb. He rolled out of the way, yelling "Duck!" to Daffer, who was standing some distance behind. But Daffer was frozen. The appearance of the strange creature had left him shaken, and he stood staring with wide eyes as the spear hurtled toward him. It struck him beneath the sternum, pushing him off his feet and carrying him toward the ground, which met him with breathtaking force. His eyes remained wide, and almost immediately the taste of blood filled his mouth. The naga moved toward him now with surprising speed, its long tail undulating in a rapid slithering locomotion.

Hutta screamed in anger, drawing his sword and rushing at the creature. With a swing of its arm it struck him across the face, sending him careening onto the ground. His head spun and his ears rang. He rolled onto his hands and knees, but could not stand.

"Fuck." Webb said as he scrambled onto his feet and like a sprinter used a hand to propel himself forward. The naga reached Daffer, and with a sadistic twist wrenched the spear from his body, tearing the wound into an even more gaping hole. It prepared to throw it again, but by the time it had turned, Webb had already reached it. He swung at it with his sword, which it deflected with the spear, but the latter was cut cleanly in two. It threw down the now useless weapon, and lunged its head toward Webb's neck, opening its mouth as it did. He raised his left arm in defense, and two huge fangs pierced straight through his forearm, their tips protruding right before his eyes. Webb growled in pain, but with this right arm kept the creature grappled tight. He grabbed it by the snout, gripping as hard as he could. It hissed and struggled, trying to pull its teeth from his arm, but it had underestimated the human's strength.

Hutta had regained his composure, and ran as swiftly as he could toward the wrestling combatants. He pierced the naga's belly with the tip of his sword, driving it as deeply as he could before leaping feet first into a slide. He twisted the sword around as he passed between Webb's legs and the creature's tail. The cut was jagged, being deflected this way and that by scales, but the blade made it all the way across the torso, and Hutta spun about and pulled it free. With a noxious smell and a high pitched scream the naga's bowels spilled forth, covering the sand in entrails and thick, green blood. Its eyes rolled back in its head as it writhed and shook, forcing Webb to continue his wrestling match. Hutta stood, and with a well aimed swing removed the creature's upper jaw from its head. Webb fell back, releasing more growls as he grasped at the snout attached to his arm.

"Leave it," Hutta told him, "you'll lose too much blood if you don't."

The naga was still twisting and flailing as Hutta walked by it, but there was no doubt it had breathed its last. He made his way to Daffer. The sand beneath his body was already stained a deep red, and the ragged hole in his torso was overflowing from both ends. Blood dripped from the corners of his mouth, and his breathing was haggard and weak. He attempted to speak, but couldn't, and he spent his final moments looking into Hutta's face with sad eyes. Hutta hung his head and sighed deeply when Daffer had passed, and for a time he could not bring himself to move. Eventually he was able to rouse himself, and using the end of the spear as best he could, he dug a shallow grave and laid Daffer in it. After covering him over, Hutta retrieved Daffer's leather cap from his pack, and placed it on the handle of the spear after driving it into the ground at the head of the grave.

Webb had sat in silence during this entire process. Despite the presence of the fangs, an unnerving amount of blood was dripping from his arm. Hutta helped him up and they made their way west, thankfully stumbling upon the roadbed after a short walk. They followed it south, but Webb began to falter after only a mile or two. Not much farther he collapsed, conscious but barely responsive. Hutta was forced to drag him by his legs. He himself could not have gone on for long, but by some grace they were found by scouts from the camp of desert dwellers who were out surveying the damage to the road. The scouts helped them to the camp, which was close at hand, and the inhabitants immediately took to healing Webb's arm. They removed the naga's snout and teeth, stuffed the wounds full of herb paste, and wrapped his whole forearm in a pungent poultice. After they finished they did what they could for Hutta's face, and then laid both of them in a spare tent. For the rest of the day and night they remained there.

In the morning Webb had regained his composure, though his arm was still in great pain. The desert folk explained the nature of their foe as they redressed Webb's wound. A sentient creature, but borderline feral was the naga. Occasionally they had to fend off raids from the nearby tribe, but for the most part the creatures were solitary hunters, ambushing whatever prey they could find, and travelers that lost the road were some of their favorite quarry.

The desert dwellers were kind enough to send Webb and Hutta off with a guide, who led them the rest of the way to the junction, but left them with a stern warning not to return by that road. They had arrived only a few minutes before their companions. Fuster sank down to the ground and put his head between his knees.

"It's my fault," Hutta said. "I shouldn't have forced him to come with us. I'm sorry, Fuster."

"What you should not have done," Enoch said, "is taken that road in the first place."

Hutta shot the man a piercing glance, but he could not deny the truth of the statement. For a time they sat there, allowing Fuster a moment to grieve, but as the day wore on they knew they must continue. They covered several more miles that day before Webb could go no farther. The grass had become softer and greener as the desert faded behind them, and even the temperature had improved. When they made camp, Enoch informed them that they were close to their goal, and should reach Deltaville around midday if they started early enough.

Fuster sat off by himself late into the night, his friends unable to offer any solace at the loss of his cousin. He sent out a prayer to the animal spirits whom they revered, but he doubted they could hear him from so far away, and he wondered with sadness in his heart whether Daffer would be able to find his way to join them. Eventually he forced himself to sleep, but the night was restless and unsatisfying.

#

At Enoch's request they set off early, and moved south at a quick but easy pace. Soon the savanna became hidden by farm fields growing all manner of crops. They still had the road mostly to themselves, but a few of the barges moved up and down the river, those going up laden with goods, and those coming down either empty or close to it. The sun passed its apex above them, but Enoch did not seem worried, and did not spur them harder. Two short hours later they reached a point where the road wrapped around the backside of a small hill next to the river. Enoch began to climb it, and beckoned the others to follow.

"Come and see," he said as he waved them on.

The group crested the hill and stood taking in the scenery, much as they had done from the top of the pyramid. Before them the river swept on straight for a couple of more miles, before it split into the five fingers of a low lying delta and poured into a great body of water beyond. Nestled all around these fingers was a city, Deltaville. It had no walls, and was shaped roughly like a triangle as it followed the natural layout of the delta. Large structures of timber and stone stood near the center, with the buildings slowly becoming more squat as they moved toward the outlying fingers and beyond. The sails and masts of ships could be seen towering over the skyline well up into the delta, and the sounds of gulls and bells were already present in the group's ears. The sun danced upon the waves of the water beyond, and only the faint idea of a distant shore was evident to their eyes.

"Welcome to Deltaville, my friends," Enoch said. "Let's go."

With that he pranced down the other side of the hill and stepped onto the road. The others followed, and within an hour they had crossed the nearest finger and stood within the city.

CHAPTER FIVE
Decisions

Hutta stood on a stone quay overlooking Leben Bay, into which the river from Artesia poured. The orange and purple light of dusk was fading. Across the water to the southwest the flickering lights of another settlement were in full glow, and far to the southeast, some twenty leagues, he could just see the rotating beacon of a tall lighthouse that marked the place where the bay rounded the opposite shore and began to become one with the sea. Large sailing ships surrounded him, and sailors and dockworkers were rushing about finishing their duties and heading for home. Hutta paid them no mind. He was consumed by his thoughts. Their profession was a dangerous one, to be sure, but the loss of Daffer had not been in the line of duty. It was unnecessary, and in his mind unfair. And the question loomed of where to go from this point. Enoch had delivered them to Deltaville as he promised, and now it was up to Hutta to decide the next move.

The light had now faded completely, and finding no answers in the lap of waves or creak of ships, he left the docks and returned to the streets. Compared with the wide thoroughfares of Artesia the streets of Deltaville were claustrophobic and ill-lit. Tall buildings of stone and dark timber seemed to bend and overhang the avenues, creating a canopy of brick and shingle over a forest of edifices. The people that passed by varied from filthy waifs to nobly dressed highbrows, but most were just common folk going about their evening business. Raucous laughter, drunken ramblings, and even the sounds of a few scuffles filled the air. In truth, it reminded Hutta of a city back home in Lovik. The apparent harmony and purity of Artesia had been comforting, but it had also been strikingly unusual. No, the rough edges of this city didn't bother him. What had him unsettled here was his now acute awareness of the diversity in the crowd. Men and fay of every color walked the streets, which in itself was not striking, but there were others, those covered in feathers, scales, and fur. At these he could not help but stare, for they were unlike anything in his experience. He thought back to the words of Enoch in the Artesian market: "you would do well to get used to them." It would certainly take time.

Through the erratic streets he moved, attempting to make his way steadily north toward the inn in which they had rooms for the night, but the absence of a main boulevard had him tracing his way back and forth in every direction, and in his melancholy he made no effort to seek out the most efficient route. His wanderings drew him close to the heart of the city, a crowded area dominated by tall buildings filled with shops, inns, and taverns. Shopkeepers had locked their doors for the evening, but patrons spilled forth from every watering hole, precariously carrying their libations as they stumbled about with no particular purpose. The air was thick with the smell of beer and liquor, and occasionally the more offensive effluvium of vomit wafted from the alleyways. Still, the odors and collisions with passing lushes did not penetrate the wall of his ruminations. It was the ruckus of a much different crowd, reaching his ears as he passed an intersection, that drew him out of his mind and once again piqued his curiosity for the outside world.

Following the sound led him to a large open courtyard filled with people. On all sides it was surrounded by what appeared to be municipal buildings, and high above rose the face of an illuminated clock tower. At the center of the courtyard a large brazier roared with flame, bathing the surrounding area and facades in a bright but variable light. The dance of shadows made it difficult to truly judge the size of the crowd, and Hutta remained on the fringe, doing his best to ascertain what the din was all about. He made his way slowly clockwise, slipping between personages whom all appeared to be angry. The more mild were snarling and shaking their heads, while the bold were jeering and shaking raised fists. His view to the apparent target of the commotion was obscured by a tree across the courtyard, but when he reached a more favorable angle he was no longer surprised by the hate in the air.

There, standing upon a crate near the base of the clock tower, was the very cultist that had appeared out of the portal just after Hutta and the others. It appeared he was attempting to proselytize to the obviously unreceptive crowd. His arms glided about, accentuating his rhetoric, while the light of the brazier cast an ominously dancing shadow high upon the tower behind him. Two large men in full plate and purple cloaks stood on the ground before him, keeping the more brazen members of the crowd from reaching him.

"Turn away," he was saying now, "turn away from your false gods, from lesser deities that are pallid and wretched in comparison to the glory of Primzahl! Turn also from the corruption of magic. That abomination that will damn your souls to the darkest pits of oblivion! Faith is the only power worth lusting after! Faith in He that leads the righteous to true glory all across the multiverse! Turn now and all transgressions may be forgiven, for Primzahl is a merciful master."

Some infuriated, and possibly inebriated, mage in the crowd now yelled out a loud "Boo!" and with it cast a fireball rocketing toward the cultist. The speaker raised and crossed his arms before him, shielding himself with a ward of clear energy that dispelled the fireball in a rapid explosion, nearly igniting the cloak of one of the bodyguards. But this distraction had left him vulnerable to the tomato that was now soaring toward him from the opposite direction. Accompanied by a cry of "Hypocrite!" it splattered against his cheekbone, eliciting a loud cheer from the crowd. He closed his eyes and grimaced, the juice and mash of the tomato dripping down from his face and onto his torso, in spots deepening the purple of his robe and staining some of the white trim red. He wiped his cheek clean with a handkerchief, and as if the incident hadn't occurred, continued with his preaching, setting the crowd back into their fit of jeering and heckling.

Hutta stopped paying attention. He had had the misfortune of hearing much of this script before, and he was not interested in reliving the experience. Instead he scanned the crowd and the courtyard, and to his relief his eyes fell upon familiar faces. Some distance away, leaning against one of the buildings that flanked the courtyard, were Enoch, Eshwar, and Kelm. Each had a disdainful look fixated on the cultist. Hutta's approach served as a relieving distraction to Kelm and Eshwar, but Enoch's gaze remained intact.

"So you stumbled upon tonight's entertainment as well," Kelm said.

"Much to my dismay," Hutta smiled. "I was on my way back when I heard the ruckus."

"We were out looking for Fuster when we were drawn to the commotion," Kelm said. "He barely ate anything at supper, and then he disappeared. He's been gone almost as long as you have. I'm worried about him."

"And what of Webb?" asked Hutta.

"Said he was going out. Obviously he didn't care to help look," Kelm replied. "Anyway, we ended up here and Enoch wanted to have a listen. It's his first sermon."

"Indeed," Enoch said, without averting his gaze. "It's sickening. I'm only glad that none of the crowd appear to be swayed."

"He's lucky they aren't more aggressive," said Eshwar. "A few more of those fireballs could make this much more interesting."

"Despite their anger, I don't think they take him too seriously," Hutta said. "And on —"

Enoch raised a hand and silenced his companion, then pointed at the cultist. He had finished his preaching and was preparing to step down from the crate, but then turned his attention back to the crowd. His tone changed, and all could tell he was now speaking for himself and not from predetermined rhetoric.

"Change is at hand," he said with conviction. "Amalgam has always resisted us, but soon the light of Primzahl will finally spread across this land and cleanse it of heathens and sinners. Repent while you can, or find yourselves judged."

With that he stepped down, and flanked by his guards disappeared down an alleyway. The crowd grew hushed and whispered nervously amongst themselves. Never had one of these evangelists broken from their usual pattern, and while the words of his affirmation seemed rather hollow, there was something in his delivery that made them ominous. The air was now tense and melancholy. Even the flame of the brazier seemed to dance with less fervor. People stood about as if expecting something to happen, but nothing did, and soon they began to disperse from the courtyard.

"What was that about?" asked Eshwar.

"I wish I knew," Enoch said. For a few moments he stroked his chin and pondered, and then spoke again, "I cannot linger here. Something tells me I must get to Bastion as quickly as I can. Come, let us look a while longer for Fuster, but then we should retire. We must have a discussion before our parting, and it should be in private."

For over an hour they scoured the streets in search of Fuster to no avail. A cool mist had begun to envelop the city. The lamplight was transformed into giant diffused orbs given shape by the fog, and the cobbles beneath their feet became wet and slippery. As the night wore on and the weather grew more inclement, the streets became more and more deserted. Windows were shuttered and went dark; the street lamps began to flicker and die. Clouds obscured the moon, turning the city into a few resilient flames connected by long stretches of thick darkness. Walking was becoming treacherous, and giving up the search they made their way back to their inn.

It stood on the northern tip of the same spit of land on which they had watched the cultist give his sermon beneath the clock tower. Its forward facade faced due south along a cross street, and was still well-lit and alive with the sounds of patrons. Before retiring to their rooms, they checked the rear courtyard for Fuster, and to their relief there he was. The courtyard was like a triangle, with its base along the rear face of the inn and its tip in one of the forks of the delta. The outer walls followed the water on either side until coming together like the prow of a ship splitting the river, as if the courtyard itself had created this fork by the force of its will, denying the river unimpeded access to the bay. Fuster sat upon this very prow, facing northward into the deepening gloom. His cloak was wrapped tightly about him, but his head was uncovered, and his hair and face were dripping from the mist. The others approached him and asked where he had been, for their search until now had been in vain.

"Oh," he replied, "I was roaming with my thoughts. I returned when the mist started, but I wasn't ready to go to my room. Sorry to lead you on a goose chase." He paused, still staring over the water, but then he turned to his friends and asked, "Did you by chance see that cultist in the city center?"

They told him they had, but that they had not known he was in the crowd.

"I was, for a time anyway," he said, "I saw the end, which I think was the most important part. I worry about whatever it is they're planning. I told you I should've gutted him back at the portal."

"Disemboweling that particular pawn would have done nothing to alter the game, I fear," Enoch said. "But their plans are precisely what I'd like to discuss before we retire. Come with me to my room."

Fuster jumped down from the wall, and they all followed Enoch back into the inn. He had rented a spacious room on an upper floor, and they were easily able to gather inside. Kelm was sent to check for Webb, but he was not in his room, and so Enoch left instructions with the innkeeper to send him their way should he return soon. After stoking the fire they sat in silence for a time, but Webb did not appear, and their eyes began to grow heavy. Refusing to wait any longer, Enoch broke the silence.

#

"I know that you have not decided your next course," he said, "due in no small part to the loss of your companion, I'm sure. But the speech we heard tonight has left me unsettled, and I am driven to make haste. I will be leaving early in the morning and moving as fast I as can to meet my friend. Even pushing myself it should take a minimum of twelve days to get to Bastion.

"I fear however, for Eshwar's safety. If the Cult has become emboldened then they would have no qualms about picking off a lone mage on the road, should they meet him and discover his nature. If I may, I would implore you to travel with him to the Magehold and ensure his safe passage. It may be completely unnecessary, but it would put part of my mind at ease."

"Noble, to be sure," Hutta said, "and a job like that might be just what we need to properly ground ourselves here, but I've been doing some thinking myself and—"

"Might I interrupt?" asked Fuster.

Hutta raised an eyebrow, slightly annoyed by being interrupted a second time in one evening, but with a wave of his hand he deferred to Fuster.

"Daffer and I joined this troupe together. You've been great to us, boss, don't get me wrong, and maybe I'm just grieving, but now this just doesn't feel quite right. And listening to that Cultist tonight, it reminded me of home, of the friends and family we've seen disappear or be executed. If I could I'd go kill every one of those motherfuckers back in Lovik, but as far as we know we can't go home. So I've decided, if Enoch will have me, to go to Bastion and be whatever help I can."

Enoch nodded slowly as he watched the fireplace. Kelm eyed Fuster, looking genuinely surprised.

"Well," Hutta resumed, "had you let me finish, I was going to say that I, too, was disturbed by the finale this evening. We've done merc work for a long time, for me it's been my entire life, but I'm sick of the shit we've just let happen. No one is going to pay us to go after the Cult, no one would dare, so we just have to take it upon ourselves, and try to make a difference. Now we know that it's not just our world that's been effected. It's Eshwar's, and this one, and who knows how many others. I'm going to go to Bastion as well, and see just what this war is all about."

"I am pleasantly surprised by this news," Enoch said. "Strong fighters joining the ranks will be as much a gift for Bastion as what I carry to my friend."

"I thought you said it was just a personal item," Hutta said.

"I'm careful what information I give to strangers, especially ones as brutish as your friend, Webb. And I would keep it secret until we reach the fortress. Now, there is still the issue of Eshwar's safety. The Magehold is in the opposite direction of our travels."

"I'll take him," Kelm spoke up. "I can make sure he gets there safely and then double back and make my way to Bastion."

"Excellent. I think we are decided then," Enoch said.

The group nodded in agreement.

"I wish I could say I could take care of myself," Eshwar said. "But I am grateful for the concern from all of you, and for the guardianship."

They were bidding each other goodnight and preparing to disperse to their rooms when Webb stumbled through the door. The smell of spirits was on his breath, and his bandage was wet and stained.

"What did I miss?" he asked.

"First, where have you been?" countered Hutta.

"Drinking. Obviously. Oooh, and fucking. Unfortunately the establishment I was enjoying doesn't allow for overnight stays, or I wouldn't be here at all."

"Nice to know someone's enjoying themselves," said Fuster.

"F-f-fuck off," Webb said. "Now what's going on? That little man downstairs said I had to come up here, but it's not really where I'd like to be. No offense."

The others stared at him. Enoch touched a finger to his temple, clearly perturbed. Fuster snorted and turned his attention to the fire. Hutta shook his head in exasperation.

"We have decided," Hutta told him, "to accompany Enoch to Bastion, and add our swords to their ranks."

At this Webb seemed to sober up. Slightly. "That doesn't sound like it pays well."

Fuster threw up his hands and shook his head.

"I shan't think it will pay anything at all," Enoch said.

"We're not doing it to get paid," Hutta said. "We're doing it to take on the Cult. It seems our days as sellswords have come to an end for now. That being said, we're not forcing you into anything. This isn't a decision I made for everyone, we all made it together. You can do whatever pleases you."

Webb stared at Hutta for a moment, then his face lightened and he grinned. "Well, let's not be hasty.

I'll tag along. Maybe I'll be pleasantly surprised and get a nice reward for my contributions."

Enoch frowned, but said nothing. Fuster let out another snort, and Kelm had joined in the shaking of heads. After a second round of goodnights they each retired to their separate rooms. Eshwar was on the same floor as Enoch, for his purse was still fat from the sale of his gemstones and he saw no reason not to afford himself some luxury. The others had settled for more modest but still comfortable accommodations on the lower floors, and made their way down through a lantern-lit stairwell. The inn had grown quiet, and no sound rose up from the common room beneath. With some final parting words the Riisgardians closed and locked their doors. Their windows showed little but pitch black night, though one final orb surrounding a lamp in the courtyard revealed that the air was still thick with mist and fog. With warm and comfortable beds and near utter darkness, sleep took each of them quickly.

#

A damp, cool morning arrived all too soon. The sun had barely crept over the horizon when the group gathered in the common room and ate a hasty breakfast. Kelm and Eshwar discreetly inquired directions to the Magehold from the innkeeper. He informed them that upon their arrival they should seek out the current chancellor. Not only would he be able to properly place Eshwar, but rumor had it he was studying portal travel and could likely answer any of the multitude of questions they might have. If he would be willing to talk to them at any rate.

After breakfast the group left together to resupply at a busy marketplace within one of the city's several port districts. The avenues were still dark, except where the occasional properly angled cross street allowed the red advance of dawn to rush through in blinding fury before being met by an unyielding stone facade. The market area was rank with the scents of fish and overripe produce, but due to the proximity of the ships and sailors there was ample and affordable supply of hardtack and cured meat. Kelm and Eshwar had a shorter journey and so provisioned more lightly and with more palatable stock. The rest chose the bare essentials and stuffed their packs just to be safe. Two weeks on the road was not out of the ordinary for any of them, but their inexperience with the land and the threat of Cult activity made them cautious.

They lingered just long enough in the market to ensure they were all sufficiently provisioned before making their way back to the courtyard where the cultist had spoken the night before. They gathered around the now lifeless brazier at the center. It was filled with saturated black ash and a few pieces of charred wood that had partially escaped the gluttony of the previous evening's blaze. Basking in the glow of the now risen sun, the face of the clock tower indicated it was only nigh eight hours past midnight. While they stood there the bells began to toll from high above, being answered by reports from the ships docked all around the delta and the bay front.

"It is here that we must part," Enoch said. "Kelm, Eshwar, I cannot promise we will meet again, but our short time together has been a pleasure. I hope that the lady of fortune casts the die ever in your favor."

He placed a hand upon his heart and bowed his head to them, a gesture which they reciprocated. Kelm and the other Riisgardians then saluted each other with two raps of a fist to the breast, and he exchanged an embrace with Hutta and Fuster. A simple nod was a sufficient parting gesture from Webb.

"I'll see you again soon my friends," Kelm said. "May your feet be as swift as Wolf and your arms as strong as Bear."

"And I hope to see you all again someday," Eshwar added. "I cannot thank you enough for allowing me to travel with you, and for lending me Kelm's sword."

"Best of luck to you, Eshwar," Hutta said. "And may the Eagle watch over us all."

With this they took their leave. The bulk of the group was to exit the city by way of the northwestern road, a road that would carry them not only in the direction of Bastion, but of the Cult's territory as well. Kelm and Eshwar were to take the easterly road, following the coast of Leben Bay until they were able to turn south into the lands of the Magehold. The two parties moved across the bridges and streets of the city until they found their respective roads, and with a long day ahead of them they left Deltaville behind.

CHAPTER SIX
The Empyrean Magehold

By the end of their first day, Kelm and Eshwar had left the farmland surrounding Deltaville behind. The fields had given way to a verdant grassland that fell quickly from the road to a rocky shoreline. The harsh climate of the desert, though in truth not that far away, was now but a distant memory, and although the days were still hot, a cool sea breeze kept them comfortable as they marched. By the end of their second day they had reached the narrowest point of Leben Bay, where it was less than ten leagues across to the point where the lighthouse stood, and that night the beacon was as clear and bright as they would see it during their journey. From this point on, the bay was more wild and rough, for far to the south its mouth opened wide into the sea. The shoreline was embattled by the crash of wave against stone, and when the road meandered too close they would be hit by stray salt spray from the clash.

The road was not busy, but neither was it deserted, and several times a day they would pass wagons or groups of travelers, mostly traders headed for Deltaville from the Magehold and lands farther east. The companions found it easy to talk to one another, and they spent most of their time telling each other about their homes.

The world Eshwar described seemed alien and fascinating to Kelm, much more so even than Amalgam. There were forests of giant fungus that at night were illuminated by all shades of bio-luminescence, trees that grew larger and taller than anything the works of man could yet equal, and cities that floated among the clouds. Eshwar himself came from a secluded corner of the wilderness, deep within a forest with some of those very trees that reached high into the clouds. His people were tribal, and far removed from the advance of civilization. It was this isolation that had caused him to realize his potential so late, and he had only been studying at the academy for a few short months before the Cult's raid. And now here he was. Few of his people left the forest, let alone traveled through portals to new worlds.

Kelm was almost embarrassed to describe Riisgard, which in his mind was mundane and boring in comparison to Eshwar's descriptions. He also hailed from a wooded area, nestled beneath the mountains that formed Lovik's northern border. The kingdom was a small one, but strategically important, as it held the only pass through the mountains to the tundra and glaciers beyond, where lived the Jokullfar, a race of pale elves who lived in palaces of ice and stone. The lands to the southeast were inhabited by banner-less men and clans of giants. It was here that they had found the portal, far beneath a ruined fortress of some long forgotten kingdom. The giants had refused to take action against the conjurer when he unleashed his summonses, for they found hunting the beasts to be good sport, and so Hutta was hired to put an end to the problem, and the rest Eshwar already knew.

On the morning of their fifth day they found themselves at a crossroads. The road continued straight to the northeast but also split off to the south. They turned and took the southerly road, soon crossing a river via a stone bridge, and found themselves within the borders of the Empyrean Magehold. For two more days they journeyed south through flat farmland under the watchful guard of windmills, their blades gently rotating in the breeze still coming from Leben Bay away some distance to their right. On their left, the fields ended abruptly at the base of rolling foothills that rose quickly into tall mountains with faces and peaks of bare stone. The people they encountered seemed like ordinary farmers, and besides the occasional plow appearing to pull itself along, nothing about the land struck them as particularly magical, until on the third day from the river crossing they reached the Magehold's first city.

They first saw the city of Velhonik when it was still many miles away, for at its center stood the tallest tower either of them had ever seen. Its base was a cylinder of solid stone, rising as high as any building in the city, forming a giant dais. Its edge was encircled by a parapet that appeared to be carved of the same single massive rock, and all the area within was decorated with trees and gardens. From this dais rose the tower proper for what seemed like the height of the nearby mountains. Of what material it was constructed, whether brick, slab, or carven stone was indiscernible, for its surface was so polished that the light of day gleamed from it in spectacular fashion. The entire height was fluted like a column, with sharp arrises whose bottoms extended well out onto the dais. The tower tapered as it reached for the sky before ultimately flaring out again to be capped by crenelations that must have been several times the height of a man. An observer standing atop it at night could likely have seen the beacon of the lighthouse across the bay though it was over one hundred miles to the west.

From the north side of the dais extended a viaduct over the streets and buildings of the surrounding city, passing between two towers that seemed like miniatures in comparison to the spire above, and angling down to form a large ramp that connected to the streets below. The buildings were bright and tall, with steeply pitched roofs poking up between the canopies of decorative trees. They were arranged in a roughly concentric pattern all around the central tower for row after row, until ending abruptly, with no walls or other demarcation of the city's edge.

"Well," Kelm said as they gazed up at the spire, "If I were in charge of a bunch of wizards, that's where I'd be."

The road on which they traveled entered Velhonik from north-northwest, transforming into a boulevard with a median lined with trees. The people here seemed to be almost exclusively practitioners of magic. Most were dressed in robes of all colors and moved about with great hurry, while manual labor was being performed by all manner of magical constructs. At one point Eshwar had to push the wide-eyed Kelm out of the way, lest he be crushed by a lumbering golem of animated rock carrying a stack of huge crates down the road.

It was not far before the boulevard met with the ramp up to the viaduct. It was dauntingly tall, but not steep. Even so, the climb to the top seemed to last forever, and once they had reached the top and were flanked by the smaller towers, the viaduct still stretched on before them toward the monolithic dais. From the edge of the viaduct they could look down on the roof peaks of houses and shops, and far, far below, tiny figures darted through the streets. As they reached the dais and approached the tower, they began to lose the sense of its shape, as it was so massive its breadth now completely filled their line of sight. Directly ahead, centered between two of the arrises, was a doorway flanked by columns and capped with a portico. In truth the structure was quite large, itself the size of a small building, but in the facade of the tower it looked comically tiny. Standing on either side of the doorway were what appeared to be two guards.

As they drew closer, both Kelm and Eshwar were surprised to find that the guards were suits of armor containing no bodies. The armor was made of some dark and pitted material that had more the appearance of stone than metal. Empty nasal helms, decorated with brows that protruded into large and impractical horns, faced directly forward, with no reaction to the approach of the companions. Below the helms were suspended crudely shapen pauldrons attached to equally crude breastplates. Beneath this was a large gap where an abdomen should have been, and then a plated pelvic girdle and codpiece, in turn connected to large cuisses, and finally sharply edged greaves and sabatons. There were no rerebraces below the pauldrons, leaving the vambraces and gauntlets suspended on their own.

When the men were at last standing just before the suits, they could see that there was some hint of shape in the empty space between plates, as if a membrane of air was filling in where there would normally be flesh. Within this space were rivers of dark blue energy, coursing throughout like a simplified circulatory system. These arteries gave off no light, but seemed to fluctuate, at times appearing as nothing more than faint blurs, then sharpening into well defined lines. After concluding their examination, Kelm and Eshwar stepped toward the doorway, but were stopped when each guard blocked their path with a large, black halberd.

The guard on the left never turned to them, but began to speak, and as it did a blue glow arose from within its spectral throat, pulsing with the sound of its grainy, metallic voice. "State your business."

A timid "Uh" managed to escape Kelm's lips, but it was Eshwar who addressed the entity.

"We're here to see the chancellor."

"The current chancellor of the Empyrean Magehold is Archmage Hague. This is the tower of Archmage Cirroc."

"Oh. Well where might we find Archmage Hague?"

"This unit is a sentry, not a guide."

"Then can we get in and ask this...Cirroc?" Kelm asked.

"Archmage Cirroc does not accept unscheduled visitations," replied the sentry.

"I don't think we're going to get anywhere with this thing," Kelm whispered to Eshwar. "Maybe we should ask around town."

"Agreed," Eshwar said, then turned back to the armor, "well...good day."

"Good day," said the guard.

The companions made their way back towards the viaduct, and when they were some distance away the sentries snapped their halberds back into a vertical position and resumed their statuesque vigil. The journey back down the ramp was not at all strenuous, but still seemed to take an inordinate amount of time. Back on street level, they began to inquire direction of passersby. Most were less than helpful, but one pointed them to a tavern along the boulevard and assured them that its keeper would be more than happy to answer their questions. The building was quite large, two full stories capped with a tall concave roof, its length filling the space between two side streets. The main entrance was at the base of a turret in the facade's center, and this led the companions into a small antechamber and then the main barroom. The room was blanketed in tables, and the second floor wrapped around in balcony fashion, leaving a clear view to the vaulted ceiling, from which hung large chandeliers. They made their way between the tables and patrons to a bar against the rear wall. Upon seeing the new arrivals, the barkeep came rushing from the opposite end to greet them.

Both of them were initially at a loss for words as they looked upon their strange host. He, or it, was more or less a keg with appendages. An inverted pail mounted to a dowel served as his head, and a hinged piece of wood made for a basic jaw. Two holes were bored into the pail, and from within came an unnatural green glow, which the companions could only assume was the barkeep's eyes. Attached to his barrel torso were a series of blocks, wheels, and dowels that formed arms, hands, a pelvis, legs, and feet. His voice was masculine and natural and came unmistakably from within the pail, though the jaw chomped along in imperfect time with his speech.

"Gentleman! Gentleman! Welcome, what can I do for you today? A fine bourbon maybe? Perhaps some wine? Oh!" he raised a hand to the side of his head and began to whisper, "Perhaps a hearty black rum? Straight from the Fliege Archipelago, very hard to come by here in the Magehold."

"Um," Kelm said, "we actually came looking for information. We were told the owner of this place could offer us directions."

"Indeed he can!" said the barkeep, "And lucky for you you're looking at him. The name's Keg. Very original, I know."

"You...own this place?" Kelm asked.

"What's the matter? You've never been in a bar run by a sentient barrel? What a sheltered life you must lead.

"Oh, don't look so embarrassed! I jest of course. If you had been in another establishment like this I would be quite taken aback. Now, I'd be glad to help you, but information is better absorbed along with a fine drink, wouldn't you say?"

Kelm and Eshwar thought it best not to argue with Keg's insistence, so they ordered an ale and a red wine and gave the barkeep the prescribed number of gold chunks. He shuffled off and poured them their drinks. His movements were inarticulate and clumsy, but he was clearly aware of his own limitations and never spilled a drop as he came and set the drinks before his customers.

"Fine choices, friends," Keg said, "now what knowledge can I impart upon you?"

"We need to find Chancellor Hague," Eshwar replied. "But I would also inquire your origins if I may be so bold."

"That's it? Anyone on the street should have been able to tell you where to find the Chancellor, but I suppose none of these enchanters are prone to idle conversation. Time is money after all. Anyway, Chancellor Hague lives in the town of Taikanìk, up in the mountains, and roughly one hundred miles travel. Take the northeasterly road out of town. It will take you to Juomanìk, and then on to Loitsunìk. There you will find a road leading northwest into the mountains. Just follow it until you reach Taikanìk.

"My origins are a longer tale. To put it simply, I was a huge mistake. My creator was attempting to make one of those magic mirrors that tell women they're pretty, but the spell reflected off the mirror and hit...me...this barrel. Everyone knows you're supposed to enchant the glass *before* you make it a mirror. But, the amazing piece of this mistake is that I immediately became self-aware, truly alive, if you would. No enchanter has been able to intentionally accomplish this feat, and my maker was never able to repeat his mistake, though he tried. Anyway, he was competent enough to be able to give me this head and re-anchor the enchantment there, but as you can see from my life-like facial features and incredibly articulate appendages, a craftsman he was not. *sigh*, I keep telling myself that some day I'll be able to reach for something beside me without turning my entire body.

"For a time I was an object of study, but even Cirroc himself, archmage of enchanting, couldn't discern how I came to be. And it didn't take long for anyone to figure out there was no money to be made creating sentient beings, unless you approve of slavery, which thankfully the Council does not, so they all went back to creating golems and flying brooms. Even I bought one of them."

He gestured to a rear corner of the room, where a broom was standing upright by itself and gyrating back and forth, sweeping the floor.

"Quite a useful purchase actually," Keg continued. "The old owner of this establishment put me to work. After all, what better bartender can there be than someone who spent most of their existence filled to the brim with alcohol? I took to the job with flying colors, and when he died he left the place to me. I've been running it ever since."

"Fascinating," Eshwar said.

"If I could smile, I'd give you grin," Keg said. "But I can't, so I won't. Now that I've given you boys my story and your directions, I'm going to get back to work. Enjoy yourselves, and let me know if you need anything else."

They thanked their host, who then sauntered off and out from behind the bar to survey his other customers.

Kelm turned to Eshwar, "So what's the plan?"

"You have delivered me to the Magehold, so I understand if you'd like to head for Bastion," Eshwar replied. "The day is not old, and our packs are still well stocked, so I plan on departing immediately."

"I'm going to see this journey through with you, my friend. Besides, I'm sure there are plenty more amazing things for me to see down this road. I don't know what to make of all these marvels."

"So I take it you don't have enchanters on Riisgard either?"

"Of course we do. But they make swords that catch fire and rings that ward off evil spirits. Not talking buckets and walking rocks."

Eshwar smiled. "So let's be off, and see what we see."

They finished their drinks and returned to the street, accompanied by a cheerful well-wishing from Keg. A few turns through the city brought them to the northeasterly road and the next leg of their journey.

#

On their left they could see that the mountains came to a point, facing due south toward the great tower behind them. To the right the land eventually fell away into the ocean. Over the next day and half they traveled with these horizons, mountains rising high upon the left and unending ocean upon the right, until after nearly fifty miles of brisk marching they reached the city of Juomanìk. It was much smaller than all the cities they had seen thus far, and rightly would have been described more as a large town. The buildings here were squat and nestled among the foothills of the mountains. Many were covered in plantings of all manner of flora, or surrounded by vibrant gardens, and close to the center of town rose a wide, vine-covered tower, but this one was not even as tall as the dais of the spire of Cirroc. It was not difficult to discern that Juomanìk was home to the alchemists who produced the Babel Brew that Byron had given them upon their arrival on Amalgam. The companions arrived late in the evening, and spent the night in one of a cluster of small cottages. Nearby was a menagerie of animals whose calls continued well into the night, forcing them to stuff their ears in order to get to sleep.

The following evening found them in Loitsunìk. The ocean was now farther away to the southeast, but two rushing rivers flanking the city made their way swiftly to its shores. This city was tiered, steadily rising in a series of walls and terraces, into which many of the edifices were built, until once again a tower rose up from the center. This one was a deep and glossy black, and had many protrusions and sub-towers poking about in seemingly random intervals. The people here were the most diverse they had yet seen in the Magehold, particularly because their clothing was not limited to robes. This was the city of sorcery, and practitioners of every kind roamed the streets, from various elementalists to eccentric seers to heavily armored battle-mages. They spent that night at the Rampart, an inn set completely inside the city's lowest tier.

When they set out the next morning the end of their journey was less than ten leagues distant, but it was not long before their road began to climb steeply into the mountains. The headwaters of one of the rivers was almost a constant feature on their left, often falling with a deafening roar through large cascades as the companions followed steep but well-worn switchbacks. The elevation rose without respite, and they stopped frequently to catch their breath and snack on what provision remained in their packs. Kelm had a more difficult time than Eshwar, his armor making every step heavy and bending his back with fatigue. His stops became more and more frequent as the day wore on, and before nightfall they were forced to make camp beneath an outcropping off of the road, where Kelm promptly fell into deep sleep without removing any of his gear. Eshwar wrapped him in his cloak before using his own to form a makeshift bed on a shelf of rock. For a time he sat awake by a small fire, listening to the howls of wolves and filling his belly with tack before himself drifting into sleep.

Their bodies begged them to stay and rest as they set off again. Each step was more laborious than the last, and the air was growing thinner as they climbed. While navigating a switchback they found the font of the river falling down a sheer rock face into a jaggedly eroded crevasse, rushing away furiously back towards Loitsunìk while the road went on ever higher. With the river gone and the tree line already left far behind them, they were left in a landscape dominated by nothing but silver stone. The air was chill, but not near cold enough for snow, and peaks rose uncapped in a roughly straight line on both the right and left. To their relief their journey met its end before midday, when they crested a final rise in the road and found themselves in a trough between two of the mountain peaks.

Within this space were spread the buildings of Taikanìk, strewn about with no order or pattern. They were built low and squat, most no more than one story tall. Some were protruding from large boulders or from the mountainsides, and looked as if they were being slowly absorbed by the stone. Breaking with the pattern the companions had observed thus far, the tower here was not in the center of the town, but rather was rising from the mountain on their right. It was perhaps the least impressive of the towers they had seen, having by far less breadth, and less relative height. At its base it was indistinguishable from the mountainside, but as it rose gray bricks began to fill in where the stone tapered away toward the peak, until it left the slope behind completely and extended upward as a cylinder of brick, capped with a conical roof of dark shingles not even as high as the summit behind.

Kelm and Eshwar made their way up to the base of the tower, which was raised above the rest of the area, and from there they could see down either side of the mountain range. To their right, southeast, they could see the black tower of Loitsunìk rising between the two rivers, and beyond that they could see the vast expanse of blue ocean fading into the sky above. To their left, northwest, like a hair draped across the land, was the road that had continued on from Deltaville, following the edge of a vast forest as it continued on to the northeast and once again out of sight.

Before them, next to a wooden door set within a threshold carved into the mountainside, a man leaned against the stone with his head hung low and his arms crossed. Dark, unkempt hair hung down just enough to obscure his face from their view. He wore dark pants and boots, and a long shirt that looked as if it should have been a robe for a child. They approached him slowly, and as they did he slightly raised his head...and disappeared. For a moment a few dim flashes of purple energy, reminiscent of the portal, occupied the space where he had stood, but they vanished almost as instantly as he had. The companions turned to each other with confused looks. Eshwar shrugged.

"Gentlemen." The voice came from close behind them. Startled they spun about, Kelm's sword half unsheathed by the time he turned, but the man raised a hand, "Take it easy there. If I was going to attack you I wouldn't have greeted you. I just wanted to get a full look at you. Now, can I ask what you want?"

The man was young, likely close in age to Kelm, but had a hard and cynical face. His eyes were sharp and pale, and seemed to be studying their every move, and although they darted about rapidly, it was clear that they did so with focus. Kelm slid his sword back down into its sheath, but his hand remained on the hilt. Eshwar spoke up to answer the man's question.

"We seek an audience with Chancellor Hague."

The man chewed the inside of his lip and nodded his head, "Hmph. Well, I am the Chancellor's steward, and vet all of his visitors. What would be the nature of your audience?"

"We have both come to Amalgam only very recently. I was sent by an instructor of mine who has studied here at the Magehold. My friend agreed to escort me due to Cult activity. We were told the Chancellor was the best person to seek out."

There was little recognition of Eshwar's words in the man's face as his eyes continued to study them, but after a moment he replied, "Seeings as your visit isn't of a...political nature, there's a good chance the Chancellor will grant you your audience. Wait here until I return."

The darting eyes now came to a fixed focus directly between the companions, and in an instant the man disappeared again, leaving behind a few brief cracks of purple. They turned back toward the tower in time to see him opening the door and disappearing inside in a much more mundane fashion.

"That's a useful trick," Kelm said.

"Yes," Eshwar acknowledged. "One I think I'd very much like to learn."

Only a few minutes passed before the door to the tower once again creaked open, and within the threshold stood the steward.

"The Chancellor will see you," he said.

The companions passed within the tower. The steward shut and locked the door behind them, and then beckoned them to follow, leading them up a flight of stairs that would serve as the true last leg of their journey through the Empyrean Magehold.

CHAPTER SEVEN
Bastion

"There it is," Enoch said.

"I've never seen anything like it," said Fuster.

"It's magnificent," Hutta added.

"Well shit," grunted Webb.

A fortnight of marching had brought them to this point. Much like their eastbound companions, their fifth day brought them to a bridge. It crossed the river Rhand, which flowed from a mountain on the edge of the desert, the last peak in a long southerly range that extended down from the very same mountains into which Bastion was set. From there it traveled south-southwest until splitting in two at the foothills of another mountain range, from which point it met the ocean to the west, and Leben Bay back to the southeast, and so it formed the entirety of the northern border of the Kingdom of Leerwandler. It also, according to Enoch, formed the border of friendly civilization. Beyond the bridge was an expanse of unclaimed territory, wild and forested. Crossing over brought them to a point where the road split in three. To the west it would follow the Rhand until crossing into the city of Nordrhanden, Leerwandler's northernmost municipality. To the northwest it led through the forested wilderness until reaching the territory which the Cult had claimed for itself, far from the other nations of Amalgam. And to the north it would lead the companions toward Bastion. The horizon to the east of this northern path was dominated by tall, jagged mountains of brown stone. Their faces were sheer and sharp, with no vegetation growing upon them, making them appear even more barren than the desert sands that fell at their eastern feet. To the west were tall and ancient trees, with a canopy so high and thick that the land beneath was locked in endless night. This road met its end at the river Euhr, but an intersection placed them upon another that followed this new water both east and west. To the west it would once again lead to the Cult, but to the east it passed through a wide rift in the mountains and into the dale in which they now stood. They had come to the valley's head. Before them was its eastern limit, and in the mountainside was the fortress which they had been seeking.

A crenelated wall of massive stone bricks extended out from the rock face, and in a wide and sweeping arc wrapped around until meeting the mountain again. Behind this wall was another, taller and even more fortified. At intervals upon its entire length were placed huge trebuchets, each flanked by a pile of projectiles. Within this inner wall was a citadel, rising up in a series of rectangular sections until being capped with a half-round turret set into the mountain, all of which was shaded by a massive protrusion of rock. From high on this outcrop the font of Euhr came tumbling down in a great mist, until after being diverted around by several smaller outcroppings it cascaded over both of Bastion's walls and met the ground below. It began its flow west in a series of angry rapids until some miles away it dumped into a large lake in the heart of the valley, and from the other end it began a much more casual flow out to the land beyond.

To the right of the citadel, rising in a series of wide switchbacks and natural stairs, the road made its way up the mountainside. Here and there masonry had replaced portions that had collapsed. In some places whole bridges had been built to cross chasms that would have deposited the unwary into open air, but by and large the way up was somehow a natural formation. And at the top, so far above that even at a distance the companions had to raise their heads to look, was another citadel. Its facade rose precariously up from the face of the mountain, and upon it sat another turret, this one fully cylindrical, large and proud. From it streamed banners and flags so large that the breeze could barely move them, and it seemed as though the clouds themselves had to split in order to pass by the unyielding fortress. The Riisgardians were enthralled by the sheer magnitude of the sight before them, and likely would not have moved on for some time but for encouragement from Enoch.

As they approached the outer wall the road turned and followed alongside it. It was decorated with niches that broke up the facade, and the battlements overhung the upper edge, supported by large, stepped corbels. Archers stood watch or paced along the top, but they largely ignored the travelers below, and their weapons remained stowed. Near the wall's midpoint stood an imposing gatehouse. Two turrets formed its flanks, each with a flume extended over the entryway that could pour pitch onto besieging enemies. The gate itself was composed of two iron doors that were swung open outwardly, and a stone header running between the turrets, nearly at the top. The road split here, with a path continuing on to the north and passing over the rapids, and another rising up to pass within the fortress. Three figures appeared within the gate, walking slowly out to meet the companions, until one rushed ahead.

"Enoch!" the man yelled. A faded black cloak streamed behind him as he ran, and the rush pulled his hood off of his head, revealing a beaming smile and happy brown eyes. His hair was dark and cropped short, and a tight but full beard hugged his jaw. His body was fully covered by plate that at once looked as if it had been dyed or stained dark but also polished to a gleaming shine. The image of a crashing wave was embossed just below the breast, and the design of his pauldrons evoked the billows and eddies of the sea. Protruding from beneath his cloak, across the right shoulder and from behind the left hip, was a greatsword with a black hilt, resting within a dark leather sheath. Enoch spread his arms and allowed the man to wrap him in a strong embrace.

"Andor!" he said with a smile and a laugh. "It is good to see you too."

The man released him but grabbed him by the shoulders.

"The sentries at the South Maw sent word you had entered the valley. Tell me, brother, do you have it?" Andor asked with excitement.

"Of course." Enoch dug his fingers beneath one of the leather lames of his vambrace and produced a small wooden cylinder, which he handed to Andor.

"Wonderful!" Andor said. "I cannot thank you enough for bringing it to me. And who are your companions?"

"Warriors from the world of Riisgard, come to offer their swords to the cause." Enoch introduced each to his friend.

"Excellent, and welcome," Andor said. "You must meet the Commandant." He gestured to the other two figures, who had now completed their approach. "May I present Josalynn Willet, Commandant of Bastion. Mistress, Enoch has brought new recruits for your consideration."

The woman stepped forward to greet them. Her torso was covered by a plate cuirass and her shoulders by thick leather spaulders, but her arms and hands were bare. A mail skirt dropped from her waist to her mid-thigh, and full plate protected her legs. A long gladius hung at her hip, and on her back rested a quiver and longbow beneath a kite shield. Braided auburn hair fell across her shoulder, and she studied them with hazel eyes. Her nose was small and sharp, her skin smooth and clear, and her lips full and colorful. But despite its beauty, her face was stern and authoritative. When she spoke her voice was confident and commanding.

"Good to see you again, Enoch," she said, "and welcome to the rest of you. This is my second, Backus, Warden of the Lower Citadel."

She gestured to the figure beside her. He was well over a head taller than her, and stood there with his thick arms crossed. His face was elongated like a canine, and boar-like tusks curved out from his lower jaw. Porcine ears pointed up from behind his jaw to the top of his head, and deep golden eyes stared out from cavernous sockets. His entire head and body were covered in a thick, coarse fur that appeared as if it would be bristly to the touch. He wore loose armor about his body comprised of leather sections strapped together, his fur protruding through the gaps in many places, and leather pants with embedded plates on the thighs, knees, and shins. Large boots covered what must have been disproportionately large feet. Two crude handaxes hung from loops on a ringmail belt buckled loosely around his waist. He grunted a sign of acknowledgment and nodded toward the new comers, and then shot a cold glance to Enoch.

"Banes," he said.

"Backus," Enoch returned the stare and gave a curt nod.

Hutta looked at the woman before him with vague recognition, an image of recent memory swirling behind his eyes. "Are you...are you the statue in Artesia?" he asked.

"That statue depicts my ancestor, Devonna Willet," she replied. "She founded this garrison around half a millennium ago. This is her bow, you would have seen it on the statue, passed down through her line as each of her descendants have assumed command of the fortress. Now come, we will show you around."

She led the group up the road toward the gate. Backus fell in at the rear. Webb moved alongside Enoch and Andor and gave the cylinder a derisive glance.

"You're telling me you traveled across worlds for that little thing? What even is it?"

"Size doesn't determine importance," Andor said, holding up the cylinder. "Though I'm sure yours has benefited you on the battlefield. This is one of my reliquaries. One that could be of great use in the days to come."

"I thought you said it was only of personal value," Webb said to Enoch.

"Forgive me for withholding my trust," Enoch replied with an unapologetic sneer.

Webb flared his nostrils and increased his pace, distancing himself from the Magnans. The group passed between the turrets and found themselves on a timber drawbridge between the outer and inner walls. The space between was filled with stray water from the cascades of the Euhr, its depth controlled by a small drain in the outer wall near the rapids outside. Another gatehouse lay ahead, larger than the first. It was once again formed by two turrets, but these were taller and capped with conical roofs. Arches on either side of the bridge connected the inner and outer turrets to one another, allowing sentinels to pass between the inner and outer walls, as well as defend the bridge from above. The bridge itself was shackled to two great chains, which could hoist it up against the inner gatehouse, which featured a much thicker header above its threshold, containing an iron portcullis.

"What do you think's guarding the moat, Webb?" Fuster asked. "Sharks? Crocodiles?" He giggled a little to himself.

"Punji sticks," came Backus's voice from behind. "I don't recommend diving in."

Passing through the second gate brought them to a flat expanse of rocky ground. The road continued on to the mountain and began its ascent, but Josalynn led them off on a side path toward the citadel. Soldiers and laborers moved about, some doing chores, some practicing in training yards, but there were far fewer than was to be expected of such a large fortification. As they approached the citadel proper, their guide pointed out a squat outbuilding near the wall, explaining that it housed the baths and latrines.

"Good, I need to shit," Webb said.

Hutta sighed and grasped his temples. "Go with him, Fuster, it's your turn."

Fuster and Webb split off from the group and headed for the building.

"This better be the last time," Fuster said. "I swear you could've taken that sling off days ago."

"Probably could've," Webb said. "But I like to see the looks on your faces when my manhood is swinging in them."

"That seems a little queer, don't you think?"

"Careful, Fuster," Webb snarled. "Even with one arm I can add a few more scars to your collection."

Fuster raised his hands defensively but casually. "Hey, don't dish it out if you can't take it back. But this is definitely the last time I'm helping you. Whether you take the sling off or not, you can remove your own armor from now on."

"Fine."

The others entered the citadel through a double iron door on the western side and found themselves in a long hall filled with dining tables. Light poured in through windows on the south face. The east side featured the Commandant's table, set before a wall of uncut mountain stone. Here they waited until they were rejoined by Fuster and Webb, and then they were led through torch-lit corridors and shown various bunkrooms, each with vacancies, leaving them with their choice of accommodation. Josalynn invited them to the evening meal in the hall which they had first entered, and instructed them to take the remainder of the day to rest and then report to Backus in the morning for assignment.

"I beg your pardon," Hutta said to her, "but we'd very much like to know what we're up against here. What is this Heart of the World and what are the Cult's plans to get it?"

She shot Andor a perturbed glance before replying, "It seems Sir Kardos included more than he should have in his letter to Enoch. Not everyone is privy to that information. I don't know yet what I can trust you with, but for now I would appreciate if you keep whatever you know to yourselves. I will see you at tonight's meal."

She and Backus took their leave. Enoch suggested that the others settle in and then followed Andor up to another floor of the citadel and to a private room. It was a modest space, but had a slit window with a view out over the fortress's walls.

"Moving up in the world, I see," Enoch said.

Andor smiled. "I've assisted with some skirmishes since last you were here, as well as assumed command of the upper citadel. It seems my performance gave me enough value to warrant my own little piece of paradise."

"Ah, but you are still far from the sea, just like our own stronghold."

"Unfortunately. And when the Euhr leaves this valley it flows on to form the borders of Cult country, where it is obviously heavily guarded. So I couldn't even make my escape that way if the mood were to strike."

"It's starting to sound even more like home," Enoch sighed.

"Why do you say that? Has something happened?"

Enoch turned to stare out the window with his arms crossed. "The conflict between Glenndronach and Umbria has worsened. The river has become contested and unsafe for travel. Had your message been sent on foot rather than air I doubt it would have reached me at all. There was even a battle around Walter's Ferry recently. Just to be safe I followed the goat paths out of the mountains and hired a ship at Whitewater to take me to Telluris. I left Jean-Baptiste in charge of the hideout, and I hope the conflict does not reach him there."

"By the Narra! I hope you've left someone in charge of *him*!"

"Don't worry," Enoch laughed, "Rhosyn has returned and is keeping an eye on him." He turned back to look at Andor, "I know that fighting the Cult has become a sort of...passion...of yours, but we need you to come home, Andor, and sooner rather than later. If things continue to escalate and our little band is somehow swept into the fray, we're going to need you with us."

Andor let out a long sigh but nodded his head, "I know I can't stay here forever, but I fear that Bastion needs me too, to counteract whatever devilry the Cult might have planned. It will not be long now before things here reach their head, and as soon as the Heart is safe, I promise I'll come home."

Enoch nodded. "What is the Heart, anyway?"

"Josalynn hasn't given me the full story. I'm not even sure she's told Backus everything. She's being far too secretive if you ask me. I think she wants to keep the Cult from finding out we know their intentions, but at this point we just need to get prepared. All I know is that the Heart lies to the east, in the realm of Amalgam's gods. That's part of the reason I sent for the reliquary. Dealing with gods too often means dealing with demons. But more so I fear what machinations the Cult can conjure up. If they attempt some sort of supernatural intervention, I'll need to be prepared."

"Yes. Well let's hope she starts trusting you with more information soon."

"Let's hope. Speaking of trust: your new friends; are they trustworthy?"

"I think so. The Cult has taken control of their home, and from the way they speak they have no love for it. I believe Fuster is especially devoted to your cause. But they were mercenaries up until now, and I'm not sure if they have any formal military training.

Though Bastion seems to house a more motley assortment of warriors all the time."

"That it does. It's difficult to keep such a garrison without open war, not to mention a tight purse. After five hundred years the coffers are running low, and volunteers are hard to come by, so your companions are welcome."

"The big one will expect to get paid. Truth be told, I don't like him, but he does seem to listen to Hutta, their leader. And a fourth, Kelm, should be joining them here. He's escorting another newcomer to the Magehold, but he said he would march this way when his task is complete."

"Good, that's good. Now, why don't you rest some, my friend. Then we'll gather for dinner."

#

Andor led the entire group into the great hall just before dusk and seated them at one of the long tables close to the rear wall. A row of braziers down the center of the room were now fully ignited, and torches along the walls chased away any straggling shadow. Josalynn and Backus were already in place at the Commandant's table, and they nodded to the group as they sat down. The other tables were partially filled with scattered groupings of soldiers, some hundred and fifty men, representing a large portion of Bastion's garrison. The remainder were on duty on the walls or at the upper citadel. A few hundred men were all that was staffing a fortress that could house thousands. Laborers were now carrying in food from the kitchens and placing it upon the tables. Wonderful aromas arose from the fresh meat and vegetables brought in from the farms on the lake's northern shore, and clean, fresh water from the headwaters of the Euhr was presented in large pitchers alongside flagons of ale. It was a meal far beyond what was to be expected at a strictly military facility.

When all the food was placed and the laborers had retired, Josalynn stood up behind her table. She had traded her armor for cotton clothing that seemed too informal for someone of her station, and her hair remained braided and draped over her shoulder, resting upon her breast. She raised a pewter goblet and the room fell silent.

"Another day past, another night the people of Amalgam will be safe."

She lifted the goblet slightly higher and then took a long draught before sitting down again. Vessels rose up around the room accompanied by cheers of "Hear, hear!" Then hands shot forward to fill plates with food, and it was clear that the evening meal had begun. The Riisgardians were not shy about joining in, and were soon stuffing themselves with all the table had to offer.

"So Enoch," Hutta said as he took a bite from a chicken leg, "your mission is complete. What will you do now?"

"I will rest here for a day," Enoch replied, "but then I must return to Magna."

"You don't want to stay and fight the good fight?" Fuster asked.

"Amalgam is not the only world with conflict, as you well know. And it's certainly not the only one that needs men willing to defend it. The Cult may not have reached Magna, but there are battles to be fought all the same."

"Well, we owe you our gratitude," Hutta said, "you offered guidance through our displacement, and led us to new purpose. And that deserves its own toast." He raised his tankard to Enoch and was joined wholeheartedly by Fuster, with Webb adding in a reluctant clink of his cup.

Enoch raised his cup in answer. "Thank you. I'm glad I could help, and I'm happy to have met you all. Best of luck to you in the coming days."

"Eagle watch over you, and us," Hutta said before draining his tankard.

"So what's with you and Backus?" Fuster asked. "There seemed to be some tension there when we were outside."

Andor began to laugh and Enoch waited for him to finish chuckling before explaining.

"Backus was my first interaction with a member of a beast race. I may have made some...inconsiderate remarks before I accepted the fact that they are really no different than the rest of us. He has never really forgiven me for my transgression."

"He loves to hate you," Andor added with more chuckling. "I think it's fun for him. You really should come around more often, I'd love to watch you two quibble."

"I'm sure you would. But if that's the case, I'd rather not give the old boar the satisfaction."

"What can we expect when we report to him tomorrow?" Hutta asked.

"He'll give you assignments based on where he thinks your strengths will be most valuable, at least in the short term," Andor answered. "And assign you a training schedule."

"A training schedule?" Webb asked with derisiveness.

"Yes. We all follow one. Keeping our skills sharp and our bodies fit is just as important as maintaining this fortress."

"Sounds good to me," Hutta said. "But we'll all be eager to put those skills to use on some Cultists."

"That'll be sooner rather than later, don't worry." Andor assured him.

At this the Riisgardians clinked their cups together once more, elated at the prospect of whatever blow they could deal to their enemy. For the rest of the meal they talked and laughed, regaling each other with stories and enjoying this precious moment of camaraderie before the morning would set them to work, and bring them closer to a horizon they were certain would have its share of hardship. When the meal was finished Josalynn stopped at their table on her way out, reminding them to report in first thing in the morning. They thanked her for the meal and bid her goodnight, assuring her they would be ready to do whatever was needed come daybreak.

When they retired they found that the bunkrooms were not crowded, and it was easy to find space away from already occupied beds. There were men and women of diverse appearances throughout the citadel, and a smattering of elves, dwarves, and bestial folk. Their chosen room was one of the least populated, and they made some short and casual introductions before settling in. Enoch chose to remain with them for the night, and Andor returned to his private room upstairs. The Riisgardians drifted to sleep, not knowing what the next day would bring, but excited to have a break from wandering, and to join a cause that was so close to home, even if home was a world away.

CHAPTER EIGHT
An Education in Magic

Eshwar reached the top of the stairs and stepped past the steward into a room that filled the tower's top floor. Kelm followed closely behind, and when both were past the threshold the steward closed a rough wooden door behind them. The windows all around were shuttered, allowing only sharp shafts of bright light to penetrate inside. Above them rose the rafters and beams of the tower's conical roof, from which hung all sorts of random trinkets and baubles. Among these were a series of glowing orbs suspended at various heights that assured the room was adequately and comfortably lit. Bookshelves and tables lined the walls, and what space was left was so plastered with diagrams, pictures, and knick-knacks that there was hardly a brick to be seen. Almost every surface around the room was overflowing with books and loose papers, with the exception of a desk in the center, which in stark contrast to its surroundings was neatly organized and free of anything that might be deemed superfluous. The companions were hesitant to step any farther into the room, fearing they might trip over a stray scroll or damage some clumsily placed apparatus.

"Come come," said a voice from deeper inside, "don't be shy, gentlemen."

The steward stepped forward, and in a dry tone, as if he were annoyed by the ceremony of introducing his master, said, "Marek Hague, Archmage of Taikanìk, Chancellor of the Empyrean Magehold, Curator of Metamagia."

Before them stood an elderly man leaning on a smooth wooden staff. He wore a very simple brown robe, cinched at the waist with a wide leather belt. Thick and wiry white hair fell far past his shoulders, and his tapered beard was so long that he had it tucked into the belt with plenty of slack left above to move his head about without tugging it. His mouth was locked into a kindly smile, and round spectacles magnified his bright, youthful eyes. He also could not have been much more than five feet tall even if he had been standing upright; both Kelm and Eshwar were already slightly looking down at him despite the distance that remained between them. The man was studying them now much as his steward had done, but with soft and kind eyes free of judgment and wariness.

The steward pushed his way between the visitors and looked across the room toward a chair on the far side. In an instant he was standing before it, and slumped himself down and propped up his feet, opening a book from a table at its side.

"Oh William," said the archmage in a huff, "do you have to blink across the room? A little walking is good for you, don't you know."

The steward simply shrugged without looking up from his book.

"I apologize for old Bill there," Hague said to his visitors. "He pays little heed to social graces, but he does an excellent job of protecting my privacy from undesirable guests, present company excluded of course. Now, who might you gentlemen be and to what do I owe the pleasure?"

"My name is Eshwar Strand, from the Fentower Academy on Agrafell." Kelm's ears perked up at Eshwar's words. It was the first time he had mentioned the name of his home world.

"Fentower! You must be one of Delwyn Leverich's students then."

"Yes. He sent me through the portal and told me to find the Magehold. The academy has been sacked by the Cult of Primzahl. I'm afraid there were many casualties."

The archmage's smile fell into a frown and his eyes dimmed slightly. "And Delwyn?"

"Alive," said Eshwar. "He remained behind to help the resistance efforts."

"That is good news, at least," Hague said. "Espousing their ridiculous beliefs is one thing, but if the Cult has resorted to open violence on a world so steeped in magic as Agrafell, I believe they will encounter much more resistance than they bargained for. Did Delwyn send you to me simply to deliver these tidings?"

"Well, uh, no," Eshwar replied, "he actually didn't mention you to me. I was the most junior student at Fentower, and with no real skills yet, he sent me here to continue studying rather than stay and fight with my more experienced comrades. An innkeeper in Deltaville told me to seek out the Chancellor of the Magehold, and we actually attempted to gain entry to the first tower we came to before we were given your name."

"Ah!" Hague exclaimed. "Tried to pay a visit to old Cirroc, did you? He hardly ever let's anyone inside that phallic monstrosity he calls a tower." The archmage lowered his voice to a false whisper and placed a thumb and forefinger close together. "Personally, I think he's compensating for something," he giggled, then returned to his normal speaking voice. "Still, he's the best enchanter I've ever seen, which has afforded him his lavish lifestyle. Even I've purchased one of his automatons." He pointed across the room to where one of the sentry armors from Velhonìk was hanging haphazardly from strings attached to the roof beams. The fingers of its gauntlets hung limply and there was no sign of its blue life force. "I find I like it better as an art piece. Less creepy. But wouldn't you know, I'm digressing. You said you've come to study? In which area?"

"I don't exactly know, I've only learned some basic spells. Master Leverich told me I wasn't inclined toward any one discipline and was free to choose anything I fancied. I can tell you I'm interested in that thing he does," Eshwar pointed to Bill.

The archmage stood up straight and his eyes returned to their initial bright beam, "Free to choose? My boy! To be a *tabula rasa* of magic is a rare gift! As for Bill's teleportation, 'blinking' as we call it, it is easy enough to learn, though it makes most people horribly ill, wouldn't you know. If your stomach can handle it, I'll have him teach you (Bill rolled his eyes). But the entire Magehold is open to you!"

"I'm not sure I'd know where to begin," Eshwar rubbed his head.

"Well, each of the five cities of the Magehold is dedicated to a category of magical practice: enchanting, alchemy, sorcery, conjuration, and metamagical studies. With cross-disciplines and miscellany scattered throughout."

"Metamagical studies?"

"Yes! My area of expertise!" The archmage began to bound across the room with a light and spry step, carrying the staff across his shoulder without using it for any kind of support. He stopped and began to lean on it once more when he reached the organized desk in the center. There he pulled a book from a stack and opened it to a marked page. "You see…," he began, but then seemed to become aware of a presence which he had forgotten. He turned and, looking at Kelm, said, "I'm sorry, my boy, but what kind of magic did you say you practiced? You have a strange aura about you."

"Me?" Kelm asked. "I'm no mage. Eshwar and I came through the portal at the same time, and I agreed to escort him here while my compatriots traveled to Bastion."

"You have no magical abilities?" Hague asked with a squint.

"No," Kelm replied. "On my homeworld I'm what's known as *verdyfir.* It literally means 'one who has been passed over.' My parents were both shaman, but I did not inherit their gifts. To be honest it's the only reason I'm still alive."

"How do you mean?" the archmage continued to pry.

Kelm breathed out a long sigh, then spoke, "About eight years ago, on Riisgard at any rate, the Cult came to my clan's village and rounded up all the magically inclined, about half of us, including both my parents. They locked them inside and burned everything to the ground, claiming that it was an unholy site. My friends and family, and my home, were the first casualties of their eradication efforts. Me being *verdyfir* is the only reason I was spared. They told me I was lucky." He looked at Eshwar and forced a grin despite the sadness in his eyes, "'For Primzahl is a merciful master.' I was seventeen years old at the time; it was the year I would have come of age and been assigned a role in the clan, given I wouldn't be following my parents as a shaman. Instead I found myself wandering through Lovik without a home or a purpose. I met Hutta soon after, and I've been a sellsword ever since."

"Kelm, I'm so sorry," Eshwar said.

Kelm smiled weakly and nodded in gratitude.

"A heartbreaking tale, to be sure," Hague said, "but do not be quick to write off your potential. Magic works differently all across the multiverse, and now that you're here on Amalgam you may discover things about yourself you never thought possible, especially in times of great clarity...or dire need." He paused, and then looked back at the desk and the open book. "Ah! And this brings me back to where I was headed, metamagia! So you see, Amalgam, and your homeworlds, and all other worlds we know of for that matter, are universes completely separated from one another but for one thing: the portal. The portal connects these worlds together, and Amalgam seems to be the hub of multiversal travel. The first time one passes through it, they will always end up here, and unless they learn the art of voidwalking, then passing back through will always lead them home. Now some of these worlds are small and finite, like Amalgam — you'll notice the distinct lack of celestial bodies — while others are vast and may themselves be infinite. Some have pantheons of deities both powerful and meek, others have but a single god, and others have none at all. And a similar statement can be made about magic and its various forms; in some cases it doesn't even exist, on some worlds mages draw their power from ley lines, some from different energies, others from divine sources, and some worlds, like here, are simply saturated with magic. This can, of course, cause problems for the voidwalking wizard; for example: if a ley mage were to enter a world without ley lines, he would find himself stripped of his abilities. It has happened to many who come to Amalgam, and sometimes it is impossible to rewire one's self to accept a different form of power. Oh, I could babble on for hours! But let me show you this."

From beside the book he picked up a small metallic pyramid intersected by a crystalline sphere. He began to shake it violently, and shafts of light shot forth from the sphere but fizzled out again almost instantly. He tried for a few more moments before going so far as to bang the object on the desk in frustration.

"Confound it all! Work you worthless piece of scrap!"

"Did you recharge the micropylonic crystals?" came the steward's voice from behind his book.

"Of course I — oh, wait..."

The archmage opened a small drawer at the base of the pyramid and revealed a vessel filled with tiny crystals. He snapped his fingers above them and sparks of small flame fell from between his fingertips. The crystals began to crackle and glow when touched by the fire, and he closed the drawer and began to shake the object once again. This time patterns of light poured forth like the sun's rays piercing through a cloud. The archmage placed the apparatus back upon the desk, and above his head the patterns coalesced to form a three dimensional map resembling a star chart.

"Ah ha!" he exclaimed. "Excellent!"

"You're welcome," came Bill's dry voice, his gaze never lifting from the tome in his hands.

"Yes...quite," Hague mumbled, then raised his voice in excitement, "This is my multiverse map! It is a catalog of all the worlds we know of so far. Here is Amalgam in the center," he pointed to a large orb floating amid the nebulous patterns of light. "And all around are the others. For some we have only a name, while for others we have documentation of whole histories." He waved his hand through the map, highlighting countless smaller orbs, each with a faint white line leading back toward the one representing Amalgam.

He chose one of these at random and raised a fist to it, then pulled his hand backwards while expanding his fingers out. The patterns shifted rapidly and the orbs disappeared, leaving the one he had chosen alone and magnified. Beneath it appeared script in a language Kelm and Eshwar could not read, and with a flick of the archmage's hand the words shot upwards, disappearing beneath the orb as more filled in from below. With every flick more lines of text came and went, as if he were cycling through a vast scroll. He then pinched all his fingers onto his thumb, and with another rapid shift of patterns the orb was returned to its initial size and resting amongst its brethren.

"You," the archmage said, turning again to Kelm, "Kevin, was it?"

"Kelm."

"Quite right. Where did you say you were from?"

"Riisgard."

"I've never heard of it." The archmage looked up into the map, and pointing with his forefinger he snapped his thumb and middle finger, and a new orb appeared at his fingertip. "How do you spell that?" Kelm told him, and with a flourish of his finger they could see a tiny line of script appear beneath the orb before fading away. "You will have to tell me all about it sometime." With that he passed his hand over the sphere, and the light faded away, leaving the air above the desk empty once more.

"You know a list on paper would have sufficed," Bill said.

Hague turned about briskly to face his steward. "And wouldn't have had nearly as much pizazz," he retorted. "A wizard is entitled to a little flair, don't you know." He returned his attention to his guests, "Anyway, Amalgam presents us with a unique opportunity to study the multiverse and the portal, but there is much more to metamagia than just that. Most of the field deals with where magic comes from and how it functions, the study of ley lines, mystical energies, and the like. It's not the stuff most people would consider 'fun', but it is certainly important."

"How did you come to study it?" Eshwar asked.

"It stems from my youth," the archmage replied, "I'm half dwarf, wouldn't you know. My father was very disappointed when he found out about my affinity for magic. He, of course, wanted me to be a craftsman. A very one-dimensional people, dwarves. But I would have none of it. I had my nose buried in books and scrolls, and my eyes pointed to the glint of the stars while most of my family had theirs enthralled by the shine of gemstones. Still, I wanted to appease my father somewhat, as young boys are wont to do, and when I discovered metamagia I figured it would set his mind at ease. If I wouldn't be an engineer or an artisan, I thought at least if I studied the 'science' of magic that I wouldn't be such a disappointment. It helped, to be sure, but he could never truly accept my path. As it turned out, I fell in love with the subject, and obviously I have gone very far with it, or else you would have found someone else entirely in this tower, if you had come to it at all."

"To be leader of a place like the Magehold is certainly impressive," Kelm said.

"Oh, the chancellorship is a load of hogwash!" Hague said. "It's just a way for the other archmages to shirk the responsibility of running a nation so they can focus on magic. 'Greatest honor in the Magehold.' My fanny! I can't wait until my term is up and I can vote my duties onto the next poor sap. I really should find a way to make Cirroc have to do it. He's been bribing the others not to vote for him for years, so he can sit in that high tower and have his automatons pour him wine and feed him grapes, but he'll find I have a few tricks up my sleeves come the next election. Ah well, at least I have sour old Bill there to help deter most of the political intruders who come calling."

"You do realize I'm probably a tenth of your age," Bill quipped.

"Maybe less even," said Hague, "but you act double it! But I do suppose that's why I keep you around." The archmage shot his visitors a wink while Bill rolled his eyes. "Well Eshwar," he continued, "I think the best course of action for you is to spend some time here. Bill can teach you to blink, and I can impart some basics of metamagia. After that I would send you down to Loitsunìk to learn some sorcery."

"That sounds like a good plan to me," Eshwar smiled.

"And you, my boy," Hague said to Kelm, "you said your friends traveled to Bastion? Will you be joining them there?"

"I will," Kelm replied. "Though I wish I myself could stay and learn from you, I need to go to them." He turned to Eshwar, "For one thing I need to know what this 'Heart of the World' business is all about."

Hague's eyes narrowed and he leaned forward forcefully against his staff. Even Bill stirred and shot Kelm a glance over the top of his book.

"What did you just say?" asked the archmage.

"Oh," Kelm replied, "the Heart of the World. We met a traveling companion back in Artesia who was on his way to Bastion to meet a friend who had sent him a summons. In it the friend mentioned that the Cult

117

was bolstering their war efforts against Bastion because they're after something called the Heart of the World. My compatriots and I are going to help make sure they don't get it…whatever it is."

The bright light of Hague's eyes turned to fear as he sighed with his entire body. His voice became low and serious, and he spoke slowly, though each word was preceded by frantic thought, "My boy, you must make haste. Bill will see you are bathed and fed, and will find you a place to sleep tonight, but come the dawn you must make for Bastion with all speed. We will provide you with a steed, and word will be sent ahead to Loitsunìk to have provisions ready for you to pick up. William, find some of those political lackeys I so loathe and have them deliver messages to the others, we are to meet at the Stone in seven day's time. And tell them that if any of them don't make it, you will be personally blinking them there. Retching out their innards should be the least of their concerns."

Bill made no argument and offered no acknowledgment, but closed his book and placed it back on the table. He stood, and in an instant was behind Kelm and Eshwar and headed out the door to carry out the chancellor's commands.

"I'm sorry," said Kelm, visibly confused, "but what did I say? This Heart is important enough to warrant a response like this?"

Hague was staring up at the trinkets hanging from the beams above, slowly rotating around in a seemingly absentminded stupor, but his mind was racing through scenarios and possible futures. "It would take hours to tell the full story," he said after a moment, "and I'm sure you will hear it when you reach your destination. But suffice it to say, the last time the Heart was tampered with it caused a cataclysm which changed the face of Amalgam forever. If the Cult were to reach it I fear history would repeat itself. We're talking about world-ending levels of damage, don't you know. But even more so I would fear something new. If they somehow were able to harness it, then who knows what havoc they could wreak. They cannot be allowed to even make the attempt. The commandant of Bastion already knows how dire these stakes are, but they will need every sword they can muster, so go quickly, and carry with you the message that I will do everything in my power to send more help."

"Perhaps I should go with him," Eshwar said, "and offer what I can."

The archmage snapped his gaze down from the rafters and onto Eshwar, "No. I plan on teaching you as much as possible in as short a time as is feasible. Tomorrow we will see how you do with blinking. If by chance you can handle it then it will prove an invaluable asset not only to your studies, but to battle. Then it's off to the black tower to study with the battle-mages. I'm afraid the finer magics will have to wait until this threat is dealt with."

Eshwar nodded. If he could not be useful right away, he was at least grateful that the chancellor had a plan to make him so.

"Now go," Hague said. "Rest tonight, for neither of you will find any come morning. I will see you both then, but for now I must be left to gather my thoughts."

Kelm and Eshwar took their leave, and with heavy footsteps and a newfound weight upon their shoulders descended the long staircase to the base of the tower.

#

They found Bill outside concluding a conversation with two men, who walked off briskly in different directions as soon as he finished speaking. He beckoned to the companions, and led them inside a low building below the southwestern slope. It was unoccupied, but furnished with a bed, desk, dining table, and stocked bookshelves, and a healthy fire was crackling in the hearth.

"There's only one bed, sorry," Bill said. "I'm going to send someone with an evening meal for you soon. In the meantime, you can bathe and rest. Do you know how to heat water?" he asked Eshwar.

"You mean with magic?" Eshwar asked.

"No, with a tea kettle," Bill said. "Of course with magic."

Eshwar frowned at the sour man. "Yes, I can handle that."

"Good. There's a basin already filled in the basement. Meet me out at the stables in the morning and I'll get him his horse, and then we'll see if your stomach can handle blinking. I doubt we'll get anywhere, but at least I'll get to watch you lose your guts a few times before you give up. Good evening to you." Bill walked outside and left them alone.

"That is one unpleasant fellow," Eshwar said after the door had closed.

"He reminds me of a smart version of Webb," Kelm added. "What a terrible combination. Well, I guess we should bathe."

"You can go first. I'll heat the water for you."

They descended a short flight of stairs against the right hand wall and found themselves in a basement with a low ceiling. The floor and walls were carved out from the mountain stone, with a few cavities filled in by brick and mortar. A few storage containers were scattered around the room, and close to the rear wall was a stone tub filled with water. They walked over to it, and Eshwar leaned over and placed his hands on the surface. For a few moments he stood there, barely moving, and then slowly steam began to rise from the water. He stood back up and wiped his hands on a nearby towel.

"That should be good, I think," he said, and returned to the main room above. There he sat in one of the dining chairs and watched the dance of the fire while letting his mind be consumed by thought.

Kelm undressed and lowered himself into the water. He closed his eyes and let out a long sigh as the heat relieved his aching muscles. After a few all too brief minutes of relaxation he began to scrub himself down with a bar of soap, a luxury he had rarely had the pleasure of enjoying in recent years. He stayed in until the water had gone lukewarm, and then dried himself and redressed in his linens, which were already yellowing from sweat and oil. Back upstairs he tossed his armor and weapons in a heap against the far wall, and wrapped himself in his cloak against the slight chill which the fire had failed to chase away.

"Thank you Eshwar," he said. "It's all yours now.

Eshwar continued to stare at the fire, rubbing and squeezing his chin with one hand. For several moments he made no move to get up.

"Eshwar? The bath is all yours," Kelm repeated.

"Oh," Eshwar said, coming out of his trance. "Yes, thanks."

He rose and went to the basement while Kelm plopped down onto the bed. Eshwar was not downstairs long when he returned wrapped in a towel, with another draped over his head. He laid his clothes neatly near Kelm's pile, and then sat back down in his chair. Presently a knock came at the door, and in walked a man carrying a tray filled with their dinner. There was fresh bread, large roasted mushrooms, and barbecued leg of goat. The aroma was wonderful, and both of them dug in voraciously until nothing remained. Afterward Kelm added more wood to the fire and then laid down on an area rug before the hearth, rubbing his content stomach.

In a few moments Eshwar, himself leaned far back in his chair, broke the silence. "Kelm, what do you make of all this?"

Kelm sat up and looked at him. "Honestly I have no idea what to think. A fortnight ago I didn't even know this world existed, or any but mine for that matter. Now, from the way Hague talked, I'm about to find myself caught up in a war for that very existence. It's all rather overwhelming."

"Agreed. I can't help thinking of home though. Why would the Cult attack Fentower if they're already planning a war here? It seems premature."

"Maybe it is. Perhaps they're overconfident in their plan and thought they could begin attempting to subjugate your world. Or they could have seen your academy as an imminent threat that was likely to send reinforcements through the portal."

"Maybe. It hurts my head thinking of all the possibilities."

"Then we shouldn't. If this is truly the hub of the multiverse then the important thing is to stop them here if we can, then worry about our homes. And I'm sure your head will hurt plenty from the crash courses Hague has planned for you."

"No doubt. Let us rest now while we can. You can have the bed tonight. I'm sure I'll get plenty of nights with a bed while I'm here, but who knows when you'll see one again."

"Thank you, my friend."

Kelm returned to the bed and Eshwar took his place on the rug, wrapping himself up in his cloak and the towels. They slept peacefully despite the news of the day, and arose before dawn. When they found the stables nearby, Bill already had a horse saddled and tacked for Kelm, and the chancellor was waiting patiently nearby. Bill helped Kelm up into the saddle and handed him the reins.

"This is Tallow," he said, running his hand over the horse's cream colored hair. "He'll get you down the mountain easy enough, but on open ground is where he'll really shine. Don't be afraid to ride hard. He should easily carry you twenty leagues a day, maybe more, and you've got roughly two hundred and twenty leagues to travel."

"And haste is of the utmost importance," Hague said as he stepped forward. "They already know to expect you in Loitsunìk, where there will be enough supplies waiting for the entirety of your journey. By the time you reach Bastion the council of archmages should have already met, and news of our aid, or lack thereof, should follow soon behind you. I'm afraid I can make no promises. Wizards can be a stubborn and complacent bunch, but I will do my best. Good luck to you, my boy."

"Good luck, Kelm," said Eshwar. "I hope we meet again."

"As do I," Kelm replied. "May Owl guide you in your training."

"Well I don't know what that means," Hague said, "but rest assured we will be cramming his head full of spells in the coming weeks. Now be off!"

Kelm spurred Tallow on, and the horse made quickly for the road with almost no direction from his rider. Together they disappeared over the crest of the mountain and down the first of the many switchbacks to come. Hague wrapped an arm around Eshwar and began to lead him back toward the tower, with Bill following behind.

"Now, my boy," Hague said, "let's see if we can't teach you a little magic.

CHAPTER NINE
An Education in History

A blue-crested pigeon with a small scroll strapped to its leg took off into the skies over Bastion. Seconds before it had been perched on Fuster's hand, and now it was rising over the mountains and flying south, its message containing a list of sundries meant for a contact in Deltaville. Fuster was standing atop the turret of the lower citadel with Backus at his side. High above them was a ceiling of brown stone, the underside of the outcropping that shaded the entire structure. Periodically they wiped water from their faces as mist from the cascades of the Euhr found its way beneath the protrusion.

On their first morning in Bastion Backus had interviewed each of them briefly and then assigned them duties. Fuster was to help care for the animals: the few horses in the stables and the birds in the aerie near the top of the turret. Webb had been passed off to Zurofel, a stout dwarf who served as siegemaster, who in turn assigned him to stock the munitions batteries along the Bulwark, the fortress's outer walls, and help maintain the trebuchets. Hutta was now somewhere patrolling the citadel, having been relegated to guard duty. They had each also already had one afternoon of training in the yards, followed by a morning off to rest. Every night they had attended the evening meal, and every night Josalynn had repeated her toast, and they joined with the other soldiers in the response.

Presently Fuster leaned against the battlements and looked down to the ground. Josalynn was walking across the yard with her hands clasped behind her back, inspecting those currently training. Even with her far below him, Fuster felt the confidence and command of her presence.

"She's really something," he mused.

"She's your commanding officer," Backus said.

"Come on, Backus, even you have to admit she's gorgeous."

"To a human maybe, but she doesn't have enough hair for my tastes."

At this Fuster smiled.

"Besides," Backus continued, "you shouldn't get your hopes up, and not only because she's your superior."

"What do you mean?"

"The Willet girls do not marry, nor do they even mate for very long. They breed, when they deem it necessary, in order to produce their successor."

"What happens if they have sons?"

"Sons are given to the father."

"And that's it? None have ever tried to claim the fortress as their birthright?"

"Not to my knowledge. But I've only been here since the time of Josalynn's mother, Beatrice. The maintenance of their bloodline is one of the few things that can be described as a 'personal life,' and I tend not to ask about other people's breeding habits."

They were interrupted by a man running up the stairs and out onto the top of the turret. He rushed up to them and greeted Backus with a salute.

"Warden Backus," he said, "the scouts have spotted a rider approaching. We assume it is the other Riisgardian."

"It seems your friend has arrived, Fuster. And quickly; the report from the South Maw that he had entered the valley arrived only just last night. Let us go to greet him."

With one last look out into the valley they saw a horse and rider galloping down the road toward the gates. By the time they emerged at ground level, Kelm had already dismounted and Tallow was resting comfortably in the stables, his tack hanging on the wall nearby. It had taken around nine days of hard riding from Taikanìk, with some hours spent sleeping in the saddle, but Kelm had made the journey across the continent with incredible haste. Fuster locked him in an embrace, and Hutta appeared from around the corner of the citadel and joined in. A whistle came from up on the Bulwark, and Kelm looked up to see Webb waving from one of the batteries. He saluted with two raps to the breast and then returned the wave. He turned back to Hutta and grabbed him by the shoulders.

"Boss, I told the Chancellor of the Magehold about the Cult and the Heart. He made the situation sound quite dire, but he may be able to send help. I passed Enoch on the road, but he wasn't able to tell me much. What have you found —"

"Well, this confirms that the time for secrecy has passed." Josalynn had appeared behind them, with Andor at her side. She did not acknowledge Kelm, but stepped around them and continued on toward the citadel. "Backus," she continued as she walked, "fetch Zurofel and meet me in the war room. We have plans to discuss."

Backus moved off toward one of the stairways up the inner wall, and Hutta turned back to Kelm.

"We've learned almost nothing at all," he said. "That was the Commandant. She hasn't decided yet if she wants to trust us."

"I need to speak with her," Kelm said, "the chancellor bid me do so."

He tried to move forward but Hutta placed a hand on his chest.

"She's not the type to be followed uninvited," he said.

"Josalynn." Andor grabbed her arm just before she moved inside the great hall. She turned around and stared at his hand. He pulled it away quickly but continued to speak. "Let the Riisgardians come. They have more experience with the Cult than some of our own soldiers. There's only four of us commanding this entire fortress. We need a larger upper echelon; more minds with more ideas."

She thought for a long moment, her face expressionless, but eventually she nodded and then entered the citadel. Andor turned around and waved to the Riisgardians, beckoning them to follow. Hutta looked up to the top of the wall and let out a whistle, and then waved Webb down when he had his attention. They caught up with Andor and followed him inside. The war room was centered against the western wall on an upper level of the citadel. A large window with iron mullions supporting the glass looked out upon the valley, before which Josalynn now stood. The center of the room was dominated by a square table, painted with a detailed map of Amalgam, and oriented roughly with the actual cardinal directions of the world. Kelm took the time to show his friends where he had been in the Magehold while they waited for Backus and Zurofel, who arrived a few minutes later. The eight of them gathered around the table, with Josalynn hovering close to the northwest corner, between the depictions of Bastion and the Cult's territory.

"I have gathered you here to discuss new tidings that have come to my attention," she began. "The newcomers are here at Andor's request. Do not presume to think this is a complete show of trust on my part, but perhaps you can offer some insight. At any rate, it is time to openly discuss the situation, especially since your friend here has informed Chancellor Hague of our plight. The Cultists have nearly finished mustering their army. I have no doubt they will march on us soon in an attempt to claim the Heart. It is —"

"Begging your pardon, ma'am," Hutta interrupted, "but we need to know what the Heart actually *is*. Why is it so important? What are the stakes?"

For a moment she glared at him, but soon softened, "Very well. You are new here. Allow me to educate you. When you arrived on Amalgam, you were in what we call the Wastes, a harsh and dangerous land that no one would care to enter if not for Artesia. But it was not always so. The lands surrounding the city used to be verdant and full of life. The river ran both north and south, and lush forests and golden fields stretched between multiple villages all around the city. Until the Sundering. The Heart of the World sat on an island in the northern arm of the river, which ran like an artery across the entire continent. Then the gods had to go and mess with it. They—"

"Gods?" Kelm asked.

"Yes. I suppose I should cover that first. Amalgam was created by an entity the Leerwandish named the Uberwesen, though it's claimed no mortal has ever seen It. It supposedly resides here," she pointed to the image of a mountainous island on the table, centered in the northern ocean, "but no expedition to the island has ever been successful.

"The Uberwesen created two others: Heil, supposedly a manifestation of goodness, and Unheil, a manifestation of evil. They were set upon each other, locked into endless combat across Amalgam. They in turn created their own armies of celestial beings, angels and demons, if you would. They had already been battling each other for untold ages before mortals settled this world, and our presence made no difference. No matter how many people pointlessly lost their lives, how many cities burned, how many mountains were leveled, They kept fighting, ignorant of the destruction They caused. Until the Sundering.

"It seems that even gods grow restless, and Heil and Unheil finally grew bored with their repetitive squabbling, and desiring the power to decide their own fate, They tried to claim the Heart of the World. They fought over it, each wanting it for themselves, and when They touched it the ground is said to have opened up, revealing an infinite nothingness. It raised these very mountains as it widened, peeling back the land like rind from a fruit. The kingdom of Norstead was completely destroyed in the cataclysm, and even Artesia was razed. Only the pyramid survived. The rest had to be rebuilt, and I doubt the land will ever be green again. It is said that the Uberwesen prevented the ultimate destruction of Amalgam, but much of the devastation was left as a reminder to the gods that the Heart was not to be tampered with. Ever since, They've continued fighting just like They always had.

"Soon after, Devonna founded this stronghold for a dual purpose. We contain the celestials, corralling them as best we can in order to keep the rest of Amalgam from burning in their wake. If they were to mount a full attack, there is likely little we could do, but they tend to only pay attention to their counterparts, and if we give them a prick here and a prod there when they stray too close then they are perfectly content to continue fighting within the mountains. And, we prevent others from entering their battleground, mostly the ignorant and the foolhardy, but presently, those who would not learn from the mistakes of the past.

The room was silent for a long time while the newcomers, as well as Andor, absorbed the information, but Kelm broke in with more questions.

"Is the Cult aware of this history?" he asked.

"Most certainly," Josalynn answered.

"Then how can they be so reckless? What makes them think they can harness it? Or do they just want to blow up the world?"

"They are arrogant," Josalynn said. "And deluded. They believe Primzahl is omnipresent, even throughout the multiverse. They would claim the Heart in His honor and expect no negative consequence. For them anyway. Now, have you brought any news from Hague?"

"Very little. He bid me tell you that he would try to send help, but that he could make no promises. The archmages were to meet seven days from my departure, so hopefully news will arrive soon."

"More mages would be a huge boon," Backus offered. "We have less than a hundred in our ranks."

"The problem is that Hague will have to convince his colleagues," Josalynn said. "The chancellor can take no real action on his own."

Zurofel was standing at the east end of the table stroking his surprisingly beardless chin. "How large of an army has the enemy raised?" he asked.

"The report I just received puts their numbers between one thousand to fifteen hundred," Josalynn answered. "Less than three to one odds."

"You make it sound so trivial," Zurofel said.

"The Bulwark has never been breached," she said.

"We've also never been this understaffed," the dwarf retorted. "The last time the lower citadel was sieged there were four times the men to defend it than the number we have spread across the entire fortress."

"Do you have an actual suggestion, Zur?"

"We should solicit any help we can get, that's all. We can't fall victim to overconfidence."

"Where are they assembling?" Hutta asked. "Is there any opportunity for a preemptive strike?"

Josalynn shook her head. "The Cult has three cities in its domain. Prophet's Gate is closest to us, and straddles the Euhr. Here. (She pointed to the map as she spoke.) But the army is amassing at Penitent's Rest Here, near the center of their territory. Any sizable force would lose the element of surprise long before reaching it, and a small force wouldn't be able to make any difference in the odds."

Hutta nodded. "Cities you say? Just how many of them live here?"

"Thousands," she answered. "They have been here for nearly three hundred years. At first they settled peacefully, and were treated like any other nation. Prophet's Gate was once a major trading hub. Many of Bastion's supplies passed through it. But eventually the Cult showed its true nature. They were shunned, and became isolated from the rest of us. For the most part only messengers and evangelists venture out now. Prophet's Gate is now little more than a front, a decaying and empty husk masked by propaganda of righteousness and opportunity. Penitent's Rest houses soldiers and the slaves that work their farms. And Cardinal's Point, here, is the home of their elite, and the Cathedral of Primzahl."

"So they're not from Amalgam, either," said Fuster.

"No," Josalynn confirmed. "Their homeworld is a closely guarded secret. None of our spies, or anyone else's, have been able to learn so much as its name."

"If they are so isolated on Amalgam, then how do they deliver armies to world's like ours?" Hutta asked.

"They teach their soldiers how to voidwalk," Backus answered.

"Hague mentioned that," Kelm said, "It let's you pass to world's other than your own...but only if you visit Amalgam first."

"Not exactly," Backus said. "An untrained individual will always end up on Amalgam, that is true, but you don't have to come here first before learning to voidwalk. The Cult now trains its troops in the art on other worlds. The soldiers can go where instructed having never set foot in the Artesian pyramid."

"Fantastic," Webb grunted.

"Fortunately it has kept their military forces here small," Josalynn added. "Having to use Amalgam as a staging ground would incite open war with the entire world. Something they're not willing to risk."

"It might have been better if they had," Kelm said. "Their propagation might have been halted if their travel was more limited."

"Perhaps," Josalynn said, "but might-have-beens are immaterial to our present situation. The spies have been recalled. We must wait for their arrival and final reports. We should have a month or so before the enemy can mobilize."

"Seems like a long time," Hutta questioned. "I thought you said they were nearly finished mustering?"

"Mustering, yes," Josalynn responded. "But they have not outfitted such a force on Amalgam before. They have few craftsmen of their own, and only black marketeers will trade with them, and you can rest assured we have done our part to disrupt their shipments. Their vanity will drive them to make their soldiers appear as stately as they are effective, which buys us time."

"Preparations on my end are complete, as usual," Zurofel said. "The trebuchets and ballistae are in peak operating condition, and the walls are as strong as ever. My only suggestion would be to collect more harvest from the farms before they are abandoned for the siege, but our storerooms are well-supplied regardless."

"I have no doubt everything is in order, siegemaster," Josalynn said. "For now we are playing a waiting game, until we have our final intelligence, and word from the Magehold. Kelm: in the meantime, you will be given assignment by Backus. The rest of you will remain at your current posts, except for Hutta. Andor advises that we need a more robust command structure, and you are the leader of your little band, I'm told, so I'm willing to test you with a little responsibility. You shall be elevated to a captaincy in the guard. Backus can brief you, and will still be your commanding officer."

Hutta nodded.

"Just remember," she continued, "I can just as easily strip you of the title and position should I find your performance less than adequate."

"Understood ma'am," Hutta saluted her with a rap on his breast.

"Do we have anything to fear from the gods?" Kelm asked.

"Doubtful," the commandant answered. "The upper citadel is always on alert for celestial activity, but as I said, they only pay attention to each other, and are largely oblivious to anything else. Andor has been at the ready and will continue to be vigilant, but I think it's safe to say he'll be with us against the Cult."

"That is my hope," Andor said. "I've noticed no change in pattern recently. Nor have my men. As far as anyone knows Heil and Unheil are always near the Heart, and there have been few stragglers from their armies near the citadel. Life up top is quite boring honestly, but some would say it's better that way."

"It most certainly is," Backus offered. "It's only a shame that your talents aren't being put to use. It's been a long time since the upper citadel had a paladin in charge, or even in the ranks for that matter."

"Talents?" Kelm asked.

Andor smiled. "You could say the supernatural is my specialty. Magnans have a tenuous relationship with gods, at best. Most of ours have been vanquished, but otherworldly threats still exist, and I have long trained to combat them. It's why I was drawn to become part of the conflict with the Cult. If Primzahl is truly a multiversal god then he may be worthy of worship, but if the tenets of the Cult are any indication, then he is a threat beyond anything that anyone has dared to imagine."

"How would you propose fighting a god?" asked Fuster.

"Discovering the Cult's homeworld would be a start," Andor answered. "And then determining if Primzahl is even real. But those are tasks for the future. For now our focus must be on the coming battle. And Heil and Unheil are more present threats than Primzahl. If the need arises, I have a few ideas for them."

"Hopefully the need will not arise," Josalynn said. "The Cult will be enough to deal with."

"Yes," Zurofel concurred, "the more resources we can dedicate to the defense of the walls, the better."

"Agreed," Backus said.

Before any further conversation, there came the sound of heavy footsteps running through the hall, and soon a lone soldier came bursting through the doorway. He was one of the men whom Fuster had been working with caring for the animals, and in his hand he held a scroll sealed with a wax stamp. For a moment the man caught his breath, and then stood erect and saluted the room.

"Commandant," he said, "this message has just arrived." He held it up so that the seal could be clearly seen. "It is from the Magehold."

Kelm's eyes grew wide, and his heart filled with hope that a legion of mages would soon be on its way to Bastion, ready to bring a swift end to a battle that had not even begun. Josalynn, too, was filled with anticipation, though hers was composed as much of fear of disappointment as it was hope. She ordered the soldier to come closer and hand over the scroll, and with a swift swipe of a knife she unsealed the letter. She rolled it out on the table before her, and leaning over it with a hand on either side began to read. Fuster could see her eyes from where he stood, and noted to himself that in the short time he had known her they had never contained such childlike anticipation. But as they scanned they began to return to a more familiar state, a cynical hardness that offered little discernment into her thoughts or character. Then her brow began to furl, and her previously expressionless lips curled downward into a frown as she chewed on the inside of her mouth. When she finished reading she stood up straight again. She picked up the letter, and, looking at Kelm, tossed it toward him across the table. It landed before him and curled back up into a loose, hollow cylinder. He looked down at it, the broken seal of Chancellor Hague staring back up at him from atop the brown parchment.

"No help will come," she said.

CHAPTER TEN
A Moot of Mages

The Lenel Stone stood near the tip of the peninsula that extended southward into the sea from the mountains of the Magehold. It was a thick, bone-colored obelisk carved on all sides with runes and symbols of various origins. Surrounding it were a series of smaller stones leaning at hard angles such that their tips all pointed toward its pinnacle. A stone stage was set in the ground before its northern face, upon which stood a podium, in turn facing toward a stone amphitheatre set into a rise in the land. The seating was arranged in a half circle divided into five wedges of equal size. At the base of each wedge was a throne, directly behind which an aisle led up through the benches to the top of the rise. Eshwar sat in the stands of the outer wedge on the western side of the theatre, which was dedicated to the city of Taikanìk. In the throne below him sat Hague, flipping through some parchment in his lap. The next wedge over was reserved for Kootanìk, the city of conjuration, and in the throne at its base sat an elf with silver hair and a purple robe, not unlike those of the cultists. This was Eledon Coman, Archmage of Kootanìk and Doyen of Conjuration. At the base of the center wedge sat an elderly but fit man with a balding scalp and sharp whiskers, wearing a short black robe and trousers, and a red overtunic. This was Ausar Marlowe, Archmage of Loitsunìk and Prime Sorcerer. Next was a heavyset man with long, curly brown hair that looked as if it hadn't been washed in quite some time, and a bushy beard. He wore a green robe with ornate lapel trim in yellows and browns, open over a more subdued khaki garment. This was Lothar O'Loghlen, Archmage of Juomanìk and Grandmaster Alchemist. Finally, seated at the base of the wedge opposite Hague was a man with dark skin wearing a blue robe and a silver circlet. Cirroc, Archmage of Velhonìk and Dean of Enchanting.

Each archmage was accompanied by a steward who sat or stood in the area immediately behind each throne. Cirroc, however, was attended by one of his automatons, an entity very similar to the sentries outside his tower, but with a much more refined finish and adorned in flowing regalia rather than horned helm. Bill Tallert was also nowhere to be seen. Eshwar looked around at the other observers in the theatre, comprised of administrative staff and particularly interested citizens. His wedge was nearly empty; other than himself only the political lackeys that Bill often curtailed occupied the benches. The others had varying numbers of attendees, with Cirroc's wedge being the fullest, given that Velhonìk wasn't too far away. Looking up and to the north the great tower could easily be seen piercing the sky. To the west and east were the waters of Leben Bay and the ocean, but they could not be seen unless one were standing at the top of the rise, and to the south the land tapered away into a craggy point that marked the eastern extremity of the confluence of the two bodies of water.

It had been seven days since Kelm had left, and now he was riding down the road somewhere, close to his destination but not quite there. It was time for the council to discuss action, but for the moment nothing was happening. The archmages were waiting patiently while Hague studied his papers, and the members of the crowd were murmuring among themselves. Eshwar thought about the days that had passed, and how quickly they had gone. When the chancellor had led him away from the stables he had been treated to a hearty breakfast and briefed on what was to come. Bill was to teach him to blink, and if he took to it he would remain in Taikanìk until he mastered it, otherwise he would be riding straight down to Loitsunìk to train with the elementalists. Fortunately he had taken to it. It took only a few short hours for Bill to impart the technical knowledge required, and then the practical training began. Eshwar violently lost his lunch after teleporting only a few feet, and on the next try he lost his breakfast. Using the spell made him more ill than when he had come through the portal, and he feared his teachers would see him as unfit and call off the training. But they allowed him to keep trying, pumping him full of water to fend off dehydration due to his continuous retching, and with every attempt he traveled farther and his stomach became stronger. For three days he trained, and by the end his innards were unaffected by the jumps and he could follow Bill anywhere he went. The steward regarded him with both resentment and admiration, for the speed with which Eshwar learned was nearly unprecedented. "Truly gifted" Hague had said multiple times when referring to the young newcomer.

On the fourth day Bill took Eshwar down to Loitsunik. It was an odd sensation, standing on a mountaintop at one moment, looking down toward the city and closing his eyes, and standing miles away and below when they opened again. Odd, and magnificently exhilarating. The steward turned him about and pointed back up the mountain, to a patch of road heading up a switchback that could just be made out. It was the safest place to aim for, should he need to make the return trip. The limitation of the spell was that one needed to see their destination, and be able to arrive with firmly planted feet, lest they find themselves bouncing off a wall or plummeting through the air. Once inside the city, Bill had introduced Eshwar to Archmage Marlowe, and then to an elemental professor who would improve his knowledge of fire. When the steward returned two days later to retrieve him, Eshwar had moved far beyond heating bath water. Flames poured freely forth from his outstretched hands, and balls of combustion consistently met their marks on the practice range. For once Bill's usual sardonic expression was replaced with one of awe as he observed the prodigy's progress. That night they met the chancellor in Velhonìk, the trip made significantly shorter when taken in a series of blinks, and a few hours of actual walking with Hague the following morning had brought them here, to the Lenel Stone, and the meeting of the council.

Bill appeared and, rather than taking his proper place behind the throne, sat down beside Eshwar, pulling him out of his reminiscence. Already the man looked bored and perturbed, and he leaned forward and placed his elbows on his thighs, supporting his chin with his thumbs.

"I was really hoping I'd miss some of it," he said.

"Where have you been, anyway?" Eshwar asked.

"Just tying up some loose ends, making sure there weren't any last minute stragglers and whatnot. And," he gave Eshwar a wry grin, "maybe grabbing a little drink while nobody was watching."

Eshwar smiled. The steward was warming up to him, if that was possible.

Presently the chancellor shuffled his papers into a neat bundle and stood up, grabbing his staff from a stand beside his throne, and began to walk toward the podium. He stopped about halfway there when Cirroc let out a loud "ahem."

"Marek," the enchanter said, "let's have some semblance of ceremony, shall we?"

Hague shuffled his feet and mumbled, "Very well." He turned about and walked back toward his chair, and with a tilt of his head toward the podium said, "William."

Bill stood, and the next moment he was behind the podium, some quickly dissipating clouds of purple the only indication that he had been beside Eshwar at all. He turned and addressed the crowd with a projecting voice that would be the envy of any orator, but not untainted by the air of his trademark sarcasm.

"Archmages, distinguished guests, citizens, (he looked toward the automaton next to Cirroc, standing unflinching and lifeless in service to its master) magical constructs! Welcome to this special meeting of the Empyrean Council. It is my pleasure to introduce to you the Archmage of Taikanìk, the Curator of Metamagia, the Chancellor of the Empyrean Magehold, Marek Hague!"

When he finished he widened his eyes and oscillated his outstretched hands in a satirical fanfare, and then turned and stood beside Eshwar once more. Cirroc made no effort to hide an audible sigh and a roll of the eyes, but he held his tongue this time as Hague approached the podium. Lothar was stifling a chuckle, and Marlowe's face underwent a subtle change of expression that could have indicated either disdain or amusement, while Coman stared on with an expressionless gaze and never so much as a movement. The chancellor laid his parchment on the stone surface before him, and after taking a few moments to think, began to address his peers.

"I have called you all here because of a plot that has recently come to my attention, that I believe is of grave importance. The Cult of Primzahl plans to claim the Heart of the World for their god, to what horrible end we need not guess. (A murmur ran through the crowd, but the reaction was more subdued than Eshwar had expected.) The only force actively opposing them is the fortress of Bastion, a garrison that we all know is not what it used to be. Though they have not asked for it, I am convinced that we should offer them any aid we can for the inevitable battle that is to come."

"What kind of aid?" asked Marlowe.

"We should send men, if we can," Hague responded.

"I was afraid you were thinking that. We can't," Marlowe stated.

"Why not?"

"We have no military. Not even a militia. A significant portion of our population is comprised of students. The Magehold is as much a school as it is a nation."

"What about all the battle-mages in your own city, Ausar?"

"What about them? Many are either students or teachers. And the ones who are already battle-hardened have no obligation to us. They are visiting from other worlds, for extra training or otherwise. Their allegiances lie elsewhere, and we cannot expect them to trudge off to fight a war of which they have no knowledge."

Hague sighed, "What about automatons? Cirroc, can we not send them your constructs? In that regard we could provide nearly limitless reinforcement."

"Send them? For free?" Cirroc scoffed. "My automatons are a product, Marek my good man. If Commandant Willet would like to *purchase* a few units I would be happy to oblige her."

A frown twisted the usual kindly expression away from the chancellor's face. "We are talking about the potential repetition of the greatest cataclysm Amalgam has ever endured, and you're worried about money!? I hoped in a time of such gravity you would not succumb to such avaricious behavior!"

Cirroc leaned forward out of the leisurely position in which he had been sitting and raised his voice, leaving behind any respect, feigned or otherwise, that he had had for the proceedings. "You are talking about ancient history, Marek! The Sundering was over five hundred years ago! Eledon is the only one here who was even alive at the time."

Movement stirred in Coman's chair for the first time since he had taken his seat. He looked at Cirroc, any thought or feeling behind his gaze still indiscernible. "And you would do well to heed the lessons of history. Long ago or not, the Sundering shaped modern Amalgam, and not for the better. The Magehold was lucky to be unaffected. The gods' mistakes cannot be repeated."

"Ah, but there's another point," said Cirroc, "Heil and Unheil caused the Sundering. There is no reason to assume that mortals could inflict the same damage."

"There's also no reason not to," Hague countered.

"Fine. But regardless, Bastion is not the only thing standing between the Cult and the Heart. There are two *gods* around it! And two armies of celestials!"

"I would hesitate to put faith in the gods, or their armies," Eledon offered. "They are not keepers. They're purpose is to combat one another, to carry out a balancing act between good and evil, to the benefit or detriment of us all."

"So your theory suggests," Cirroc countered with a raised finger.

"Regardless," Coman continued, "they have always been indifferent to the actions of mortals. I myself have walked in that land, in the midst of the struggle, and I was paid as little heed as an ant crawling on the battlefields of men. I have even conjured their thralls for use in my studies. They are mindless and indifferent. Mere suggestions of the forms they emulate. In fewer words, mortals can pass them by easily with proper care."

"Speaking of conjuring," Hague said, "could we not conjure reinforcements?"

Eledon shook his head. "I'm afraid not. Deals with devils aside, we could only conjure creatures and spirits over which we ultimately have no control. Or worse, we could summon sentient beings and in essence be conscripting a slave army. At that point we would be no better than the enemy."

"Is there not something we can do?" Hague pleaded to his peers. "And think of this: we have assumed during this conversation that we are looking at a second Sundering. But what if something new happens? What if the Cult is successful and claims the Heart? It has never been studied, we have no idea of the power it could contain. Their control of it could be a far worse calamity than the physical decimation of Amalgam."

The amphitheatre was silent. This was a notion to which there was no quick response or immediate answer. The threat to Amalgam was one piece, but Hague's suggestion had implications for the entire multiverse. Even Cirroc had settled and was lost deep in thought.

Marlowe was scratching his chin and slowly shaking his head. "There's simply nothing to be done, Marek. We cannot send students and civilians to war."

"Cirroc, please."

"I'm sorry, Marek. If the day comes that we are drawn into war then my constructs will be ready, but for now we are speaking in what-ifs and making predictions with no precedent. I will not float such an expense without more surety."

"I can offer some small aid," Lothar spoke up for the first time. "We alchemists can provide the fortress with a supply of potions. Draughts of healing and stamina. Hopefully we can make one of their men worth several of the Cult's."

Hague nodded. "That is something, thank you, Lothar. Please begin production immediately when you return home. The sooner the shipment can leave, the better."

"Hmph, always one for charity, you alchemists." Cirroc's tone was more wistful than sarcastic. "You could be making a fortune off that Babel Brew."

"We are scholars first, Cirroc, and we live fine lives," Lothar said. "I have no need for a tower that rakes the moon or servants to carry me in a litter."

"No, it looks like you could use a walk." Again Cirroc's comment could have been biting, but his tone was flat and his gaze empty. He stood and walked up the aisle behind his throne. The automaton turned to follow its master, its unnaturally loud footsteps filling the space as it climbed to the top of the rise.

"Well, unless anyone has more to add, I suppose that means we're adjourned." Hague was looking down at his papers. The top two were placed side by side, one a map of Amalgam pre-Sundering, the other post. The chancellor ran a finger down the second map, along the cavernous gash and jagged mountains surrounding a tiny dot labeled "HotW."

The silence remained, accompanied by airs of guilt, embarrassment, anxiety, and contemplation. Each archmage had his head down, looking away from his peers, except for Eledon, who was again locked into a statuesque stare, his eyes pointed to the Lenel Stone. In time the audience began to stir, and in a quiet procession the theatre emptied. The three remaining archmages and their stewards were the last to vacate, leaving Hague standing at the podium, his eyes still cast down on the maps, but not really seeing anything. Eventually he gathered the papers and his staff and walked toward the Taikanik wedge, his spry step replaced by a tired, aged gait. He walked right past his throne and slumped onto a bench near Bill and Eshwar, releasing a sad and exasperated sigh.

"William," he said, "prepare a bird. I have a letter to write. Not the one I was hoping to send, wouldn't you know."

"I could've told you they weren't gonna go for it."

"Save it," Marek hissed. "There's no need to kick an old man while he's down. I had to try."

"At least Archmage O'Loghlen offered the potions," Eshwar said.

"I doubt the commandant will be satisfied with those," said Bill.

"No, she won't," Hague concurred. "Her faith is in steel and strong arms. So it has always been with the ladies of Bastion. But her men will be glad to have them."

"Is there no one else we can appeal to?" Eshwar asked. "What about the other nations?"

"There simply isn't time," Hague said. "To convince anyone to dedicate the resources, and then to mobilize, well it could take a year, if it happened at all! No one worries about anything until it's already on their doorstep. The Cult will be moving very quickly. And I don't know how long Miss Willet has known about their plans, but she should have informed all of us immediately! Not left us to find out because your friend happened to mention it in passing, and he only had the information by chance. Ah, so much could've been done differently...and I'm not only talking about recently."

An unlikely but insidious thought entered Eshwar's mind. "You don't think Bastion will surrender, do you?"

"Oh no," Hague said with confidence. "They will win or they will die, but they will never abandon their charge."

This helped to put Eshwar at ease, but his mind now went with melancholy to Kelm and the others. "I should go."

"No. Bury that thought," the chancellor said. "Your training must continue. The aptitude you have shown cannot be wasted by rushing into that fight. I'm sorry Eshwar, but your four friends are the only swords Bastion is going to get."

Eshwar sighed. "Very well. So what's next for me then?"

"You must return to Loitsunìk. There are more elements to master, and the battle-mages can teach you combat spells for if you ever do find yourself on the field. But I want you to check in with me from time to time. As often as you'd like really. You can even stay at the house in Taikanìk if you want, given that now the towns are only a blink away."

"I'd like that very much," Eshwar said.

"Good, then that's settled. Now, let's return to Velhonìk. I plan to send word to Bastion before day's end. And in the morning the two of you will rush east. I'll be taking the long way home; I'll prefer my breakfast stay in my stomach, don't you know."

The three of them made their way up the aisle and out onto the high ground. In the distance the rough waters of the Leben were crashing into the stony shore. Cirroc's tower dominated their vision as they walked north, its upper extremity hidden in a rolling bank of thick clouds. It took almost the remainder of the day for them to reach the city, but there was enough light left that the chancellor was able to quickly write and seal a letter, explaining the outcome of the council meeting and promising the arrival of the potions. Bill tied the letter to the leg of a large pigeon and sent it on its way, watching it disappear into an orange and violet sky. Two days later it would land in Bastion, and its cargo be carried directly to the war room, to be placed in the hands of Josalynn Willet.

CHAPTER ELEVEN
Caught

Braoin Dunne entered his cell and closed the door behind him. It was a tiny room, furnished only with a writing desk and a bed so uninviting that a dog would have chosen to sleep on the floor. He lived in a building that housed ten clergymen, each with a cell identical to his own. It was situated mere feet from the outer wall of Cardinal's Point, and his cell's location on the first level meant the sun's rays never graced its tiny slit window.

He moved to his desk and retrieved from within a drawer a piece of black armor, the majority of a vambrace. He turned it over in his hands. Braoin knew the object had to be at least six centuries old, but time had not touched it. Someone who did not know its history would have thought it fresh from the forge. He wrapped it in a chunk of cloth and hid it inside his robe, then took one last look at his cell as he exited, glad that he would never see it again.

Down the hall and out into the street he moved, briskly but casually, so as not to arouse suspicion. The day was bright, but Cardinal's Point felt no less ominous than ever, with its darkened edifices and glum denizens. Braoin wondered how the Cult of Primzahl was able to inspire loyalty when all of its citizens always appeared so depressed. He passed off of the side streets that led from his dormitory and onto the main thoroughfare, at which point he turned east toward the city's gate.

He could see it there before him, standing open and ready for him to pass through. Commandant Willet had recalled the spies from Cult territory, and Braoin was eager to shed his purple robes and look upon Bastion once more. It felt like years he had spent with the Cult; daily life in their ranks was slow and dreary. He had chosen to infiltrate in the guise of a clergyman, rather than a soldier, because he thought it would give him more access to the Archbishop. It had, but it had also subjected him to nearly continuous sermons and lectures, besieging his ears with scripture dedicated to the glory of Primzahl. He wished that he could selectively turn off the effects of Babel Brew; hearing a string of gibberish would be preferable to the monotonous pontificating he was subjected to on a daily basis.

When he wasn't attending a service, his assigned duties kept him in and around the library and scriptorium, near the rear of the cathedral complex. Before leaving Bastion he had practiced copying script as part of his cover, and by now he had become a veritable expert. The tomes and scrolls he produced were then passed off to other clergymen who illuminated them with illustrations and decorative calligraphy. Braoin was glad he had not included illumination as part of his falsified background. He had a steady hand, but he was no artist, and the level of embellishment the Cult expected on their manuscripts would have quickly seen him outed as a fraud.

He spent every spare moment he had, precious few, engaged in his real work of spying. The library offered him some insight into the Cult's motivations, but the texts were just as guised in tales of milk and honey as were the sermons, making it difficult to discern any fact within them. His main focus was keeping his eyes and ears open, absorbing every piece of information he could from passersby and loose-lipped monks. Hardly ever was anything of substance said, and the Archbishop was particularly careful with what passed his lips in the presence of more lowly clergymen. Braoin had managed to steal the piece of armor only recently, right from within the Archbishop's private quarters after eavesdropping on a conversation while delivering scrolls to the offices. It had been no easy feat, but if it prevented the item's use for some evil purpose, then the risk had been worth it. The vambrace was a relic of Unheil's army, and the Cult's possession of it could mean nothing good.

"Brother Bols."

Braoin stopped and gritted his teeth at the sound of his alias. What distraction was this? He was so close to the gate, he thought about ignoring the voice. But he could not simply make a break for it, he would be shot or chased down easily. He put a mask of pleasantry on his face and turned around.

"Yes?"

"The Archbishop has requested your presence."

"Now?" Braoin asked. "I was just leaving to journey to Penitent's Rest. I have been assigned to help bless our troops." This was a lie, and not a very good one, but Braoin was nearly shaking with the desire to see the city disappear at his back.

"The Archbishop was quite clear that you were to be fetched and report to him immediately. Follow me, please."

The man turned and walked away, and Braoin let out a visible but silent sigh. Fighting every urge to run to the east he followed the man back west, straight along the thoroughfare that led to the cathedral. Eventually the buildings fell away to either side and they passed into the square that stood before the cathedral's door. They did not raise their gaze to look upon the building; it was customary to keep one's eyes low near the building, so as not to offend Primzahl. Walking to the right led them to an outbuilding, connected to the cathedral by an arcade, that served as a vestry. The man opened the door and beckoned for Braoin to step inside.

He found himself in a long room, lined with racks of extra robes and crates that contained items rarely used. Why the Archbishop would have him brought here was a mystery to Braoin, but perhaps there was no reason at all. Convenience, as it turned out, was the driving force, as at the far end of the room, amid bolts of fabric, the Archbishop was standing and being measured by a small woman who served as a tailor. He was wearing a white undertunic and had his arms outstretched for the woman's benefit, and was facing away toward the far wall.

The man who had led Braoin urged him forward, navigating through the mess of clothing and containers until they stood in a clear space near the Archbishop. Another man, wearing a black robe, was leaning against the wall near the corner of the room, his face stern and his eyes fixed on the newcomers. Braoin began to feel uneasy. Black raiment meant a member of the Inquisition. He hoped the man was not there on his behalf.

"Brother Bols," the Archbishop said without turning around, "kind of you to join us."

"It's my pleasure, Archbishop," Braoin said, trying to sound normal, "how may I serve?"

"I believe that you have something of mine."

"I'm not sure what you mean, Your Worship."

"Come, come. No need to waste either of our time feigning ignorance."

"Your Worship," Braoin sputtered, " I assure you, I don't know wha—"

"Enough lies!" The Archbishop spun around, causing the tailor to squeal and stumble backwards. His eyes were fierce and his nostrils flared. "Do you not think that I have sneaks of my own? Men that I trust to sniff out cockroaches such as yourself? I know that you are a spy, Bols. One sent by that foul woman of Bastion, no doubt. Now, give me what is mine."

Braoin panicked. He saw no use in trying to talk his way out of the situation. Even with a solid alibi and the most deceptive of tongues, the Archbishop seemed to be in no mood to be convinced. Braoin turned and ran, but armored guards had emerged from within the muddle of the room and stood between him and his freedom. He had no weapons, and his brief struggle was in vain. They subdued him and carried him back to drop him on his knees before the Archbishop.

"Find it," he said to the guards.

They peeled back Braoin's robe violently, and underneath they found the cloth-wrapped bundle. One of the guards unwrapped it, revealing the glossy black vambrace, and with a bow presented it to the Archbishop.

"Was that so difficult?" he said. "I always knew there may be subversives in our ranks, but when this went missing I could no longer ignore the possibility. It's very important to our plans, you see. Your mistake, of course, was not making your escape as soon as you stole it. The past few days, which you were no doubt using to avoid suspicion, gave my investigators all the time they needed to reveal your treachery.

"You will of course need to be punished. You are not truly one of us, and I'm sure Bols isn't even your real name, but all the same, I hereby charge and find you guilty of treason, the punishment for which is death."

"What use do you have for that trinket?" Braoin asked, unfazed by the sentencing. "Its very existence must offend your god."

The Archbishop grinned and spun the vambrace playfully in his hands. "Perhaps. But ends often justify means. As for its purpose, you have no right to ask."

"You've condemned me to die, there would be no harm in satiating my curiosity."

"You still have hope to escape. You want me to expound my grand scheme in the comfort of knowing it will never leave this room, only for you to make your dramatic getaway and deliver the information to your master. I won't waste my breath. Take your curiosity to the grave." The Archbishop looked to the man in the black robe, "Justiciar, if you would."

The man stepped out of his corner and approached the prisoner. He knelt down and grabbed Braoin by the jaw, and for a few seconds stared intently into his eyes. When he stood again he looked to the Archbishop and shook his head, then returned to the corner and leaned against the wall once more.

"A pity," The Archbishop said. "I was hoping to make you the centerpiece of a burning, it would have been good for morale. But there's no reason to waste such ceremony on a non-mage. Still," he tapped his chin as if in thought, "beheading is so quick and clean, it's really not like punishment at all, and I wish to see you suffer for your crime. Hmm. What to do? (Braoin thought the man's display rather melodramatic.) Ah yes! Guards, take him down into the crypts and deliver him to Confessor Paxton. Tell him there's no need to extract information, just do as he sees fit. But keep the prisoner alive, his execution must still be used for the entertainment of the public."

The guards hoisted Braoin to his feet, and half-dragged him out of the room by a rear door. From there they would find the nearest stairway and carry him down into the network of crypts that ran beneath the cathedral complex. The Archbishop handed the vambrace to the clergyman who had led Braoin to the vestry.

"Take this back to my chambers," he said. "And lock it up."

"Right away, Your Worship," the man bowed and took his leave.

The Archbishop straightened his tunic and returned to his previous position, allowing the tailor to resume her measurements.

"I don't like this plan of yours," the black-robed man said. "That spy might be right, it is offensive to Primzahl."

"And I am not impressed with your army, Barrett," the Archbishop retorted. "Had we had a true military presence on Amalgam, I'm sure the Inquisition would not have been blessed with such a responsibility. Open war should be the domain of the Commandery, but I realize that the siege is *your* assignment. However, the Heart of the World is to be my responsibility, and I will do what it takes to see it in our possession. You worry about your troops, I'll deal with Unheil. I suggest you go Penitent's Rest and check on the progress of the outfitting. But I will expect you back here for the execution."

"Very well. I will leave immediately and return when summoned. Do what you will, but be careful, Archbishop."

"Come come, Barrett, everything will be fine. For Primzahl is a merciful master."

#

An indeterminable number of days later, Braoin was hauled up out of the crypts and into the harsh assault of daylight. He could not walk, and instead had guards carrying him by either arm, what was left of his lower body dragging along on the ground. One of his feet was gone, the stump wrapped in a dirty bandage, and the other was devoid of toes. His remaining fingers had no nails, and as far as he could tell his left arm had lost all function. His eyes were sunken and dim, and his lips sucked in, wrapped loosely around his now toothless gums.

Confessor Paxton had been delighted with his guest, and being under no obligation to extract information, had used their time together to experiment with new ways of inflicting pain. The chamber where Braoin was kept stunk of bodily fluids and every surface seemed to be stained with the remnants of the Confessor's victims. The torturer's various tools, saws, knives, axes, chains, and things Braoin could not, and cared not, to identify, were in diverse conditions. Some were clean and sharpened to pristine edges, others were rusting, dirty, and notched from neglectful use. Braoin could not decide which ones unsettled him more.

Save for his teeth, the Confessor had largely left his face alone. The display of the execution would be better served if the spy's face were not turned into a bestial monstrosity. But the rest of his body was open to the machinations of the torturer's sadistic mind, and Paxton set upon it at once with both the savagery of a barbarian and the deftness of an artist. Beneath the sackcloth rags Braoin now wore, there was little left that could be described as human. His torso was a patchwork of gashes, incisions, abrasions, burns, and spreading infections. It was incredible that there was any blood left in his body, but the Confessor was as skilled at keeping his victims alive as he was at causing them pain.

For a time Braoin's screams and moans had filled the crypts. Even clergymen who had to venture through were unsettled by the cacophony of horror. But eventually he stopped responding to any stimuli, and was subdued into a nearly comatose state of shock. His eyes looked at nothing in particular, and seemed to stare straight through the walls and ceiling of the chamber. Paxton was no longer amused by his victim, and sent word to the Archbishop that the execution could commence at his leisure.

They were now dragging Braoin through the arcade between the cathedral and the vestry. Emerging from beneath its canopy subjected his weakened eyes to another barrage of unforgiving sunlight. To the center of the square they brought him. A stage had been set up there, before the cathedral, and atop it was a well-used chopping block. Beside it stood a man in a black robe, his head covered by a black executioner's hood. The guards hoisted Braoin up onto the stage. His head bobbled limply as he turned it to look at the executioner. Was this the Justiciar? Braoin decided it really didn't matter.

He was placed on his knees, body draped across the chopping block. They tied his hands off on either side, even though he could not run even if he had desired to. His head hung over the front edge of the block. He was staring into a stone bowl that would catch his head when it fell and collect his blood. No doubt they would keep what was left of his life-force for some ritual or dark alchemy.

Presently the Archbishop burst forth from within the cathedral's main hall. He was wearing a splendid robe of deep violet, trimmed all over in gold. The eye of Primzahl, also in gold, stared out coldly from above his forehead. He approached the stage and climbed up, outstretching his arms to welcome the gathering crowd of onlookers.

"Brothers and sisters," he began, projecting with a strong and clear voice. "This man," he gestured toward Braoin, and a guard grabbed the prisoner by the hair and raised his head, allowing the crowd to see his face, "this man you see before you has been found guilty of treason." Jeers arose from the crowd. "He stole a relic from my very chambers to be delivered into the hands of our enemies, and in so doing stole from Primzahl Himself!" There were more jeers as the Archbishop paused for dramatic effect. "But not to worry! The Great One delivered him into our hands, and the time has come for him to receive his punishment!" The crowd cheered now. "I hereby sentence this traitor to death, to be carried out immediately!"

The crowd let out a series of loud cries, a mixture of hateful condemnations targeted at Braoin and worshipful praises to the glory of Primzahl. Braoin ignored both. Just as his body had shut itself off from all sensation but that of numbness, so his mind was operating in a state of disinterested observation. He was not afraid of the axe that would soon end his life. He was not even offended or angered by the hate being shouted in his direction. Nor was there any notion of the disdain he normally felt for the Cultists and their worship. There was only the sense that the whole affair was dragging on longer than he desired.

Finally, when the crowd had somewhat quieted, the executioner hefted his large axe and moved into position beside the chopping block. It was a dark, gruesome looking thing that would have been quite frightful to someone who had not already accepted their doom. The guard let go of Braoin's hair, allowing his head to flop back down and face the stone bowl. A hushed anticipation fell over the crowd as the axe was raised up into the air, a communal deep breath as its weight fell downward. It might have been a violent scene to the casual observer, repulsive even, but as the blade separated his head from his body, all Braoin felt was relief.

CHAPTER TWELVE
Preparations for War

Nearly a month had passed, and the Riisgardians once again found themselves gathered around the map table in the war room. Josalynn had called another meeting, and they now stood waiting with Andor and Zurofel for the arrival of the commandant and Backus. Kelm had been assigned to guard duty under Hutta's command, a position he found quite comfortable given he had taken orders from his friend for the better part of a decade. The others had remained at their previous posts, and their training schedules weren't aligned, but every night at the evening meal the four former mercenaries joined each other in fellowship. Andor ate with them frequently, but sometimes his duties at the upper citadel kept him on top of the mountain. Fortunately celestial activity had still been normal, and so only their enemy to the west was on their minds. They had heard no more intelligence, though they were aware that at least one spy had returned, and there was an unsettled air about the fortress. Had the enemy army begun to move? Were they still waiting for something? The uncertainty was causing a mixture of fear and the anticipation of taking the plunge into battle.

The commandant entered the room, followed closely by her fur-covered second, and took a position at the far side of the room, between the table and the window. Backus moved in with the others, distributed on the remaining three sides of the table. Josalynn's hair was loose and unkempt, and bags were apparent beneath her eyes. For a time she stared at the map, seemingly unaware there was anyone else in the room. Finally she spoke, but her eyes remained lost in the imagery of her mind.

"Two of our spies have returned. One, you know, arrived over a week ago. The other has been back nearly a week himself, but the third is still out there. There has been no report from him since before the Riisgardians first arrived. He was stationed at Cardinal's Point, and very likely could have had vital information, but we cannot afford to wait any longer. The enemy force should be close to mobilizing, and we must make final preparations. Backus."

"The final harvest has been brought in to the stores, as Zur suggested at our last meeting. As we speak the farmers are securing their homes and will then move into the fortress for the remainder of the conflict. This will leave the valley empty between here and the outposts at the mouth." Backus moved around the table in order to be able to point out the relevant locations. "We will assume the enemy will march down the road, coming directly past the South Maw. As soon as they have been sighted, the garrison there will abandon it and rush back here, providing us with a final numbers report and adding to the defense of the Bulwark. The North Maw, however, will remain manned. Its marriage with the mountainside makes it a more defensible location, and we will need fair warning if a splinter force attempts to enter the valley north of the river. A final supply run will need to be made as soon as possible to make sure the outpost is provisioned for a siege of its own. Webb, the squad making that run will need strong backs, and Zur has agreed to let you join them. You will be moving out tomorrow morning. Zurofel."

"As per usual, the siege equipment is being tested at regular intervals and maintained daily. I'm happy to report that all the machines are up to snuff. I can have men cook batches of pitch starting immediately, and the barrels stocked on the outer gate turrets. I'll have relief batteries set up at the base of the inner wall with enough ammunition to resupply each trebuchet at least once. A medical unit for minor wounds will be set up in the stable, where we'll keep the potions from the Magehold. Everyone down here will take a stamina draught when the enemy approaches. Hopefully that gives us an edge. The great hall will be converted into a field hospital the day before battle, for the injured who won't be able to return to fighting. Andor."

"The celestial armies have remained far to the east, and it is my hope they won't have a change of habit. One hundred men from the upper citadel will be brought down to bolster the ranks down here. The remainder will stay on alert, just in case there are any problems up top. I still plan on being on the Bulwark for the siege. Hutta."

"The guard units are already being outfitted with full combat gear, and that will be complete long before the battle begins. The archers will be placed along the outer wall, with infantry and pikemen spread throughout to counter any ladders or grappling attempts. The rest of the melee boys will be posted behind the inner gate, just in case there's a breach."

Josalynn rubbed her eyes and nodded her head. "Good. Good. But what of the mages?"

"Oh. Sorry," Hutta said. "Mixed in with the archers on the outer wall. And some of them are working on some surprises for the trebuchets."

"Yes," Zurofel said, "some exotic ammo, if you please."

Josalynn nodded again. "Then we're ready. But for now we're blind. Without the spies we have no idea when the enemy is going to come. We won't know until they enter the valley. I wish Braoin was back, or that we at least had a report. I can't shake the feeling that there's information that failed to escape Cardinal's Point. Especially if he's dead."

"I could go," Fuster spoke up. "I can move quickly alone, and sneaking about is my specialty. Half these scars are from being whipped for thieving as a boy."

"If you got whipped, it means you got caught," Backus said.

"Only means I had to get better," Fuster countered.

"But what will it accomplish? Especially this late in the game." Hutta was skeptical.

"One final report of troop movements would help us," Josalynn said as she turned to look out the window. "Fuster could go and send a bird back telling us if the army has moved."

"Uh, no offense, Commandant," Fuster said, "but it would be more than a little difficult to sneak about while carrying a caged pigeon."

"You wouldn't have to," she replied, "we have a dead drop near Penitent's Rest. We can send a bird there to wait. You get there, send back your report, and get back."

"That's well and good, but I beg you, let me go on to Cardinal's Point. I wouldn't be missed in the siege, and any information I can gather could help."

"The probability of you returning before the battle begins might as well be zero," said Backus. "I'm not sure what good information will do if we don't have it in time."

Josalynn was still staring out the window, with her hands clasped behind her back. None of the others could see her face, but had they been able to they would have found it expressionless, with no indication of the thoughts behind it. She could see that Fuster's request was nearly pointless. She had just recalled all the spies from enemy territory, there was little logic in inserting another at this stage, but something was nagging at her. A voice that she could not quiet, like a mosquito that hovers near one's ear, buzzing back and forth obnoxiously and avoiding every attempt at dissuading it.

"Go," she finally said. "Anything you can learn could benefit the struggle, even if the fortress were to fall. This battle isn't going to end the war."

Backus and Hutta looked at her with surprise, but said nothing critical of her decision. With their briefing concluded, she dismissed them, and they left the war room to see to the final preparations.

#

Hutta let the others leave him behind and stood in the hall waiting for Josalynn to emerge. He leaned back against a wall and ran his fingers over the roughly hewn stones. All the halls of the citadel were dark, lined with torches that cracked and popped but cast an inconsistent and shifting glow that was as much shadow as it was light. The shaft of daylight pouring in lazily from the door of the war room offered a comforting alternative to an otherwise gloomy atmosphere, but the torches at least would remain vigilant long after the sun had left the valley.

As he waited he thought back on the last month, which had been far longer than he and his friends had expected. On Riisgard time had been kept according to the phases of the moon and the passage of the seasons, but on Amalgam it was not so. Here a month consisted of fifty days, and there were ten months in the year. That system seemed easier than the one he was used to, but it was still hard to reorient his mind. To him this new world was both simpler and at the same time more mechanical. Something about it felt unnatural, arbitrary, but Hutta couldn't quite put a finger on it. Kelm was the philosopher of the group, after all; Hutta had never had much reason to look beyond what his eyes could see. He could not claim that the entire idea of Amalgam had not overwhelmed him, but it did him good to focus on the Cult, a tangible threat that he was familiar with.

Josalynn was released from whatever prison of thought in which she had been, and stepped out into the hall. Hutta fell in beside her as she walked toward the stairway.

"Ma'am, might I speak with you as you walk?"

"You may."

"Are you sure about this business with Fuster?"

"Would you rather have him here for the battle?"

"It's not that exactly." Hutta scratched his head and ran a hand through his hair. "He's right that he probably won't be missed; open battle was never his forte. I suppose I'm just worried about him. We already lost his cousin to this world, and I fear that loss may have made him reckless. I don't want to lose another man, not for nothing."

"Who's to say it would be for nothing? He could bring back something invaluable, but if he were to die, it would be in a valiant cause. You have been his leader for a long time; do you have confidence in his abilities?"

"Of course."

"Then trust him, and let him do what he's good at."

"Yes ma'am," Hutta nodded.

They had moved into a hall on a lower level and were heading toward Andor's room. The same dancing torches lighted their way, and they found his door cracked enough that they could see inside. Andor was kneeling before a small table, upon which was a random assortment of trinkets surrounding a bronze figurine. It depicted a female form rising out of a wave, arms outstretched toward the sky, hair flowing backwards to become one with the water. Andor's head was bowed and covered by his hood, but his hands were bare and clasped in front of him. No sound came from within the room, not even the sound of his breath. Josalynn moved farther down the hall and beckoned for Hutta to follow. When they were some distance away she stopped and waited.

"What's he doing?" Hutta asked.

"He's praying," she answered.

"I thought his job was to fight gods. And that his world didn't have any."

"Apparently they still have some, although most Magnans choose not to worship. Andor, however, has sworn himself to some sea goddess. He believes that his power comes from his faith, and Her grace. I've tried to tell him that She isn't here, that he draws his power from within himself, but he goes on praying anyway."

"Faith can give a man courage where he would have none, or purpose, or, in some cases, great power."

"Or it can turn him into a radical and a zealot. Just look at our enemy. Given the chance they persecute anyone of differing views."

"True. But their extremism is no reason to begrudge Andor's choices. My men and I all have our own faith, though it is not in gods per se. Have you no faith of your own?"

"What need have I for faith? The Uberwesen is so absent as to be nonexistent, and the other two are little more than brats. Irresponsible children who were given too much power and not enough discipline. And what has it gotten them? They are locked in a pointless battle with no end. They are prisoners of their own existence. And my family has been at odds with them for generations, making sure they are also prisoners of these mountains. So no, I have no faith."

"Adamant, isn't she?" Andor had appeared from his room and was walking toward them. "This is an argument you can't win, Hutta. 'To each his own.' Best leave it that way."

"I'd appreciate your company, Sir Kardos." Josalynn said, ignoring his comment. "I want to go topside and make sure every contingency is accounted for. Just for my piece of mind."

"Of course, Commandant," Andor said.

"Hutta, I trust you have duties you can attend to?"

"Yes ma'am," Hutta said, and made his way toward the armory to check on the outfitting.

#

A lean, gray horse was tacked and ready to go, standing in the preparation bay of the stables. Fuster had gathered what little he needed as quickly as possible, with Kelm shadowing him, pleading, but to no avail.

"Are you sure you want to do this?" he kept asking.

"Yes, Kelm, for the upteenth time, I'm sure." Fuster said as he hoisted a saddlebag onto the horse's hindquarter. "You're wasting your breath."

"I just don't see what it will accomplish."

Fuster turned to him, his eyes fiery. "What it will accomplish? It will make me useful, that's what it will accomplish. I've stopped trying to count the days we've been here, but all I've done in that time is take care of animals. Picked up horse shit down here, gotten covered in bird shit in the aerie up there. I thought I was done dealing with others' shit once Webb's arm healed, but no, the spirits have decided that Fuster is to be the steward of stool. When I said I wanted to be whatever help I could, this isn't exactly what I meant. I came here seeking retribution. I need to take action."

"There's a battle coming! You'll have that opportunity!"

"Oh please, Kelm, what good would I be in that battle? I can't shoot a bow, can't shoot fire from my hands either, so that means I'm not needed on the walls. So that leaves me sitting inside, possibly never even seeing combat. But then, what if the walls get breached? Say the enemy comes in and I get to fight? I don't wear heavy plate, don't swing giant swords and clash shields, kicking and screaming with eyes red, full of lust. I sneak around. It's what I'm good at. I slit throats so that the clashing and the screaming never have to happen. Quiet, clean, quick. A siege isn't the place for me. But slipping in right through the gullet of enemy territory, stealing their secrets, maybe wetting a silent blade along the way, that's the place for me. It's why Hutta hired me in the first place way back when, and it's how I'm going to be of use now."

Kelm sighed and leaned back on a stone brick post. Fuster was right. It was how things had always been. Daffer had tracked their quarry or made sure they got where they were going. Fuster gathered intel, assassinated, and culled enemy ranks. He, Hutta, and Webb handled the hacking and slashing. It was a system that had worked well for a band of mercenaries. It didn't translate when they became part of a garrison. Andor had secured them special treatment, somehow appealed to Josalynn to allow them to join the meetings in the war room, but Hutta was the only one that had been given a position of any authority. The rest of them were little more than cogs in a machine. It was mundane and regulated. And they had all been used to a life that was spontaneous and free. The anticipation for the battle with the Cult was the only thing that was keeping any of them from coming down with cabin fever, but Kelm could see that the siege would not satisfy Fuster.

"Alright, I'm done arguing. You're right. Just please, please, be careful."

"Don't worry," Fuster said, finishing preparing his mount, "I don't plan on seeing my cousin again just yet."

"So what's the plan?"

"The horse will get me as close as possible as quickly as possible. Then I have to find a way across the river, and then it's on foot, skirting the towns until I get to Cardinal's Point. Then I do what I do best: be patient and listen."

"Seems straightforward enough."

"Were it so easy as saying the words. I'm ready. I need to be fast, I have many leagues to go and not a lot of time. Goodbye, Kelm. May Bear watch over you and the others, and all of Bastion."

Kelm wrapped Fuster in an embrace. "Serpent hide you, my brother."

Fuster climbed up into the saddle and spurred the horse on without hesitation, across the yard and out through the double gate of the Bulwark. On the road he begged the mount for all the speed it could muster, and like the rush of a river they were gone.

#

"Why do you trust the Riisgardians, Andor?"

"For the same reason you don't."

They stood now on a high rampart of the upper citadel surveying the walls and craggy landscape to the east. The turret rose at their backs. The sound of the huge banners occasionally flapping in the breeze was almost deafening. Andor had his black cloak and hood wrapped tightly about him against the chill air, and Josalynn had donned a thick, fur-lined robe that left only her head exposed. Andor had given the order for the one hundred men to reinforce the main garrison, and they were gathering in the rocky yard below and making ready to march down the mountain road. The remaining men had been divided into day and night shifts, and those currently on duty were spread across the eastern wall, keeping their vigil against the ever-present but unseen celestial forces.

"They're new here," Andor continued. "No offense, but this place has gone stagnant. If it were a ship, it would be like being stuck in the doldrums. The Riisgardians bring fresh ideas and perspective. Hutta has proved to be a capable commander, I think you'll agree, and beyond that, they have experience with our foe. Much more than me. My history with the Cult consists of a few guerrilla skirmishes, but they've actually *lived* this struggle. I'd say they have more to fight for than even your seasoned men. I consider that an important asset."

"Sometimes I wish I could see things with the same trust and optimism that you do. My mother always taught me that it was safer to be rigid."

"A closed mind exposes us to as many dangers as an open one. But you'll find the experiences afforded to you by an open one to be far more rewarding, most of the time."

"I wouldn't have called my commanding officer close-minded," she said, shooting him a chastising glance, "but I see your point."

Andor smiled. "You know I don't hold my tongue," he said with a shrug.

Something down in the yard caught his attention, and without another word he began hopping down the nearest staircase to the lower ramparts.

"I haven't dismissed you, Sir Kardos," Josalynn called after him.

He stopped and looked back at her, saw that she was smiling, and smiled back. "Come on then," he said, and continued his descent.

She followed. Since first arriving at the fortress Andor had deferred to her authority, but had also always treated it, and that of anyone else, with a casual disregard. It was not that he meant any offense, but he clearly had little respect for most of the conventions she was used to. Whatever driving principles were behind his conscience, he followed them with little care given to institutional precepts, rules, or chains of command. At first she had found it to be a rather annoying trait, but over time she had come to be amused by it, and now more and more she could not deny the wisdom and objectivity that his nonconformity had brought to her stronghold.

Together they walked down the stairs and crossed a short distance on a lower tier of the citadel and down another stair into the yard. The ground was hard and uneven underfoot, and bare of even the hardiest of weeds. Beyond the wall the landscape was jagged and sharp, dangerously so, full of stones akin to spear tips and axe blades. A fall down a crevasse would likely shred an unfortunate soul before they could die of impact. But within the wall the yard was at least somewhat level, and its deadly edges had been dulled by the foot traffic and industriousness of its inhabitants. They passed by the group of men filling carts with gear to be moved below and made for the eastern gate. A group of guards were gathered there, huddling beneath the gatehouse. They called up to a comrade in one of the turrets, who proceeded to lower the portcullis, once again cutting the citadel off from the harsh land beyond. One of the guards heard the commanders approaching and spun around.

"Andor!" he cried, "you need to see this!" Then immediately upon realizing he was in Josalynn's presence, he straightened up and saluted. "Commandant Willet."

She once again shot Andor her authoritative glance. His own insubordinate behavior was something she had come to abide and expect, but promoting informality in the lower ranks was not something she was keen to allow. Still, she held back her criticism for the time being, and simply acknowledged the soldier with an "At ease."

"What's going on?" Andor asked.

"Scout Harborough has just returned, he's in the group here. Come see."

The guards parted and saluted as the commanders stepped forward into the group. A dark skinned man wearing the black leathers of a scout was kneeling near the wall. Set on the ground before him was a severed hand and forearm. Its skin was gray, with lacerations along its length leaking a thick, pus-like substance. The point of amputation was suspiciously dry, but some of the same substance was crusting in globs around the bone. The hand was twitching slightly, and featured unnaturally long fingers and sharp, yellowed nails. Andor reached down and picked it up. It recoiled violently at his touch, causing all the guards to jump in surprise, and the group became uneasy, as if the breeze were carrying some unheard but tortured scream. Andor squeezed, as if crushing the life out of a rodent, dripping more of the foul fluid onto the ground and releasing a pungent odor of rot and decay. The hand writhed in response to his grip, but soon succumbed to its unknown pain and went limp.

"Where did you find this?" he asked, turning it over and studying it.

"A couple miles out, to the northeast." Harborough said, standing up. "It would've been in sight of the wall, if not for the topography of the area."

"Was anything else there?" Andor asked.

"Nothing but more of this…blood. It was lying there, shaking somewhat, but nothing like what just happened."

Andor grinned. "This belonged to some fiend, some manner of ghoul, if I had to guess. My touch is

179

like fire to such things. This is closer than any celestials have been for some time, but it seems one of Heil's army has taken care of it. That's my hope at least. Keep an eye on that area. I will likely be down below until after the battle, but if there are any other sightings send word to me." He dropped the arm on the ground and began wiping his gauntlet off with a rag. "And burn that."

"I don't like the celestials being so close when we are distracted by our foe to the west," Josalynn said once they had walked out of earshot of the guards.

"No," Andor replied, "I was hoping they would stay far afield for a while. Pray we end the coming battle quickly in case we need to turn our attention back east."

"I'll leave the prayer to you. But I certainly don't want to be torn between two fronts. Come, let's go back down." She stopped and put a hand in front of his chest, "and Andor, don't tell the lower garrison about this. They have enough to worry about."

He frowned, but nodded, and they began their downward trek.

CHAPTER THIRTEEN
The Cathedral of Primzahl

Night was falling over Cardinal's Point, and an uneasy feeling was falling over Fuster. The city was like the maw of some great beast, full of sharp, misaligned teeth of various lengths, ready to swallow him up as soon as the moonlight woke it from its slumber. Everything was dark; the stones and bricks, the indigo shingles, even the windows, almost all devoid of light, were dark. Fuster wondered if the whole place would just disappear with the passage of the sun, becoming one with the starless sky.

He was climbing now, up the side of the great cathedral at the rear of city. It stood at the pinnacle of Amalgam's northwestern peninsula, an arrowhead of land that rose steadily out of the sea on the backs of cliffs so steep that in places they climbed at an outward angle, suspending the land and city above over an empty drop that hid them from the assault of the crashing waves below. But even on flat ground the cathedral would have towered over its neighbors, unrivaled by even the tallest buildings of the city. Its arrogance pointed toward the empty sky, as if one day it would launch from its perch and take its rightful place among the sun and moon, and its condescension was cast wide, enveloping the town and daring its subjects to try to escape its shadow.

The only consistent light source came from the cathedral itself. A stained glass window rose along the entire height of the steeple, from just above the tympanum up to meld into a circular window just below the belfry. A yellow luminescence evenly filled the entirety of the window, but it did not seem to actually cast any light. It drew the eye to its glorious and imposing glow, but did not allow the viewer to bask in its comfort. The only way to escape the shadows of the streets was to pass inside through an ebony door, but Fuster guessed that in reality there would be no solace found there.

He continued to climb, past fixed barriers of stained glass, grasping protrusions, grotesques, gargoyles, anything within reach, until he came to an eave. Hoisting himself up onto a low roof, he found a window that he could pry open with his dagger, and slipped in to find himself on the thin balcony of a clerestory. Easy. Maybe a little too easy, he supposed. He had expected infiltrating the territory of an organization like the Cult to be more difficult. But now here he stood.

He had ridden hard for two days before releasing the horse back to Bastion. Prophet's Gate straddled the southern fork of the Euhr, and at its heart stood the only bridge across. Guards were stationed all around the city's walls, but under cover of night Fuster had been able to swim slowly across the river north of the city. He skirted it, giving it a wide enough berth that the guards would not catch him passing, but he had to admit that from the outside the place looked splendid. Well lit, clean, and maintained, with streamers happily flapping from ornate spires. But it was all a lie. The walls and outer rim were nothing more than a pretty coating on an empty husk. The streets inside were quiet and mostly abandoned, the buildings dilapidated, and its denizens little more than empty shells themselves, forced to stay and keep up the appearance of Primzahl's glory.

Penitent's Rest had been worse. With no obligation to evangelize with its appearance, it was more a collection of hovels than a city. Fuster walked all through the night after passing Prophet's Gate, moving as fast as he could once he was on open ground and away from watchful eyes. He crossed over the main road, a wide thoroughfare of large cobbles, and approached this second city from the south side before noon the following day. He could see the military tents, neatly organized in rows juxtaposed to the haphazard town, but he knew he must wait until nightfall to gather information. The waiting killed him, for he so wanted to get to Cardinal's Point, but he also knew he must do his duty to Bastion. He found the dead drop, a tall tree that had been struck by lightning and cloven in two, just as it had been described to him by the stable master. A pigeon was contentedly perched on a branch, ready to carry his report. He hid himself as best he could and tried to sleep most of the day away.

When darkness fell he infiltrated the city. It had no walls and might as well have been unguarded. A few soldiers patrolled the streets in pairs, but nothing that he couldn't slip by. The streets were dirty, full of mud and excrement, and the whole place had an odor of filth. The houses were squat, made of timber, the people here not worthy of stone. Fuster peered into some of the windows, and found nothing but the sad faces of slaves and impoverished farmers, forced to work the surrounding fields to provide for those who were fortunate enough to call themselves clergy or soldiers. The priests and guards lived in a stone barracks on the city's edge, with a clean yard and a cobbled road leading out to connect to the main thoroughfare. And just outside the perimeter of this fortification were the tents. There was no way Fuster would be able to sneak through them unseen, so he hid among some carts near the road. Fortunately the passing soldiers were quite talkative, it never occurring to them that a spy might be in their midst. After a few hours of a grueling wait, Fuster had heard enough. The army was to move out in five days time. He was struck with relief that he had been nowhere near too late. He moved like a mouse back to the tree, scribbled a report and sent it off on the leg of a groggy pigeon, then he moved as fast as he could to the northwest, eager to be clear of the enemy army.

From here the land had begun its steady rise out of the sea. It took him twenty-four hours of continuous walking before he saw the walls of Cardinal's Point, their charge perched upon the rise of land like a raptor upon a fresh carcass. Along the way he had passed a henge of obelisks, and at their center a stone altar coated in the ruddy brown stains of blood. For what unthinkable rituals it was used he had chosen not to guess, but upon seeing the cathedral, dark and angular, decorated with razor-sharp pinnacles and other protrusions, the altar seemed rather benign. The guard here was much more lax than it had been at Prophet's Gate, and the Cult's propensity for architectural flair made scaling the wall an easy task. Fuster had followed the rampart straight for the cathedral, slipping past only a few sentries. There were people moving in the streets below, clergymen most likely, but their heads remained bowed and their eyes on the ground, afraid to meet the damning gaze of the glowing window, and he moved along unnoticed.

Now here he was, moving along the balcony in the clerestory. Below him ran a long nave filled with pews, covered by a fan vault high above. Across the nave he could see an aisle running beneath the roof opposite from which he had entered. It was filled with busts and artifacts on display, but they were too distant for him to make out any details. He reached the end of the balcony, where a claustrophobic stairwell disappeared into the wall in a downward spiral. But rather than move down into the halls and crypts, he found himself a shadowy alcove among the pilasters and positioned himself with a view of the apse. There stood a gilded altar, bare but for a purple runner displaying the minimalistic symbol of the eye.

His strategy proved fruitful after a short wait when he heard footsteps and voices coming from a side hall whose threshold was between the apse and the far aisle. There were two men, from what he could tell, one light of foot, the other heavy. He could not yet make out words, but the conversation was mostly one sided, though he heard enough to know that the voice with less to say was deep and harsh.

"You will of course be given a steed," came the voice of the talkative man as the footsteps approached the mouth of the hall. His voice was smooth and soothing, but contained a hidden venom. "And will ride to Penitent's Rest tomorrow to join with the army. Take this letter, it contains instructions for the quartermaster to outfit you with much more befitting garb than that simple getup. You are to be Justiciar Barrett's second in the coming campaign, you must look the part."

The footsteps were like beats of a drum now, echoing through the aisles and the nave. The first figure passed through and turned to the altar. He was a tall, slender man, dressed in the typical purple robes of a Cultist, but trimmed in gold instead of white. His face was aged, covered in deep wrinkles and sharp whiskers, but his eyes were bright and proud. He carried himself fully erect, his stride purposeful and graceful. The second figure, with the heavy feet, came next, following the first to stand in front of the altar. Fuster nearly gasped out loud at the sight. *No, no, it can't be*, he thought. But it was.

"And what of your true plans, Archbishop?" said the deep, familiar voice.

"Ah yes," the robed man replied in his serpentine tone, "my communion with Unheil went surprisingly well. He has dispatched a splinter force that is lying in wait. Not enough that His brother would take notice, but enough to provide us with the necessary cover. And He claims the mounts He has promised are faster than any horse of the land, and will be able to climb the sheer cliffs north of Bastion with ease. My personal guard and I leave first thing in the morning, to get a head start before the army mobilizes. We will cross the Euhr and travel through the Splintered Coast, north of the mountains, and meet our escort there. I must admit," he stopped to run his fingers along the runner and altar, "I cannot help but feel excited. Soon Primzahl's light will pour over this world like a cleansing wave, a rejuvenating fire. Ah! It will be glorious!"

"And what of Unheil?" asked the harsh voice, the source of which Fuster was still refusing to accept.

"Ha! A pawn in the plan, nothing more. He is a pathetic, lesser deity, but He will serve His purpose. Our deal was that the Heart will be His to command once we have secured it and nullified its more...apocalyptic...tendencies. His greed made it an easy sell. The fool! He and His brother will be the first abominations to perish when Primzahl takes Amalgam, and their distant patriarch will soon follow." The Archbishop's mouth was contorted into a cruel smile and his dark eyes twinkled with images of fire and brimstone. He stood at the center of the altar and took a deep bow, his arms outstretched in praise. Then he straightened himself slowly, his face returned to a contented grin. "Go and get some rest. Oh! And I must thank you again for informing me of our other visitor. His welcome has been prepared, and the guards are looking for him as we speak. I do so hope to meet him soon."

\#

Fuster was running along the roof. What an unfortunate turn of events this had turned out to be. It had taken every ounce of discipline inside him to sneak back along the balcony and out the window quietly, but now caution was an afterthought. He had done exactly what he had come to do: gather vital information. But now he must get out, and they knew he was here.

He reached the eave and plunged over the side, catching himself on the snarling head of a grotesque. After a series of drops from handhold to handhold he was standing on the wall again, but he could not simply plunge over the side. Here the wall rose straight out of the edge of the cliff, and there was no escape there but to plummet hundreds of feet into the sea. The city that had seemed so quiet and subdued when he entered was now alive with activity. Patrolling torchlight was everywhere, glowing worms moving between the teeth of the great beast. There were guards heading straight for him along the rampart. Night had him hidden, but their lights would reveal him and there would be nowhere to run. Behind him was the gable end of one of the cathedral's outbuildings, and the terminus of the wall. To his left was the climb from which he had come. To his right, the plunge. He was beginning to panic, looking back and forth, no escape, no good option.

He charged. The guards staggered, surprised by the figure sprinting toward them from out of the shadows. They began to draw their weapons, but Fuster barreled between them, knocking them to the ground.

But their cries drew the attention of their comrades farther ahead, and the next pair were prepared well in advance for Fuster's charge. He saw this, and turning to the left he leapt from the rampart and grasped the eave of the nearest building. He hoisted himself up and clambered along the roof, knocking shingles loose and sending them crashing to the street below. There were cries from every direction now. The streets and alleys were filled with dancing flame, as the worms slithered this way and that, converging on their prey.

A black crossbow bolt whizzed past. Then another. A third right between his legs, ricocheting off the roof and disappearing into the night. He clambered faster, did his best to follow a random path while still maintaining his footing on the steep, slippery surface. A leap across an alley put him on another roof, perpendicular to the first, and he scrambled up to the ridge. Without bothering to take in the view he slid down the opposite side and launched himself into the air again, catching the next island of his journey as more bolts arced overhead. Finally he came to a gap he could not cross.

The main road was below, as bright as daylight. The worms were running by, clad in their mail, flaming eyes searching, trying to pinpoint him based on the calls and reports of their comrades. He could feel their hatred, their hunger. Their dreadful voices filled his ears. Smoke assaulted his nostrils and drew tears from his eyes. There were shingles cracking and falling somewhere behind him. They were on the roofs, coming for him. He froze, thoughtless, hopeless, driven by the will to survive but left with no road to take.

And then he saw his salvation. Far to the right was a gatehouse crossing the main road. A dividing wall stood between two districts of the city. If he could get to it he would be able to cross this horrible river of steel and fire and get back on the outer ramparts. With fresh resolve he took off again. His footfalls shattered many of the shingles, making loud clangs and raining shards down onto the hunters. They spotted him. Bolts began flying toward him from a new angle, up out of the now bright and fiery throat of the monster. There was still too much distance between him and wall, one of the projectiles was sure to find its mark. He turned back right, up over a ridge again and out of sight of the monster's gullet.

He was being chased up here now as well, but he was far more agile than his pursuers, and except for the occasional launch of one of their own stingers they posed little threat to him. He kept on, running, leaping, running, leaping, slipping, scrambling, running, leaping. Too many times he nearly surfed into the air on a displaced shingle, but fortunately every time he found new footing or caught an eave and hoisted himself back up, but his muscles were fatiguing. His legs would carry him as long as he had the will to live, but the same could not be said for his arms. Eventually they would give out if he had to keep scaling ridges and catching himself after barely making it across a too far gap. Fortunately the end was in sight, just a couple of more jumps and he would find his feet planted firmly on the stone bricks of the dividing wall. The whoosh of a bolt filled his ear as he scrambled over the final ridge. A barely controlled slide translated into a graceful launch, and he passed between two crenelations and rolled onto the wall, landing on his hands and knees.

"Hey!" One of the worms was there, sword drawn, eyes filled with bloodlust beneath his mail cap.

He plunged in and swung at Fuster, but the Riisgardian rolled out of the way and back onto his feet. Fuster rose up, drawing his dagger and running it across the guard's throat. The man grasped at his neck, muffling a gargling sound, and quickly collapsed onto the floor. But Fuster did not have time to catch his breath. There were more cries. Men to the south were running his way from the junction with the main wall. And they had crossbows. Soon they would be raising them and letting fly a swarm which he could not escape. He sheathed his blade and turned north, sprinting as fast as he could, eyes wide with fear and lungs burning with every breath. He was across the gatehouse now, and the outer wall was in sight. To his relief there were no men between him and the intersection, but how many would be around the corners? To the left? To the right? How could he hope to stampede his way through the sentries that remained between him and his freedom? Surely he had not yet come far enough that there was solid ground beneath the wall; he would be forced to make the right turn and continue along the rampart. And if he did make it to the ground, how many would pursue him? And for how long? They would send horses after him, no doubt, and he would not be able to outrun those. The junction was close at hand now, just a few more strides.

He felt a sting, a burn. A bolt was flying away from him, out over the battlement and down to the sea. But it had gotten a piece of him, left a clean crevice on the outside of his left arm. There was nothing to do but ignore it. A close call was better than a direct hit. But after a few more steps he stumbled. A few more and a darkness was encroaching upon his eyes, then more stumbling. He looked down at his arm. A black tar was filling his wound. It writhed and undulated like some vile invertebrate, mixing with his blood and penetrating into his flesh like a ravenous leech. The longer he stared, and the more of the substance disappeared into his body, the weaker he felt. The darkness was steadily closing in around him, wrapping his vision in a vignette even blacker than the night. He could still hear the cries, though they seemed far away. The tone had changed; it was joyous now, for the prey had been maimed. He was a wounded deer, ready to collapse after making its final adrenaline-fueled run through the trees, only to collapse from the shot of a smug hunter and be made into a meal, a coat, a trophy.

But Fuster knew his fate would not be so kind. Whatever this poison was, he did not imagine it would kill him. There was not enough sport in that. He would awake, be tortured, not for information or strategy, but for the sadistic pleasure of some Cultist. Or, possibly a worse fate yet, he would be sacrificed to Primzahl on that foul altar, his blood adding to the stain left by countless victims, his essence used for some diabolical invocation. He could not allow it. He would not allow it. If he had to fail his mission, if his life had to end, his enemy would have no further satisfaction. His soul would remain pure and unmolested, and he would see Daffer again among the trees of the Eternal Forest.

There were footsteps nearby now, more vibrations in the rampart than sound, drawing ever closer. The high-pitched draw of swords from steel scabbards. He was swaying, nearly unconscious. Shapes were moving around him, blurry and amorphous. Five? Or a thousand? They would not have him. With one last act of will Fuster threw himself toward the battlements. He climbed up between two crenelations, and with the last of his strength propelled himself as far as he could out into the sky. He lay there, floating in the air, the darkness drawing ever closer around his eyes. The cliff rushed by in an avalanche of crags and crevices, scars and barnacles. He spun peacefully, barely breathing. And behold, the sea was traveling up to meet him, how kind and welcoming. The crests and troughs reached out, offering him their embrace. Finally, accompanied by a deep and utter silence, the darkness closed completely on his eyes, and his body broke against the waves.

CHAPTER FOURTEEN
The Call

The sky was clear and bright over Taikanìk, but a cloud seemed to be hanging over Eshwar. He was sitting outside the base of Hague's tower, his elbows digging into his thighs and his head resting in his hands. His hair had now grown out to some extent, but his face was still as smooth as a babe's. The simple clothes that had covered him since fleeing Agrafell had been traded in for a pale orange robe, the garb of all the students in the Magehold, and a black sash reflecting his current placement in Loitsunìk's college of sorcery. He had elected, however, to keep his old leather moccasins, for they were comfortable and reminded him of home.

The mountain air was cool and dry, and the sun's rays warm. Anyone else would have been quite comfortable, but Eshwar was restless. His studies had been going better than anyone could have expected. Hague had insisted that his primary focus be the elemental branch of sorcery, for it was most easily applied to combat. He had requested some martial training to go along with his magic, but the chancellor would not hear of it.

"A good wizard has no need for such crude and rudimentary skills, don't you know," he had said.

Still, Eshwar thought some training with a sword couldn't hurt. And it would provide him with a challenge. Magic seemed to just…come to him, with little effort at all. After returning from the council meeting, it had been a matter of days before his pyrokinetic teacher had passed him off to study another element. Now his flames would be the envy of a dragon, his lightning the envy of the sky, his fluid locomotion the envy of a river. *But ask me to chop wood and I still wouldn't be able to swing an axe,* he thought when his professors praised his abilities. There was still more to learn from the elementalists, but they thought he knew all he needed for combat, and so he was shuffled to a different wing of the tower to learn about wards. Just like the rest he had taken to the concept quickly, and could conjure an aegis about himself that could deflect the strongest steel, but he was still learning, and was not quite at the point where he could dispel a powerful magical assault.

The sorcerers were beyond delighted with the progress he was making. He was a teacher's dream. But he was also a peer's nightmare. His aptitude would have made social bonds difficult enough, with him never spending much time around any other students before being moved to another discipline, but it had also made him a bit of a pariah. The forces of nature were not the only thing in which he inspired envy. Most of his fellow students were not happy that all the praise was going to this scrawny newcomer. He felt isolated.

Every night he returned to the little house in Taikanìk, which had become a comforting retreat. He often dined with Hague, who was even more elated than his teachers by his progress. Eshwar would have been happy to spend every day with the old man. It was true that the use of magic came naturally to him, but he couldn't say that he actually understood what he was doing, and he readily admitted that that bothered him. His time in the Magehold had led him to a place where he was less excited to learn to *do* magic, and more excited to learn *about* magic. But the archmage was adamant that he focus on his sorcerous studies, which at present meant his wards. Apart from a few tidbits that answered some simple questions, Hague was irritatingly tight-lipped, but he promised that once Eshwar could defend himself, and the current crisis, of which almost no one was aware, was over, then he would be free to study the finer points of academia, or anything else he desired for that matter. This abated his restlessness for a time, but it soon returned, starting as an itch which could not be scratched, and growing into a battery of undirected energy that he thought would soon cause him to burst.

As he sat by his fire or lay in bed at night, he thought often of the Riisgardians, especially Kelm, whom he felt was his only friend. Hague was kind, and a mentor, but also distant, and an authority. Bill was Bill. And he spent no time of substance with anyone else. But he had become attached to the others in the short time they had spent together. They had been kind to him when there was no obligation for them to do so, and Kelm most of all. Eshwar was concerned for their well-being and wanted desperately to hear some news of their plight. Had the battle started? Was it over? Who had won? And the most pressing question of all: was this world, which he had not even come to know, about to end? These thoughts and questions kept him awake far too long into his nights, and they were with him now, as he sat outside the tower.

He picked up a rock and began to fidget, seeking some relief from the anxious tremors in his bones. The high-pitched cry of an eagle sounded overhead. Eshwar felt as though it was taunting him, flaunting the freedom afforded by its wings while he was relegated to the hopeless ground. A dark thought crossed his mind. One zap of magical lightning would silence the winged bully, knock it from its airy pedestal and bring it down to share his prison. But the thought quickly passed, and he was ashamed of himself for allowing such a thing into his mind. This burgeoning irritability was just one more thing to add to his list of worries. From behind him he heard the sound of the tower door opening and closing, and footsteps approaching and stopping at his side.

"Eshwar, what are you doing here?" Bill asked.

"Master Borkheim wasn't feeling well. He said he wanted to rest and resume tomorrow, so I came back. I was hoping the chancellor might have some time for me, but the door was locked."

"He's working on a few things, and had me doing transcriptions, but then he got irritated and kicked me out. I wouldn't go disturbing him now if I were you. The old man can get cantankerous."

"He has a right, at almost three hundred." Eshwar looked up at Bill and grinned, "I'd hate to see you at that age."

"Hey now, don't you start with me, golden boy. Marek gives me enough of that."

"Are you allowed to call him that?"

Bill shrugged. "He's not here is he? I'll call him what I want."

Eshwar supposed that was fair.

In a most uncharacteristic fraternal gesture, Bill took a seat at Eshwar's side. "So why are you sitting here, of all places? Doesn't seem like the most comfortable choice."

"I've got a lot of thoughts distracting me. I figured this was as good a place as any to sit and stew. It's nothing you would care about."

"Try me."

"What?" Eshwar asked, surprised.

"Tell me what's on your mind. If I don't care, I'll just leave."

"Um. Okay." Eshwar paused for a few moments to articulate his thoughts.

"Speed it up."

"Fine. I'm worried about my friends at Bastion. And about the Heart, and Amalgam. The council meeting did nothing, and it feels like we've just given up. We're just waiting to see if the world ends. Waiting to find out if my friends are dead. I can't fucking stand it."

"Whoa, I think that's the first expletive I've heard you use. I like this side of you." Bill's dig elicited no response from Eshwar. The steward scratched his chin and thought for a moment. "So what do you want to do?"

"I don't know. Go join them. Find out what's happened. I hate just sitting here. And my studies aren't offering any respite."

"No wonder. They're not studies if you only have to be told one time and then you're an expert. You're a savant. It's really annoying."

This time Eshwar smiled, but his head remained hung. "What would you do, Bill?"

"Go."

"That's it? Just like that?"

"Yea, why not? If it's bothering you that much."

"But what about Hague? He's forbidden it several times now."

"And?"

Eshwar looked up and gave Bill a quizzical look. "What do you mean, 'And'? I don't want to blatantly defy him."

Bill scoffed. "Come on Eshwar, grow some balls. Look, Marek is old and wise and an archmage and all that good stuff, but that doesn't mean," he poked his finger repeatedly into Eshwar's chest, "that he knows what's best for *you* all the time. We can't always follow the path our mentors lay down for us, because it won't always get us where we need to go, despite the best of intentions. If your gut is telling you to go to Bastion, then you need to go to Bastion. It's probably the only way you'll find any solace."

Eshwar looked at the steward with dumbfounded eyes. He was blinking his eyes erratically, with his his lips slightly parted.

"What's that look? You look stupid."

"That advice…it was actually incredibly helpful. No offense, but I never expected something like that from you."

Bill grinned and stood up. "Tell anybody, and I'll cut your tongue out." He patted Eshwar on the back and walked off. "Give it some thought," he said before he was too far away.

The little rock began dancing between Eshwar's fingers once more. The eagle called again overhead, but this time he paid it no mind. Bill had essentially given him permission to consider an option that he hadn't dared to before: to make his own choice, to ignore Hague's wishes. He had fantasized about going, true, but thinking about the chancellor always quelled the daydream. Now he considered going to be an actual possibility, but it almost made him feel more torn than he had before. The tremors returned deep within him. The rock danced faster. His feet tapped so hard that they almost left the ground. The rock danced faster. The world began to fade away from his eyes. The rock danced faster. The world was gone, and Eshwar's eyes looked upon nothing but the recesses of his own thoughts.

There was Fentower, rising before him. It stood atop an area of hard, rocky ground in the midst of a wetland, the low lying marshes all around the mouth of the river Saad. He was standing on the causeway that stretched down out of the academy and went off to find higher ground. Every bit of the little island was capitalized by the complex, with dorms and academic buildings huddled together inside the low wall that delineated the hard from the muck. And at the rear, behind the beautiful college green, was the seemingly monolithic tower that the professors called home. It could not rival the scale of the great towers of the Magehold, but it was impressive to behold nonetheless. It was composed of three wings of equal height, on the sides and rear, that were littered with balconies and porticoes. The center section doubled these wings in height, and its forward facade was flanked by two smooth pilasters that reached from the ground to a lintel just below the roof. The roof itself was a smooth pyramid, reminiscent of the pinnacle of an obelisk.

Eshwar felt as though he was seeing it for the first time, but then…something was wrong. Fire. Smoke was rising now from the buildings, wrapping the tower in a choking cloud. People were pouring out of the gate, students and teachers being corralled by men wearing purple. There were stakes rising out of the swamp now, piles of wood at their bases. The purple men were tying people to them. Burning. They were burning his friends, his instructors. The non-magically inclined were forced to watch the display before being set free. "For Primzahl is a merciful master." Then Eshwar saw himself and others, hands bound, being led outside. But there was Master Leverich as well. He summoned a ferocious wind that turned the fire back on its masters. Then Eshwar's group disappeared, and under the cover of a magical veil they escaped into the marshes.

Now he saw the camp surrounding the Agrafell portal. Fortifications had been built on every side: angled stakes to protect against cavalry, wooden sentry towers, and fortified trenches. Master Leverich passed Eshwar off to a man whom he swore the boy could trust, despite the fact that he was wearing purple. The man led Eshwar through the camp nonchalantly, but casually avoiding most patrols. The place was dismal, dotted with cages filled with magic users who for one reason or another were not yet to be executed. Eshwar's body trembled with the fear that at any moment he might end up locked inside one of the cramped little prisons. The people inside looked at him with sad and pleading eyes, and he had to look away and down at the ground just to keep moving forward, deeper into the hellish collection of doomed men.

After an eternity they reached the portal. It had once been safely hidden inside its own little house of rock, but now it had been excavated and was floating out in the open at the base of an escarpment. It billowed and swirled peacefully with a low drone, blissfully unaware of the horrors being carried out in its vicinity. A makeshift square had been set up in front of it, with a row of iron stakes that were covered in ash and char. A line of the condemned was being spurred forward, their heads hung low, the will to fight gone. It seemed no one was spared from Primzahl's judgment; there were people of all races, human, fay, beast, and men, women, and even children. They were bound in groups of four to the stakes and offered up to the violet god, whom Eshwar imagined was relishing in their screams. The inside man led Eshwar up to the flank of the portal while the sentries were distracted by the spectacle and pushed him in, and the next thing he knew he collapsed onto the floor of a huge pyramid, heaving as if he would lose what little food was in his stomach.

And now he saw something different, something that did not come from the stream of his memory. A great fortress standing in the midst of mountains, with high walls and fearsome defenses. But it was surrounded by purple men, and like Fentower, it was burning. Clouds of smoke floated up from within the walls and grew so huge that Eshwar did not know what was mountain and what was ash. And now, like Fentower, people were being tied to stakes and burned, but this time they were soldiers instead of academics, though that made their screams no less horrible. A stake appeared before him, and strapped to it was a man in heavy armor. The plates glowed and danced with the heat and light of the flames that licked the man's boots. Eshwar looked up and into Kelm's face. Then beside Kelm was Hutta, and Fuster, and Webb, and even Enoch, all bound and burning. But his friends were not screaming. Their expressions were resolute and defiant, even as the sweat poured down their faces, and their flesh began to redden as the flames grew higher and hotter. Eshwar tore his gaze away, but all around him was the sound of laughter and celebration, the purple men singing the praises of their god, even as skin was melting before their eyes and the effluvia of a sickening barbecue filled the air. Eshwar's stomach turned, and he felt he might retch, and tears began to flow from his eyes. Finally he could take no more. He shook his head violently, and the calm, clear day over Taikanìk appeared before him again.

He rubbed his eyes and slapped his cheeks, making sure he wasn't still trapped in some vision, where the Magehold itself was about to go up in flames. Thankfully the sight before his eyes was real, and with a few moments of deep breaths, his heart rate began to normalize, and his stomach felt less likely to forcefully expel its contents. But the visions stayed with him, hanging there in his mind and on the outskirts of his eyes, faded and dreamlike, but present. The screams and laughter remained in his ears, muffled, but too loud for him to have peace. He rubbed his arms, fending off a chill that was not warranted by the ambient temperature. The third scene bothered him the most, for it was new to him. The others were memories that he had lived with every day, and he was slowly becoming desensitized to them. Or he was starting to repress them. Neither seemed healthy. But this new vision terrified him. Had he seen the future? The past? Was it happening right now as he sat here? Or was it just a manifestation of his anxiety? It was gnawing at him, like a canine caught in a trap gnaws at its own leg.

Eshwar looked to his left. There, far off toward the sea, the black tower stood, its turrets and projections both gleaming and absorbing the sunlight. He was supposed to be there again the following morning, ready for Master Borkheim to assault him with all manner of spells until his wards were effective enough to repel any attack. He looked to his right. A thread was lying across the ground, between the mountains and the forest. A thread that, if he pulled on it, would unravel the world before him until he stood at the gates of Bastion. He had seen Hague's maps, he knew the route. Normally the trip would take several days, weeks on foot, but Eshwar could blink, and find himself there faster than any steed could carry him. He craned his neck around to look behind. The unassuming door into the mountain was shut fast, and the chancellor's tower appeared out of the rock above it, with all the windows shuttered, confining Hague to the self-imposed isolation in which he preferred to undertake his research. Eshwar thought he heard him, high above, cursing some apparatus that wasn't performing quite right. Would the archmage be mad at him if he went to his friends? Did it matter?

He thought of breaking into the tower. A locked door was an obstacle he could easily handle. He would climb to the top and plead with Hague to let him go. But he realized it would be no use. Hague would only deny him, and seeing as he was already irritated, his denial would likely be more harsh than usual.

Eshwar sighed, but afterward his face hardened with resolve. He stood up, looked at the black tower once again, and then up to the chancellor's study, and then down to the road. He blinked, and when he opened his eyes he was standing on the rutted dirt of the thread that would carry him to his friends. Taikanìk was miles away and above, only the tower visible from this angle. He took one last look up to the peaks, and then turned to look down the road to the southwest, and blinked again.

CHAPTER FIFTEEN
The Siege of Bastion

Horns were blowing and echoing through the mountainside over Bastion. The enemy had been sighted. The garrison from the South Maw had arrived in the wee hours of the morning, providing an updated numbers report. They had been allowed a few precious hours of sleep before they joined the rest of the defenders in the yard and on the Bulwark. Andor, Hutta, and Kelm were briskly crossing the yard, having emerged from the great hall, where the field hospital was ready to receive any injured. The infantry men, several hundred, were gathered in the yard behind the portcullis, waiting to welcome the visitors should the gatehouse be breached. They were outfitted in mail and plate, many with tower shields and shortswords; but there were some, those who had been soldiers and adventurers before swearing themselves to Bastion, who were geared with their personal armor and weapon choices, unique islands in an otherwise monotonous sea of flesh and steel. Andor and the others passed by these men and climbed up to the inner wall, then crossed from the inner gatehouse to the outer, and found the other commanders standing together on the outer wall.

Backus was standing with his arms crossed, looking out at the incoming force with fiery eyes. Josalynn stood beside him. A mail shirt that covered her arms, as well as leather gloves and vambraces, had been added to her armor. And past them both was Zurofel, clothed in a loose mail hauberk. A serrated axe hung at his hip, but it looked to be more a tool than a weapon, and he was holding a battered spyglass up to his eye.

"This doesn't make sense," he was saying, "there are no siege engines. There doesn't even appear to be any archers. And many of them seem to be wearing ill-fitting armor. This is not a force with which to attack a motte-and-bailey, let alone a fortress of this size."

"What about the numbers?" asked Josalynn.

"Six squares of two hundred, just as the sentries from the South Maw reported," the dwarf replied. "Twelve-hundred men. Better odds than we had hoped for."

Josalynn nodded. "You're right though, something doesn't seem quite right. Even the Cult of Primzahl can't be so arrogant as to think they can defeat us with that bunch. There's been no more word from the North Maw?"

"No," Backus interjected, "at last report the north side of the river was quiet. There's been no activity since the supply caravan was raided."

Hutta and Kelm frowned at his words. A report had come in from the North Maw not long after Webb's departure that the caravan had been sacked by Cultists. There had been no survivors and the bodies and supplies had been burned. On top of that, there had been ample time for Fuster to return since his report had arrived, but he had not, and Hutta feared the worst. The absence of their friends had left the two remaining Riisgardians feeling somber and lost.

"Well, we'll see what they'll offer in parlay," Andor said. "No doubt they'll feign diplomacy before the fighting starts."

"I'd cut one of those trebuchets loose right now," said Hutta.

"This isn't some disorganized mercenary operation, Hutta," Josalynn countered. "We'll hear what they have to say. But I assure you they won't say anything that we can take seriously. You'll get to drop a rock on them, if that's what you want."

"I can't wait," he replied.

From behind them a horn sounded again, but this time it originated from above, and fell down the mountainside like an avalanche. Two long reports. Celestials. Then two short ones. Unheil's. With surprised expressions the commanders spun about and looked up into the sky. Black wings were visible sweeping over the upper citadel, back and forth like birds of prey circling their quarry.

"Shit!" Andor yelled. "I've got to get up there." Without another word he took off running, back across the bridge to the inner wall and disappearing down the stairs.

Josalynn made a move as if to follow him, but hesitated, and looked back at the approaching army.

"Go, Josalynn," Backus said, "we can handle things down here."

She nodded, and disappeared after Andor. The remaining four turned back to look out from the wall and await the advance of the enemy. The army stopped a short distance away, three squares in front, then a knot of unarmored clergymen, then another three squares. From within the ranks emerged three horsemen. On the right rode a standard bearer, supporting a pole that rose out of his saddle, from which hung a white banner, trimmed in a wide border of regal purple, with the simple device of the eye in its center. In the middle, slightly ahead of the others, upon a steed clothed in ornate finery, was a figure who was the apparent commander of the force. Encased in full, fuchsia-dyed plate, it rode forward with its head held high within a winged sugarloaf helm. A black cloak flowed from beneath its pauldrons, trimmed with thick, white tassels, and featuring the device of the eye, also white, but rotated ninety degrees, the symbol of the Cult's Inquisition. And riding beside this figure, looking resplendent in purple-hued plate that was trimmed in gold, was Webb.

Hutta leaned forward and wrapped his fingers over the edge of a crenelation. His eyes saw red and his knuckles turned white within his gauntlets. Kelm's mouth fell open, and he shook his head in disbelief. Even Backus and Zurofel could not remain stoic at the sight, but composed themselves by the time the trio reached the base of the wall.

The leader craned his neck back and a masculine voice came from within the helmet, "I am Justiciar Barrett. Open your gates and surrender the mages in your ranks, and the rest of you will be free to go."

A guttural hocking sound arose out of Backus's throat, and he released a large and discolored glob of saliva directly at Barrett's head. A breeze caught it and it landed harmlessly on the ground at the horse's feet, but the message was clear.

"Now here's my deal," the warden retorted. "Hand over that traitor, then turn around and leave this valley, and we won't rain boulders down on your heads."

The justiciar stared up at him for a moment, then silently turned his horse about and headed back toward his army, and his companions moved to follow him.

"What? No speech? What kind of Cultist are you?" Zurofel called down.

"Eloquent speeches are the domain of the evangelists," the man called back, without turning his head, "I'll let my actions speak for me."

"Webb! WEBB!" Hutta screamed, but the big man made no answer.

"Zur," Backus said, "get ready to unleash the first volley."

As if anticipating the impending assault, the three riders sped up to a cantor. Barrett stood up in his saddle, and waved a hand toward the army. In response, the clergymen, five of them, formed in a line, still in the center of the array of troops, and began to chant. An amber energy began to swirl about each of them, swirling around their bodies like a dancer's dress. Then it rose up, and the five streams joined together, becoming a violent maelstrom above their heads. Once it reached a certain height, it began to bloom like a fungus, and stretched out into a sprawling canopy. The farther the energy stretched from the source, the more it seemed to solidify and define itself, until it appeared as though a great upturned bowl was covering the army. The three riders moved beneath its lip, which settled still some distance off the ground, and turned about once more to look back toward the fortress.

Backus slammed a fist onto the crenelation before him. "Fucking hypocrites! Loose a trebuchet. Now!"

Zurofel looked to one of his crews and raised an arm. They prepared themselves, and when his arm fell the machine's counterweight fell with it, pulling the sling around and releasing a boulder into the air. It flew out from the walls and across the valley until it slammed into the massive ward. There was a deep boom, and a wave of reverberation traveled across the amber surface, but the projectile crumbled and slid down the cap of the mushroom, its pieces dropping to the ground and coming to rest, safely away from any enemy troops.

Backus' nostrils flared. "Well, no need to waste arrows I suppose. MAGES! Cast at will!"

A volley of conjured elements shot forth at intervals from amid the ranks of archers, but every bolt of lightning, every ball of fire, icy shard, and ray of raw energy was dispelled against the mystical shield, with even less reaction than the stone projectile. When it was clear there was no use, Backus raised a hand to stay the onslaught, then rubbed his eyes and snout in frustration.

"They're plan was always to draw us out," Kelm said. "That's why there are no siege engines."

Backus scratched at the fur of his jaw for a few moments, then said, "If they want to meet us on the field, then we will give them the pleasure."

"What?" Hutta cried. "With all due respect Backus, that's a terrible idea. We can't win a war of attrition. Let's wait them out, they can't keep that thing up forever."

"I'm inclined to agree," Zurofel said.

Backus let out a deep growl. He pointed up to the dark creatures in the sky. "Do you see that!? That's no coincidence. This is a coordinated effort, one that we never could have anticipated. We need to end this quickly, and then concentrate on the celestials."

"Let's just send the infantry to the upper citadel," Kelm offered. "The walls can be held without them."

"There are thousands of celestials, Kelm," Backus countered. "They will keep coming, until none of us are left. But, if we win on this front, down here, then I have a feeling we win on both. It's the best chance I see."

Hutta shook his head. "I think it's a mistake."

Backus shoved a furry finger in Hutta's face. "A decision has to be made, and I'm in command. If you want to disrespect my order, then go out there with your friend. Otherwise, file in with the infantry. We're taking the fight to the field. Zurofel, you have the Bulwark."

He stormed off toward the gatehouse, leaving Hutta and Kelm a little dumbfounded. Zurofel sighed and shook his head, but encouraged the Riisgardians to follow the warden. Down in the yard, they took places beside Backus at the head of the column. He had calmed down, slightly, and acknowledged them with a nod. A second draught of stamina from the stables was distributed to each soldier, and the overdose was like a surge of adrenaline. Their skin reddened and their muscles bulged. Men began to bang their shields in wild anticipation for the coming fight.

"This Cultist army is little more than a conscripted militia!" Backus yelled to the infantry. "Each of you is worth ten of them!" Manic cheers rose out of the ranks. "Let's show them why this fortress has stood for five hundred years, and why it will stand long after they rot!" More cheers. Then he addressed Kelm and Hutta, "We just need to get to those priests. Take out that shield, and Zur can rain fury down on them."

The Riisgardians nodded, and Backus gave the signal for the portcullis to be hoisted up, and the outer doors opened. Kelm felt the potion coursing through him. He drew his sword and gripped the hilt so hard his fingers cracked, and in his other hand he held his buckler. Hutta drew his sword as well, and Backus's axes left his hips. The gates swung open, and the soldiers of Bastion poured into the valley. When they were close to the enemy Backus halted them and raised an axe.

"Shield wall! Arrowhead formation!"

The entire phalanx shifted and formed into a large wedge, the men with tower shields forming the perimeter. Backus and the others stayed in the vanguard near the tip, and as one unit they marched beneath the brim of the ward and right into the middle square of enemy troops. The cultists fell on them like flies, but they were repelled almost effortlessly. The perimeter men thrust out from behind their shields with shortsword and spear, pushing ever deeper into the enemy ranks. And for every defender that did fall, another moved in to take his place, keeping the formation tight and strong. The grass was already turning red with blood, and the stench of death began to fill the air beneath the amber canopy.

The arrowhead had reached the center of the square when Webb and Barrett appeared, riding at a charge with weapons drawn. Their horses leaped over the perimeter of the formation and they proceeded to wreak havoc, trampling, slashing, and impaling anyone in their path. They burst out and back into the line in several places, leaving openings in the shield wall for their troops. Backus yelled orders, tried to rally the men back into formation, but the damage was done. The arrowhead was broken. From there the battlefield fell into disarray. The defenders were divided into small groups, striking down enemies in wild fury, but more cultists moved in wherever their brethren fell.

Backus grabbed Hutta and Kelm and pulled them close. "Take a squad. Push forward and get to those priests. I'll keep trying to reorganize our ranks."

The Riisgardians grabbed a few men and formed into a flying V and continued to push forward, ever closer to the swirling column of energy ahead. Backus moved backwards, burying his axes in the throats of several cultists as he went, until he was roughly at the center of his forces. He called out again, trying to tighten the men back into close order. His men moved toward him as best they could, but they were slowed by the influx of the enemy, and more of the defenders were falling all the time.

Backus heard hoof falls behind him, and he spun about to see Barrett riding toward him, a long spear held between his arm and body, pointed at his foe. Backus tried to dodge but it was too late, and the spear passed through him between his clavicle and his heart, spinning him around and breaking one of his ribs. His natural strength, augmented by the draught, kept him standing. His eyes grew wide with fury and he let out a feral yell. With one of his axes he chopped at the spear, leaving a portion lodged in his body, but knocking the majority to the ground. He dropped his axes to the ground and picked up the spear shaft. Barrett was coming around for another pass, this time with sword held high. Backus stooped low and swung the shaft into the horse's legs. The spear splintered and cracked, and the animal tumbled over, throwing its rider into a dazed heap. The warden retrieved his axes, but his enemy managed to compose himself and stumble to his feet.

They met in a frenzied clash. Backus pushed forward in a flurry, and the justiciar fell back while desperately parrying. When he had fully recovered from his fall he halted his retreat, and retaliated against Backus with slashes and stabs. But the boar was lost in a rage. He continued to flail wildly, with little thought to defense. He dented his foe's plate with a few glancing blows, but Barrett managed to knock away one of his axes. Backus made a wide swing with his remaining weapon, but Barret moved in close and grabbed the wood protruding from the warden's chest. He twisted and pushed, and the pain brought Backus to his knees. The justiciar drew back his sword, ready to make the killing blow. Backus dropped his axe and reached up, grabbing the side's of the cultist's helmet. He pulled the man in, and with an upward thrust of his head, drove his tusks up underneath the helm. The sword fell to the ground and the man's arms began to flail. A muffled scream and gargling sound came from within, and blood poured out, down Backus's chin and both of their chests. The warden held the justiciar there until the flailing stopped, and then he pulled his face away and pushed the body to the side. He grasped at his axe and tried to stand back up, but he staggered and lost his balance, and collapsed beside his foe.

#

The squad led by the Riisgardians continued pushing forward. Men had been falling at their feet, and they had only lost one since beginning their charge. Some of the untrained cultists began to flee when Barrett fell, but most were lost in the lust of battle, and the fight was raging on all around. As they neared the rear of the infantry square, they saw Webb to their left. He had lost his horse or dismounted, but he still towered over the men around him. He had a sword in each hand, and was cutting down friend and foe alike, laughing maniacally as the blood of his victims rained onto his face. He continued wading through the combatants until he caught sight of his old companions.

"Hutta!" his voice bellowed across the field. The men around him took note of where he was looking, and they cleared out of the path of his sight, leaving a swathe of open land between him and the others. He dropped the two blades, and then reached behind him and drew a huge claymore from his back. He raised it and pointed it at Hutta, holding with one hand what many men could not have held with two. "You know I can't let you go any farther."

"Kelm, you've got to get to those priests," Hutta said. "Our boys can't hold out much longer. I'll keep this traitor distracted, and with Eagle's guidance, I'll get us some justice."

Kelm nodded. "Bear give you strength, Hutta." The squad continued on, leaving Hutta to advance toward Webb.

"We mourned you, you know," he said to the big man. "When the report came in that your caravan had been raided. Your armor was found in the pyre!"

"Well, I had to make it look convincing, didn't I?" Webb said. There was something different about his voice.

"How could you do this to us? How could you defect? How did they even get to you!?"

Webb laughed. "You sound so desperate, '*boss*'. But the truth is, I've worked for the Cult for a long time. Long before we left Riisgard." There it was again, a refinement that wasn't there before.

Hutta was dumbfounded at the depth of the treachery. He struggled to find words. "How...but...how could *you* pledge yourself to their god? You barely acknowledge our own faith! And how could you even be capable of deceiving us like that?"

"Oh please, I don't give a shit about their god or their cause. There's one thing that I've always made clear: it's all about the money. And the Cult of Primzahl has the deepest coffers I've ever seen. As for the deception, well, playing the dumb brute has always served me well. It worked on you like a charm. But now, as much as I like the confounded look on your face, how about we get down to fighting."

Hutta's temper flared, and he rushed at Webb. The big man's eye's filled with lust and his face stretched into a huge grin, and he bounded forward like a stampeding animal. His strikes were forceful and erratic, and the huge sword gave him more reach than his height already afforded him. Hutta had to deflect the blows to the side when he parried or risk Webb smashing right through his defense, or worse, his sword breaking. He ducked and dodged the wild swings, dancing around the mountainous man as best he could. He went low and slipped behind Webb's legs, and ran his blade along the back of his thigh, hoping to hamstring him, but this new armor was too thick, and Hutta's effort was rewarded only with the grating sound of metal slicing into metal.

"You'll have to do better than that," Webb laughed. He reached behind and grabbed the braid of Hutta's beard, then swung him around and threw him back down in front.

Hutta wailed in pain, but gathered himself quickly. He rolled to the side, causing a narrow miss from the claymore, and was back on his feet and continuing the dance. He tried to stay in as tight as possible to prevent Webb's wide slashes, but even in combat the big man was frequently handling the claymore with one hand, as if it had no weight at all, and a blow from his fist was like being hit with a warhammer. Hutta's breath started to grow heavy. Despite his enhanced endurance, fighting such a ferocious opponent was wearing him down.

"If you were working for them, why'd you even come on that job?" Hutta asked, hoping to distract Webb, even slightly.

"Oh, do you have to ruin a fight with talking?" Webb asked as he aimed another swing at Hutta. "They wanted me to come, of course. I told them you had taken the job, and they wanted me to follow along. That conjurer was no such thing, he was a cultist." He grunted and swung again in between sentences. "They didn't want to occupy the old fort, because that would imply it had some value, and it would identify their supply line, so they had the 'conjurer' put on his little masquerade to keep the place secure. He was bringing creatures through the portal, not summoning them." Hutta managed to sweep Webb's legs and knock him over, but he recovered quickly and avoided the followup blow. "The fool started having too much fun, got sloppy, and so you were hired to take care of it. The Cult still didn't want to reveal their stake in the situation, so they sent me as a double agent. But the cave-in, coming to Amalgam, that was never part of the plan."

Hutta's face swirled in a mix of anger, confusion, and disappointment. "And why stay with us after? Why wait this long?" He took a stab at a joint between Webb's curaiss and waistcoat, but the claymore deflected his sword to the side.

"You still just don't get it, do you Hutta? I've been under orders this whole time. I was going to defect in Deltaville, slip away in the night. I wasn't really out getting drunk and fucking whores, you know. Well, I was doing some of that. But I met with that evangelist that night, and he instructed me to stick close to Enoch, to infiltrate Bastion. I was having a hard time formulating a plan to make that happen, but then the rest of you took care of it for me. Too easy." He backhanded Hutta with a free hand, sending him twirling away. "Then, once I had enough intel, I had to come up with a plan to get out of here and report to the Cult. And Backus sends me away! Really, it's like the lot of you fools didn't want to challenge me at all. And slaughtering the rest of the caravan was wildly entertaining." Hutta moved back in with a flurry of slashes and thrusts, but Webb deflected them all, and then raised a leg and delivered a heavy kick to Hutta's torso, knocking him on his back. Webb raised his sword and brought it down in an overhead slash, but Hutta grabbed his own sword by the blade and caught the claymore with a perpendicular block. The traitor stood over him, pressing down, slowly overpowering the smaller man. "I was going to kill you in that desert, you know. Get you alone, leave you to bake on the sand, and the others never would've been the wiser. Instead we just lost that fool, Daffer. Which wasn't a total loss; out of all of you, he annoyed me the most. And then," he laughed, "and then *you* saved *me*! How ironic life can be."

Fury flared in Hutta's eyes. He pushed Webb's blade up and aside, and then rolled back onto his feet. But he had been baited successfully. He raised his sword and charged forward in a rage, and the tip of the claymore met his abdomen. There was the sound of metal on metal as it pressed through his curaiss, then a disquieting liquid sound, then metal on bone as it scraped against his spine, then metal on metal again as it emerged from the rear of his plate. The wrath was gone from his eyes, but they remained wide with shock, and his mouth hung open, a series of weak gasps escaping as he exhaled. He dropped his sword to the ground and his arms fell to his sides. Webb put a hand on his shoulder and leaned forward to whisper in his ear.

"*Primzahl is a merciful master,*" he breathed. Then he pulled back, staring at Hutta. The horrible grin returned to his face, and his eyes were filled with a morbid sadism. "But I'm not."

He grasped the hilt of his claymore with both hands, and with a strenuous grunt hoisted Hutta into the air. Hutta hung there, struggling through short and haggard breaths, until gravity did its job. His body slid down the blade until it was stopped by the crossguard, and then sank toward the ground as it sliced through his torso and the weakened plate until the motion was halted again by his ribcage, creating a gaping canyon in his torso. Webb laughed maniacally again, bathing in the blood of his former comrade. He held him there until the last breath escaped his lips, and the light faded completely from his eyes, and then he dumped him unceremoniously onto the ground.

#

Kelm and his squad pierced through the final ranks of the square, and before them, atop a slight rise in the land, were the five priests. Their arms were outstretched, their fingertips just touching those of the next man in line. They were chanting loudly in unison, but their voices were nearly drowned out by the magical wind swirling about them like a storm. The violent maelstrom coalesced and twisted over their heads, feeding the apex of the ward and flowing out to form the canopy. The squad formed a line just outside the square, facing back the way they had come, allowing Kelm to break away and cover the last stretch of ground. He stopped as he reached the row of men, bewildered by their hypocrisy. Could they be so naive as to think these priests were no different than the very mages they burned at the stake? Did they really believe this incantation was pulling some divine power from a god on another world? He did not have time to ponder very long. Behind him, men were screaming and dying, the numbers of the defenders were continuing to dwindle. Despite the obvious disparity in training between the defenders and their foes, the difference in numbers was overwhelming. The four hundred men at the flanks were steadily pressing in. And there were six hundred more in front of him, and the men of the middle square had noticed his presence. They were starting to advance, knowing they must defend the priests.

Kelm ran up to the left end of the line of clergy. The amber wisps began to whirl around him, and the energy felt strange, like fog given form, but it did not impede his progress. All of the priests' eyes were blank, like clean eggshells. He approached cautiously, and drove his sword through the belly of the first man, and twisted. The priest's pupils and irises reappeared briefly before rolling back into his head, and Kelm pushed him backwards off of the blade. The stream of energy originating from the man faded, its last tendrils traveling up into the greater tornado. The energy had not hindered Kelm's sword, and he thought that it must only be effective in its more petrified form up above. He quickly decapitated the second priest with a swift swing, and his energy faded as well. The remaining three began to show signs of strain. Their bodies shook and sweat started to run down their foreheads. After the third man hit the ground, the other two began to shake even more violently, and streams of blood appeared from their nostrils. Kelm felled the penultimate priest, and the final man succumbed to the strain of trying to maintain the spell. He fell to the ground on his own, either dead or unconscious, and the last of the energy sources dissipated. The maelstrom maintained its violent rotation, but its lower extremity began to recede upward, until it disappeared into the apex of the shield. And then Kelm could see blue skies above him. From the center outward the canopy began to recede, until after a few moments the amber had evaporated completely.

The advancing troops stopped and looked upward. Fear transformed their faces as they watched their safety disappear before their eyes. Kelm heard a call go up from behind him, "Fall back! Danger close!" Over the din of the battlefield, he thought he could hear Zurofel's voice call a drawn out "Loose!" and then the whipping of slings as counterweights fell. From over his head boulders appeared in the sky and slammed down into the enemy's rear squares. The fortunate victims were crushed instantly. Others were screaming as their arms and legs were transformed into gelatinous stains beneath the stones. And then men were catching fire. Balls of flame were issuing forth from the mages on the wall, magical missiles that shot straight into the ranks. The archers on the wall stayed their hands, as their volleys would have been too random with their allies still on the ground, but the enemy was routing. And the defenders were rallying. Great cheers and battle cries were rising along with the screams of horror, and the soldiers of Bastion were easily dispatching their discouraged foes and falling back toward the gate. Kelm turned around, ready to join the retreat, just in time to see Hutta's body hit the ground.

His eyes widened and his mouth fell open. He tried to call out, to scream, but no sound would come. Webb was standing over Hutta, skin and armor alike covered in blood, his teeth bared in a triumphant and sadistic smile. Kelm sprinted toward him, but Webb saw him coming and knocked him aside with a swing of his arm. Kelm tumbled across the ground, coughing as he tried to regain his breath.

"Ah, Kelm," Webb said as he turned toward him and outstretched his arms in greeting, "it's just you and me now. Fuster is dead, I should let you know, food for the fishes. And in a few moments, it'll be just me."

"You've lost, Webb, can't you see that. Look around." Kelm wiped his mouth and stood up. "Just surrender."

"And then what? You execute me? I can see in your eyes that you want my head on a spike. I'd much rather finish you off and be on my way."

"I'll cut you down for what you've done, traitor. And I hope you never see the Eternal Forest."

"Oh I hope not too," Webb smiled. "I'm not eager to see any of you again. But we'll see who's going to cut who down."

Webb swung his claymore, and it sundered Kelm's buckler when he blocked. He dropped the now worthless shield and wrapped both hands around his sword hilt. He parried blow after blow from Webb's weapon, but like Hutta, he had to hastily deflect if he hoped not to be overpowered. He attempted to run in and slam the larger man, but to no avail, he simply bounced off of his target, and narrowly avoided having his scalp removed. He out-finessed Webb's brutal style several times, but the heavy suit of plate brushed off every strike. They continued to clash until Kelm, like Hutta before him, began to tire. Eventually he made a mistake, and with a wide sweep Webb knocked the sword from his hand, sending it careening through the air to land some distance away. Webb spun back around from the follow-through of this swing with an arm outstretched, slamming it into Kelm and knocking him to the ground once again.

"Goodbye, Kelm," he said, raising the claymore behind his head with both hands. "Say hello to the others for me."

He leaned forward into a reckless fall and began to swing the sword forward. Kelm raised an arm before himself and squeezed his eyes tightly shut, bracing for a strike that was likely to rend him in two. But the blow never came. He waited another moment, but still nothing. Was he dead? Had it happened so quickly that he felt nothing at all? He opened one eye. There was still a blue sky above him, though it seemed dulled and grainy. He moved his arm aside, and there was Webb, diving at him through the air, the claymore bearing down on him. But he was frozen, suspended there before him. His faced was locked in a hungry snarl, his eyes fierce and full of hate. Then Kelm noticed something. Webb was moving, ever so slightly, toward him still. Fear took him and he scrambled away, but calmed himself when the motion remained slow, like sap traveling down the bark of a tree. He stood up and looked around. All around him at some distance was a gray haze. He thought he saw the shapes of men beyond the veil, moving slowly by, and he could hear muffled, drawn out screams and cries. Above him, round blobs, both gray and red, were drifting by through the sky. What was going on?

He retrieved his sword, which still felt solid and real. He swung it around and it moved normally. Then he tossed it into the air. As soon as it left his hand, it came to an almost complete stop, floating in the air. It was still moving upward but at a barely noticeable rate. Kelm grabbed it again and its weight fell fully into his hand, and with every motion of his arm it moved at full speed. Confusion and wonder mixed together in his mind. Was he dead? That really wouldn't make sense, given the circumstances. Had someone saved him? There was no one in sight, save for the hazy shapes and Webb, and this certainly wasn't *his* doing. And then, from within his memory, he heard Marek Hague's words: *in times of great clarity...or dire need.*

Possibilities flashed through his mind. Was he a wizard now? Surely his parents hadn't been able to cause something like this to happen. His thoughts went in a million different directions, and as they did things began to change. The noises from beyond grew louder, and Webb began to fly faster, the claymore continuing to slice forward through the air. Kelm sprung to action, and raced back over to the traitor. Webb looked like the figurehead of a ship, his arms and sword forming the bowsprit. Kelm stepped around him, and he could see

Webb's eyes slowly tracking after him, and the spiteful expression morphing into confusion. The bowsprit moved slowly down, and Kelm raised his sword above Webb's now exposed neck.

"Goodbye, Webb," he said. "I hope you don't get to say hello to anybody."

Kelm brought his sword down, slicing it cleanly through Webb's over-sized neck. He pulled it back when it began to glance off of the traitor's upper arm. A ragged curtain of blood hung from across Webb's throat, like a sheet of ice hangs from the eave of a roof. Blood ran freely down Kelm's blade, but when it dripped off the droplets paused in the air, floating toward the ground like tiny balloons. Kelm breathed out a long sigh, and suddenly his senses were bombarded with input. The hazy veil vanished, and soldiers were running all around, some crying in victory, others screaming in death. Balls of fire and stone soared through the air and crashed down in explosions of dirt, flesh, and steel. The curtain of blood liquefied and splattered on the grass, and Webb's body crashed down on top of it. His head rolled forward a few feet, his final expression one of bewilderment.

Kelm shook his head and gathered himself, then rushed to Hutta's side. He dropped to his knees and began to weep. Hutta was staring blankly into the sky, his mouth still hanging open. The blood had almost completely drained from within his abdomen, and his mutilated innards were clearly visible through the canyon in his gut. Kelm embraced him and kissed his forehead. Again the sounds of death and destruction faded from his ears. There was only him and Hutta, all alone and far from home. Kelm rocked back and forth, weeping into his bloody hands. He wiped his nose and took a deep breath.

"May Raven guide you into the Forest, brother, ' he said. Then he ran his fingers over Hutta's face, closing his mouth and eyes. He pulled his friend's hands up and clasped them together, resting them on his chest. He squeezed them tightly. "Until I see you again." He let go and took a seat beside Hutta's body, and watched the fury of Bastion rain down on the Cult of Primzahl.

CHAPTER SIXTEEN
The Upper Citadel

Andor and Josalynn were running as fast as they could up the mountain road. Had it not been for the stamina draughts they would have already run out of breath, and it still felt as though they would expend all their extra energy by the time they reached the upper citadel. They were almost at the top of a switchback when they heard a thunderous boom. They stopped and looked down in time to see the shards of a boulder tumbling down the canopy of a massive amber ward. Josalynn's eyes bulged and she felt distraught. She started to move back down the path, then hesitated and took a few steps back up, then shifted again in her indecisiveness.

"Josalynn, take a breath," Andor told her in a calm and soft voice.

She looked back toward him, and for the first time since he had known her, uncertainty was painted all over her face. "What do I do, Andor? I can't be in two places at once!"

He took a few steps towards her, and pointed down toward the Bulwark. "You have three capable men in command down there. Between them, they'll be able to handle whatever the Cult has brought into play. But those men," he now pointed upward, "despite the purpose of this fortress, many of them have never even seen a celestial, let alone whatever devils Unheil has sent. They will be afraid. But seeing you, having you with them, that will bring them courage. They need you, Josalynn. Come."

She nodded, resolving that he was right, and they took off running again. The journey upward seemed to take forever, but eventually they rounded the last bend and sprinted up the final rise. The first thing they noticed as they mounted the top of the cliffs was the archers on the walls facing inward, loosing arrows down into the yard. The soldiers were in disarray. The majority were near the center of the yard, but other groups and individuals were scattered all around. Creatures with sickly gray skin, the same as the forearm that Scout Harborough had found, were attacking the soldiers with tooth and claw. They were unnaturally lean and gaunt, as if all the cavities in their bodies were devoid of fluids, and their faces were flat, with orifices that looked as if they had once had noses but they had been sliced off. Their pointed teeth were as yellowed as their nails, though many had already turned red with blood. No clothes covered their bodies, and they did seem to have nipples and navels, but there were no genitalia between their legs. Instead their pelvises resembled the smooth codpiece of a suit of armor, and their bowed legs were set farther apart then those of a human. Harpy-like creatures with leathery, bat-like wings were swooping overhead, dropping in more of the gray creatures, as well as setting them loose on the walls and ramparts. The men of the upper citadel were quickly becoming overwhelmed and succumbing to fear, many attempting to seek retreat.

"What are these things?" Josalynn asked. "They are unlike Unheil's usual filth."

"Like I said before, probably some sort of ghoul," Andor said. He reached back and grasped the black hilt protruding from behind his right shoulder, and from beneath his cloak he produced his greatsword. It was polished to the same darkened shine as his armor, and an ornate fuller ran nearly the length of the blade, featuring alternating crescents in a wave-like pattern. "Go to the men in the yard. I'll try to secure the ramparts." He ran off to the left and climbed the nearest stair to the next level of the citadel.

Josalynn strapped her left arm into her kite shield and drew her gladius, then sprinted toward the center of the yard. A soldier who was about to turn and run saw her coming, and cried out to the others.

"The Commandant! The Commandant is here!"

She reached the mass of men and moved in among them. "Circle up!" she yelled. "Shield wall! Spears, then archers!"

Without hesitation the soldiers formed concentric rings around her, men with shields huddling close on the outside, then men with spears, then the few archers who had been down in the yard. The men began to cheer, and all around the yard they began to rally to cries of "To the Commandant!" Soon every living man on the ground had made his way to the central formation, and smaller groups began to form rings of their own, until the yard looked like some choreographed dance floor. The ghouls bashed into the shield walls and were met by quick stabs from the soldier's blades. Some tried to leap into the groups, but were skewered by the spearmen. Their disgusting, pus-like blood slopped down in globs on the shield bearers, but this did nothing to dampen the men's renewed vigor. Their commandant was with them, and they would fight with her to the last.

"Archers, concentrate on the fliers! And take some pressure off your comrades on the wall!" Every command she issued seemed to give the men more courage. The ghouls were falling all around in stinking heaps, and some of the airborne creatures were letting out disturbing wails of pain and crashing into the rocky ground.

A ghoul managed to clamber into her formation. It pushed its way through the men, heading straight for her, as if it knew she was the harbinger of this fresh valor, and killing her would cause the men to once again run in fear. She welcomed it with several short slashes across its torso, and then a clean stab between its ribs, where she assumed it might have a heart. The soldiers only cheered louder as she struck the creature down, and inspired by the sight they continued slaughtering the unrelenting horde.

But suddenly there came a flap of wings like a hurricane. A huge, shadowy thing passed over them, and from black talons it released a new challenge. The delivery landed before them, near one of the smaller formations. It had the same gray skin as the ghouls, but it towered over everyone around it. Its knees were bent at an acute angle, leaving it standing in a perpetual squat, and above its ankle was another joint, making its lower legs like the hind legs of a cat, and its feet were oversized and flat. Lanky, elongated arms reached nearly to the ground, and ended in disproportionately large hands with sharp, black nails. It was square-jawed, with an underbite that revealed rotting, blocky teeth. Its nose was wide and snubbed, and featured nostrils that looked perpetually flared. Its eyes were similar to a human's, but set deeper and too far apart. Its head was bald and the skin tight, accentuating the ridges and contours of its skull. In its left hand it held a giant wooden club, inset with jagged pieces of metal and stone, the whole thing stained with various colors that were presumably all blood.

Josalynn's eyes widened. This was a foe she knew. One of Unheil's demons. Her men had never laid eyes on one, and she knew she must keep her composure or risk losing them to terror. She squared herself to face the demon, and then, careful not to allow any fear to enter her voice, began to shout out more orders.

"Fan out, keep the shield wall tight! Archers, loose at will!"

A volley of arrows flew toward the creature, and it raised its free hand to protect its face. The arrows stuck in its arm and torso, but there was no reaction, no cry of pain. The projectiles were little more than an annoyance to the demon. It drew its club across its body and sent a back-swing into the nearest group of soldiers, sending several of them careening through the air. The club swung back like a pendulum into another group on its right, cracking armor and bones like chalk, its surface now glistening with a fresh coat of red paint.

A brave soul rushed the demon and began slashing at its legs, releasing streams of black blood. This elicited a response, but the cry was composed more of rage than of pain. The demon reached down with its right hand and grabbed the man around the abdomen. Its hand was large enough that it wrapped fully around the soldier's body. The man struggled, pushing and writhing, even stabbing at the demon's fingers, but to no avail. The creature squeezed and the man began to scream out in pain, until all the breath was gone from his lungs. His armor folded and split, his innards lost all form, and his spine severed. He became a ragdoll in the creature's hand, and it swung its arm and cast him aside. The torque of the throw put too much pressure on what little was holding him together, and as he left the demon's grasp, his torso stretched and split in twain, sending his upper body on one trajectory and his lower on another, and his bowels became a vile rain. This amused the demon, and it laughed a deep and disturbing laugh.

The soldiers recoiled in disgust and horror, and a few even retched at the sight. Their bodies were tense, and courage faded from their eyes, making way for terror to fill the empty space. Josalynn knew she would lose them if she did not act quickly, but she also had never fought one of these demons, and she hadn't the slightest idea of how to bring it down, especially since both arrow and sword had bothered it little. There were no mages in the upper citadel, the few in the garrison

were all down on the Bulwark. All she had was Andor.
Andor!

She looked around desperately until she spied
him above her, and then called out at the top of her
lungs, "Paladin!"

Andor was on an upper rampart relieving a
ghoul of its head when he heard the cry. He looked
down into the yard and saw the demon lumbering
toward Josalynn and her line. It was flailing its club,
crushing or launching the men who had fallen out of
formation. The ramparts were still overrun, with ghouls
climbing all over, and the harpy creatures were even
swooping in to grab men and lift them into the air, only
to let them fall screaming from lethal heights. Despite
this, Andor ran toward the stairs without hesitation. He
descended as fast as his feet would allow, leaping down
a few steps whenever he could, until he reached the
lowest rampart. From there he jumped onto the shed
roof of a storage area on the citadel's eastern face, then
onto some crates, and finally to the ground.

"Get behind me!" he cried, waving everyone
aside as he approached the center of the line.

Josalynn and the men fell back, and left Andor
standing alone between them and the demon. He turned
to face it, and as it continued lumbering forward it
began to laugh that disturbing laugh, a laugh that would
have been sadistic if there had been any intelligence
behind it. The ghouls hung back in a semicircular
fashion, sneering and snickering, as if seeing this black-
hooded man being crushed was going to bring them
great pleasure. The soldiers, and even their
commandant, trembled with unease, uncertain of how
this one man was going to make any difference against

a foe that had already singlehandedly killed nearly two dozen of their comrades.

Andor stood before the approaching giant without flinching. His right hand let go of his sword, and his left twisted down, allowing the blade to rest on the ground in front of him. This made the men even more uncertain, and the demon only laugh more ominously. Then he raised his right hand. His thumb and forefinger were extended, sightly bent, and his other fingers hung loosely. He began to trace a circle through the air, and as he did, a line of white energy appeared and followed his finger. It crackled and vibrated violently, as if it were highly unstable. Once the circle was complete, he traced a vertical line, bisecting the circle, then a horizontal one, and then two more at forty-five degree angles from the others, until floating in front of his hand was what looked like a wagon wheel made of white lightning. The demon stopped laughing, looking slightly confused, but continued forward, undaunted by the tiny man and his tiny spell. Andor pulled his hand back now until it was even with his chest, extending all his fingers out as far as they would go, then he leaned forward and sent his hand back toward the energy with a mighty push. Although his hand never touched it, it began to fly forward. It rose up, and grew in diameter, until it was nearly as big around as the demon's torso was tall. It came into contact with the creature and passed into it, its upper extremity passing just below the level of its nose. The crackling sound intensified, and everywhere the energy had touched, it left behind an incision that was black with the demon's blood. The energy emerged from the creature's back side, and quickly dissipated, and the demon collapsed to the ground in a disorganized pile of severed parts.

Now it was the ghouls' turn to recoil in fear, and the soldiers were cheering once more. Triumphant cries of "Andor!" and "Paladin!" sounded in the ranks, and the eyes of the men were once again filled with courage. Without taking any time to bask in the revelry, Andor raised his sword and fell upon the ghouls once more. Josalynn was soon at his side. They fought back to back, him using strong, two-handed sweeps to sever limbs and roll heads, her bashing and blocking with her shield and impaling with thrusts of her gladius. Watching their commanders together made the men feel nigh invincible, and even though some of their comrades continued to fall, they fought on with reckless abandon.

"Thank all that is good that you were here, Andor," Josalynn said between kills.

"If only that had ended it," he replied, "but these ghouls just keep coming. The ramparts still aren't secure. I should get back up there." He brought his sword down in a vicious overhead slash and split a ghoul from shoulder to hip. "We need to try to bring the fliers down before they can drop the ghouls in."

"The yard shouldn't be our focus. Take some of these men and go back to the ramparts. I'll take the rest and secure the wall, hopefully take all the pressure off the archers and let them clear the skies."

Andor signaled several men and led them back to the citadel and up the stairs to the ramparts. Josalynn divided the rest into squads and instructed them to assault each of the wall's several stairways. Every one of them was occupied by groups of ghouls. They leaped onto the men from above, biting at them like wild dogs, but the men pushed through until they had mounted the tops of the stairs and were able to fight on level ground at the top of the wall. The ranks of the archers had been culled to dangerously low numbers, but the fresh influx of troops soon transfered control of the wall back into the hands of the defenders. Josalynn found Harborough sitting against the battlements, breathing erratically. His black leather hauberk was ripped open and claw marks were visible on his side, but there was much more of the ghoul blood covering his body than there was his own. He spoke, but his sentences were accentuated with moans and grunts of pain.

"Commandant," he said, "I...I don't know where...they could've come from. There was no sign...of these numbers...when I was doing re...reconnaissance."

"It's okay, Harborough," she knelt down and placed a comforting hand on his shoulder. "These are celestials we're dealing with. The gods provide their armies with many tricks. Let me see this wound." She peeled the leather farther back, revealing deep lacerations that ran from his chest to his hip, but had not penetrated through his muscle tissue. "You'll live, as long as we end this soon."

He moved to stand up, but fell back again. "I...can fight."

"No, you can't," Josalynn ordered, "Sit here and rest. We'll protect you."

She sheathed her gladius and placed her shield down near the injured scout, then removed her ancestral bow from her back and joined the line of archers. They concentrated their fire on the harpies, causing several to drop ghouls to their deaths, and felling many to the ground. But the situation beyond the wall looked bleak. Hundreds more ghouls were gathered around the boulders and jagged rock formations outside, waiting impatiently to be airlifted into the fray. The stream of harpies seemed to have no end; every one that was brought down was immediately replaced, from where, no one could tell. Andor and his men were holding their own on the ramparts of the citadel, but they were forced to press their backs against the stonework to ensure the fliers couldn't grab them and deliver them to the bottom of the mountains in spectacular fashion. Over half of the defenders were lying dead or injured. As long as the fliers continued adding more ghouls to the fight, attrition would eventually cost the men of Bastion the upper citadel.

But just in time, like a beautiful song, the sound of horns rose up from the lower citadel, reverberated over the edge of the cliff, and echoed through the upper yard. The horns of Bastion. Horns that sang a song of victory. The ghouls looked around with bewilderment, and then fear, as if they knew that the sounds meant defeat, and that at the very least more troops would be free to join the defenders of the upper citadel. The gray creatures scattered and ran, attempting to clamber over the walls, or latch onto passing harpies. The flying creatures made no effort to save their comrades and immediately began flying east. The ghouls beyond the wall followed, leaping and sprinting across the rocky landscape.

The soldiers cheered and celebrated, and moved through the yard clearing out what remained of their now-timid foes. Josalynn and Andor met in the center of the yard, and with sighs of relief embraced each other before moving off to help finish the slaughter. Incredibly, the day was won.

CHAPTER SEVENTEEN
The Heart of the World

Kelm still sat beside Hutta, stoically watching the destruction on the battlefield. The cultists were trying to retreat in every direction. Those who attempted to cross the rapids were being picked off by the archers and mages on the Bulwark, and those that sought cover in the mountainside to the south were hunted down by the infantry still outside the walls. Zurofel had unleashed his exotic ammunition into the enemy's rear squares; projectiles that had been enchanted and exploded upon impact, ripping through the ranks as thousands of shards of stone. One trebuchet had also been outfitted to launch the barrels of pitch, which, when followed up with a fireball from the mages, created a pool of fire so hot that it melted the bodies of those caught in the inferno. The outer extremity of the battlefield had become a red lake of shattered stone and amorphous flesh.

The bulk of cultists that had escaped annihilation were racing down the road to the west, but the men of the South Maw garrison had regrouped and were chasing after them, determined to secure the valley. It was unlikely that any cultists were going to see the end of the day. But there was no revelry in Kelm's heart. He was the last Riisgardian on Amalgam. All of his friends were gone, and Hutta, the man who had saved him from his sorrows and taught him to be a warrior, was lying desecrated before him, slain by a man who was supposed to have been a friend.

"I'm so, so sorry, Kelm."

The words were accompanied by a hand grasping his shoulder. He looked up to see Eshwar standing beside him.

"Eshwar," Kelm said, both confused and relieved, "what are you doing here?"

"I came to help, to make sure you were alright. It seems I was too late." He saw the confused face on the disembodied head close by, "No, Webb too."

"I killed Webb. He betrayed us, Eshwar. He did this to Hutta."

"By the gods. And Fuster?"

Kelm shook his head. "He went to spy on the Cult. Webb told me he's dead. I'm the last one."

Eshwar squeezed his friend's shoulder tighter, but could find no words to say. He looked around at the horror of the battle. The only comparison he had were the atrocities he had seen the Cult perform, but the scene before him was far worse. There were men crawling, legless and hemorrhaging, but desperately clinging to life. Some were still fighting, blood pouring and splattering, limbs and heads falling. Many were crying and screaming. And the smell. A pungent mix of excrement and iron. For a moment Eshwar wished desperately that he had not come, that he had never had to witness such a scene.

"This is horrible," he said, "how do you ever get used to this?"

Kelm stood up. "If you get used it, you've been doing it for far too long."

To their right, a litter was being carried toward Backus, who was still lying motionless next to Barrett. Kelm led Eshwar there, and helped the men lift the warden onto the stretcher. The spear was still protruding from his chest and back, but faint breath was escaping his muzzle. The soldiers carried him back toward the gate, with Kelm and Eshwar following in guard, ensuring no straggling cultist decided to make a last desperate strike. As they approached the gate, they noticed a horse-drawn cart coming from the north, crossing over the rapids. It reached the intersection before they did, and turned up to head inside the gatehouse. Another litter and a body were resting inside, covered in white blankets.

"Kelm!" a cry came from the cart.

Kelm and Eshwar abandoned the men carrying Backus, who were now safely under the watch of the archers on the Bulwark, and ran up to the vehicle. Their faces became ecstatic when they recognized its cargo. It was Fuster, bruised and broken, but alive. He smiled weakly and tried to speak again, but calling out to his friend had sapped his strength. After a few moments of painful breathing, his face became grave, and he was able to get out a few words.

"The siege ... all a feint ... Webb a traitor ... Archbishop on way to the Heart ... must ... tell Josalynn."

Kelm's eyes widened. "A feint? We'll tell her, Fuster, don't worry. We'll find her right now. And Webb is dead."

Fuster nodded. The men leading the cart explained that he had been found by scouts from the North Maw. He was slowly dragging himself, half dead, through the woods from the direction of the sea. They had given him healing draughts to stabilize his condition, but he would need much more extensive care. When they finished their story they spurred the horse on and steered the cart toward the great hall.

"Come on, Eshwar," Kelm said, "we've got a long climb ahead of us. Josalynn is at the upper citadel."

Eshwar stopped Kelm from running off. "Wait," he said. He scanned the mountain road, looking for a place to which he could blink. His eyes landed on a stairway attached to the upper citadel. It was the only good option. "Lean forward," he told Kelm, "we don't want to fall backwards."

Kelm looked at him, confused, but did as he said. Eshwar wrapped his arm around his friend, looked up at the stairway, and blinked. They stumbled forward and collapsed on the treads of the stairs, and Kelm immediately retched.

Eshwar stood and extended his hand. "Sorry, I should've warned you about that, too."

Kelm coughed and shook his head, then took Eshwar's hand. He scrambled to his feet, slipping in his own vomit, but recovered, and looked back, down at the battlefield far below.

"How did we…?"

"I've learned a few new tricks since you left the Magehold," Eshwar said.

"Obviously," Kelm replied. "Now let's find Josalynn."

They descended the steps and rounded the corner of the building to find themselves in the yard. Josalynn and Andor were in the midst of their soldiers, slaying some frightful gray creatures that looked as if they were attempting to escape. Kelm and Eshwar ran toward Josalynn, who had just finished extracting her gladius from one of the creatures.

"Commandant Willet!" Kelm called. "Andor!"

The commanders spun about at the sound of their names. Josalynn awaited the arrival of the two men rushing toward her, and Andor ran across the yard to join them.

"Who is this?" she asked, gesturing toward Eshwar.

"My friend, Eshwar," Kelm replied, "but there's no time for introductions. Fuster has just returned, badly injured. He said that the siege is a feint. He said that 'the Archbishop is on his way to the Heart.'"

"That can't be," she said, "they couldn't have slipped through this."

"They must be working with Unheil," Andor said, "this whole thing has been a destructive distraction."

"The Heart is around eleven leagues to the southeast," Josalynn said, shaking her head, "if they have a head start, there'll be no way to catch them before they reach it."

"I can help with that," Eshwar offered, "I can teleport."

"Thank the Narra," Andor exclaimed. "Can you take others with you?"

"Yes."

"Then we must leave at once," Andor said, turning toward the gate.

"You should drink some stamina draught first, and bring some water," Eshwar cautioned, "your stomachs aren't going to like the trip."

"Wait just a moment," Josalynn said. "Let's take a minute to think. What's the situation down below, Kelm?"

"We've won, but at great cost. The cultists are in retreat but there's still some fighting going on. Hutta…Hutta is dead, and Backus is gravely injured."

The commandant took a deep breath and a moment to think. "I need to stay. Zur can't command the entire fortress on his own. I trust the three of you to stop the Archbishop."

Andor and Kelm did as Eshwar had suggested, and then the soldiers opened the portcullis and let them step outside before lowering it again.

"Andor," Josalynn called out. He looked back at her. "Be careful what you bring back."

He nodded. Eshwar stood between Andor and Kelm and wrapped his arms around them. He blinked, and they disappeared from Josalynn's sight.

#

When they reappeared after their first jump, with the upper citadel far behind them, Kelm and Andor immediately keeled over and sprayed the rocky ground with vomit. Eshwar gave them a moment to recover, bid them drink, found his next target, and they disappeared again. And so it went, blink to blink. Eventually the two warriors stopped retching, but they continued to dry heave and lose their breath with each round of teleportation. A faint but evident path snaked between the boulders and protrusions of the landscape. Eshwar used it as a guide, but as much as possible he kept them above it, on top of small rises and rock formations, thereby maximizing his line of sight and minimizing the number of necessary blinks.

Despite its jagged teeth and pockmarked skin, the base of the land was actually relatively flat. Any peaks were far away on the southern horizon, and had it not been for the close proximity of the clouds, they could have forgotten they were traveling across such a high elevation. So far the barren land had been devoid of all life. There was no vegetation, no birds, not even any celestials in sight. But that changed when they found themselves less than a league from their destination.

After reappearing and recovering from their last blink, they became enthralled by the scene laid out before them. Slightly below them, on a wide, open expanse of ground, war was raging. Tall, featureless men with pale skin, some clad in black and others in blue, were locked together in fierce combat. Their ranks were so thick that the ground could not be seen beneath them, and although warriors on both sides were constantly falling, the forest never seemed to thin. Each man was indistinguishable from every other, with lifeless eyes and primal voices, the color of their armor offering the only delineation between them. But that meant little, for there were hundreds, even thousands of them, spread over the entirety of the plain. Wading through the lake of warriors were multiple of Unheil's demons, smashing their gruesome clubs into the blue-clad men. In contrast, muscular giants with bare chests and massive swords were slicing through the men in black, and clashing with the demons in impressive displays of raw strength. And above all of this, the harpy-like creatures were swarming, met by their counterparts, griffin-like creatures with feathery wings. And higher still, far above even this, dashing in and out of the clouds, were large creatures that were too far away and flew too fast for the companions to discern their form.

In the midst of the chaos, floating through the sky, were two ovular clouds. One was dark, almost black, like a storm cloud, and was shot through with flashes and strikes of green and red light. The other was a pale but pleasant blue, and periodically flashes of white and gold erupted from inside. The clouds billowed and rotated, seeming to repel and draw each other in a tug-of-war of will. Heil and Unheil.

"What the fuck is all this?" Kelm asked, his head swiveling as his eyes darted all over the battlefield before them.

"The Fields of Ruin," Andor said, almost to himself. "Josalynn has described them to me, but…there's plenty she left out. Now I can see why she doesn't allow the scouts to come this far out."

"Why?" Eshwar asked.

"Because this makes Bastion look like a farce," Andor replied. "If the men knew that this is what they were guarding against, they'd abandon the fortress in an instant. Even if it were fully staffed, I doubt it could hold against these forces, certainly not if the gods joined together and decided they wanted to leave these mountains. It's like a cruel joke. Even I feel fooled."

"But Bastion *did* serve a purpose today, Andor. We kept the Cult out," Kelm said.

"Yes, you're right. And speaking of, we still have a duty to fulfill. We can't remain distracted here. Look to the east."

Still around a mile away to the east, the ground ended abruptly and gave way to a great chasm that seemed to be miles wide, and extended as far as they could see to the north and south. And near the end of the path, riding along on strange mounts, were three humanoid figures. They were heading for a series of natural steps and bridges that extended out over the chasm, ending on a suspended island of stone that, to the surprise of the companions, appeared to be covered in trees and other plants.

"There they are!" Eshwar cried.

Andor and Kelm took long swigs from their canteens, then did their best to prepare themselves for one final jump.

"Get us there, Eshwar," Andor said, "there's no time to waste."

Eshwar wrapped his arms around them once again, and in an instant their enemies were only a few feet away.

#

"Stop right there!" Andor shouted, after he had fought off a bout of heaving.

The three figures looked back, then spun their mounts around to face their pursuers. The creatures appeared reptilian, with serpentine eyes and frilled manes, but in place of scales they had chalky white skin. Their feet were large approximations of humanoid hands, and their tails were tipped with bony points, as if they were meant for stabbing. Sitting atop them in simple saddles were three humans. One was unmistakably the Archbishop, clothed in his golden-trimmed robe. The other two were his large personal guards, clad in tinted plate reminiscent of Justiciar Barrett's and barbute helmets. The men scowled and the mounts revealed forked tongues as they hissed at the companions.

"Deal with them," the Archbishop said, then turned his lizard about and spurred it toward the end of the path.

There, across the steps and bridges, on the small island, which could not have been suspended naturally, beautiful silver trees sprouted from lush grass. A font of clear water babbled over the side, disappearing into the chasm below. It was an idyllic display amid a hellish backdrop, and looking at it seemed to drown out the chorus of steel coming from the Fields of Ruin, making the world peaceful and quiet. And in the center, floating and bobbing in a blissful rotation, was an unassuming stone, shaped like a polyhedral cylinder with pyramidal ends, no bigger than a man's forearm. This was the Archbishop's target. His eyes locked onto it and he kicked and spurred his mount to go faster, but he soon found himself tumbling forward through the air and rolling across the rocky ground.

Eshwar had released a gout of flame toward the fleeing man, and as it burned the creature's rear haunch, the mount let out a hissing scream and bucked its rider, then retreated north along the edge of the chasm. The other two creatures were rushing toward the companions, and their riders had drawn their weapons. One leapt from the ground and clasped onto a nearby rock formation, then launched itself toward Andor. He stood his ground, and as the creature fell toward him he drove his greatsword up through the underside of its head, through its open mouth, and out from the top of its skull, then jumped clear just before being crushed beneath it. The other charged toward Kelm, who dodged to one side and sliced at its leg, ducking beneath the sweeping sword of the rider. The creature hissed and doubled back for another pass, but this time the rider leapt from the saddle and tackled Kelm. The lizard continued on toward Eshwar, but a few streams of fire that left charred, black blemishes on its white skin sent it into a terrified retreat. Andor was squared off with one of the guards, his sword still lodged in the dead creature. Kelm had managed to kick the other off of him, and both were on their feet exchanging sword blows.

Andor's opponent managed to land a strike on his curaiss and knock him to the ground, then moved in to perform an overhead slash. But before he could deliver a fatal blow, the man began to violently shake, his teeth chattering so forcefully they might break, lightning coursing over his body and arcing between the plates of his armor. When Andor stood, both guards had collapsed to the ground, writhing as lightning danced between them, until they finally fell still. Kelm had let his sword fall limply in his hand. Eshwar was standing there with a hand outstretched, the last sparks of electricity still dancing across his fingertips. Kelm looked over to his friend, who was slightly trembling.

"Are they dead?" he asked.

"I…I don't know," Eshwar replied. "I've never killed anyone before."

Kelm placed a hand on his shoulder and squeezed. "Not to be insensitive, my friend, but I hope you just did. And I think you saved Andor's life."

"You most certainly did," Andor said, clasping Eshwar's hand. "You have my thanks. Now, for the Archbishop."

The remaining cultist had recovered from his fall and was on his feet, climbing and running as fast as he could up the first stones leading out to the island. Andor had retrieved his sword from the reptilian carcass, but laid it on the ground at his feet. He clasped his hands together, and they began to vibrate. The motion grew more violent, until his whole body was quivering, then he began to draw his hands apart. A point of the crackling white energy appeared between his palms, and as he drew them farther apart, the point formed into a line. It grew until his hands were as far apart as he could reach, then with his right hand he clutched the energy like a javelin. He took aim toward the Archbishop, and let the spectral projectile fly. It missed its mark, ricocheting off the rocks and careening into the chasm. Andor prepared another, and this time the javelin found its target. It pierced through the Archbishop's calf and caused him to fall to the ground. With a wail the man rolled over onto his rear. He grasped at the energy protruding from his leg, but recoiled when it burned his hand. He looked up toward the billowing masses floating above the Fields of Ruin.

"Unheil!" he called. "Help me! Our hour is at hand! Dispose of these heathens!"

There was a thunderous rumble, and the dark cloud rotated faster at the sound of the Archbishop's invocation. A comet of smoke issued forth from the cloud, heralded by a resounding crack and a flash of green. It hurled past the blue cloud, its shadowy form undulating like the waves of the sea, and impacted the ground a short distance from Andor and the others. A figure emerged from within the smoke and debris of the impact. It was of average height and size, with skin so ghostly pale it was almost luminescent. It was clothed in tattered black clothes with dark red lapels and dark green accents, with black boots and bare hands. A dark hood shadowed the upper half of its face, but its eyes, red globes with yellow irises, glowed so fiercely that they could be seen within the shadow. Its lips were so thin and pale as to be nonexistent, giving its mouth the appearance of abnormal size, and when it smiled, black gums were revealed gripping its snowy teeth. The figure stretched and flexed, and made a motion with its head as if cracking its neck.

"Ah, I have not produced an avatar in this form for quite some time," Unheil said.

"Go. Get the Archbishop, he won't stay pinned forever," Andor said to his companions. "I'll handle this."

"Handle *me*?" Unheil laughed. "Arrogant mortal. I can sense the *righteousness* (he spat the word with particular disdain) coursing through you. But I am not some lowly fiend, no demon that you can dispatch with your parlor tricks. I am Unheil. God of darkness and shadow! God of chaos and...what are you doing? Gah! What foul witchery is this!?"

While the god had been proselytizing Himself, Andor had removed his reliquary, the same one Enoch had delivered to him, from a band around his neck that had suspended it beneath his breastplate. He had opened it, and from inside he removed a single chain link. He had grasped it lightly and raised it to his face, whispering an incantation into the cusp of his hands, and a white glow from within illuminated his face. More links began to appear, composed of white energy, and as he lowered his right hand, grasping the first link, the chain steadily grew. He had swung it over his head and whipped it toward Unheil, and it wrapped itself around the god's torso, pinning His arms to His side, and shooting extensions down into the ground, locking Him in place. The avatar struggled and flexed its muscles, but the chain only squeezed tighter.

"Let me go, mortal!" Unheil cried.

"I don't think so," Andor said.

"Very well," the god said, ceasing his struggle. "Prepare to meet your end."

More of the smoky comets shot forth from the dark cloud, rocketing straight for Andor. But now Heil was aware that something was amiss. Blue lightning snapped forth from the blue cloud and dissipated the comets while they were still high in the air. Still more issued out, but each one was zapped out of existence almost immediately.

"Heil! You sanctimonious fool! Can't you see I'm trying to free us from this monotonous existence?"

But no sympathy came from the bright cloud. Heil continued to destroy the fresh avatars as quickly as they appeared, until Unheil relented. He sighed and rolled his eyes, then closed them and extended himself straight upward, but nothing happened. He tried again. Still nothing happened. He opened his eyes and stared at Andor with flared nostrils and a vexed expression.

"Right," Andor said. "As long as the binds are in place, you won't be able to recall that avatar."

Unheil's lower lip trembled with fury. His fists clenched tightly and his muscles flexed once more, but still the chain grew tighter. Andor left the god to His ensnarement and took off after his friends.

The Archbishop managed to crawl almost all the way to the island, but Kelm and Eshwar were almost upon him. They moved along the rock formation as quickly as they could, being careful to avoid the edges. The walls of the chasm disappeared below into empty space, a void of the darkest blackness either of them had ever seen. To their left and right it extended as far as the eye could see, and seemed to absorb any light that was unfortunate enough to be cast upon the darkness. The sight was dizzying, and the air seemed to thin the farther out they ran. They reached the Archbishop just as he grasped the first blades of grass, and Kelm flipped him onto his back and pressed a sword tip against his breast.

It truly was quiet here. Even the rumbles of the divine clouds could not be heard. There was nothing but the trickling of the water and a pleasant hum from the gently floating stone. The silver trees emitted a comforting glow, and some sort of appetizing fruit hung from their branches. The entire world around this little island seemed to dull and fade from view, but the emptiness below remained, still casting an uneasiness into the air.

"Come now, gentleman," the Archbishop said with a charming and diplomatic tone. "Don't you know where we are? That stone is the Heart of the World. With it, we can rule over all of Amalgam. All I need to do is claim it, and this realm will belong to Primzahl. Then the two of you could be greatly rewarded, become men of nobility and wealth, or great power. Any past sins can be forgiven. For Primzahl is a merciful master."

"I don't think so," Kelm said. "Your Cult killed my family; I will not betray their memory. And now my friends have shed their blood to prevent you from getting the Heart; I'm not about to betray them either."

"And I've watched you burn countless innocents, offering them up to your 'merciful' god. I was almost among them myself," Eshwar added.

"Fine," the Archbishop's tone changed to condescension and irritation. "Once Unheil deals with your friend He will take care of you. And when Primzahl's glory washes over this pitiful world, He will cast you into the void, far from His light!"

Eshwar took a few steps toward the edge and pointed at the darkness. "Oh, you mean like this void?"

The Archbishop's eyes widened as his gaze followed Eshwar's finger down into the chasm.

"You know, Eshwar, I think that's exactly what he means," Kelm said.

He sheathed his sword and grabbed the cultist's robes at his chest, then hoisted the man to his feet. He pulled him toward the edge and held him precariously at the precipice. The Archbishop was beginning to sweat, and his legs were quivering, and not from the pain of the javelin wound.

"Please," he said, his voice now trembling with terror. "Please don't deny me His light, I beg of you. Have mercy on an old man."

Kelm's face contorted with fury. "Mercy? How many people begged you for mercy before you set them on fire? How many begged you to spare their loved ones while they were allowed to live, because 'Primzahl is a merciful master'? How many more would have died if you had claimed the Heart? You don't deserve mercy."

Kelm let go of the man's robe and gave him a stiff-armed shove. The Archbishop toppled backwards and fell into the endless pit below. His wailing scream echoed long after the darkness had swallowed him up, until it finally faded away, and Kelm and Eshwar both released long sighs. They looked toward the Heart, still peacefully bobbing as if no threat had existed, as if there hadn't been any calamity to avoid. They felt drawn to it, a silent call that tugged at their minds, but they tore their eyes away and the magnetism subsided. They made their way back toward solid ground. Andor met them part way and congratulated them on averting the catastrophe, and the three of them headed west.

Unheil was struggling once more, and called out to them as they passed.

"Free me, mortal! And we shall forget this whole thing. I might even be willing to reward you!"

"No thanks," Andor said. "I don't make deals with devils. But I promise you, the binding will wear off."

"Insolent fool! When it does, I will find you and have retribution! Maybe I'll finish what I started on that pathetic fortress of yours!"

"We'll see if your brother lets that happen," Andor quipped.

Unheil shook with rage, and continued to shout expletives while the companions climbed up to a rise that gave them a decent view to the northwest. They smiled at each other, and Eshwar placed a hand on Andor and Kelm, and they were gone.

CHAPTER EIGHTEEN
Divergent Paths

Kelm and Andor were almost too weak to stand when they stumbled, supported by Eshwar, beneath the portcullis. Josalynn was there to meet them, and after relaying their success, they were loaded onto litters amid fanfare from the soldiers and carried down the mountain road to the great hall. There they were laid on the makeshift beds of the field hospital and given more water than they could drink. Nearby were Backus and Fuster. The spear had been removed from the warden's chest, and, although he was still unconscious, his breathing had normalized.

Fuster was being attended by several healers who were stabilizing bones that had been reset and dressing his various wounds with salves and poultices. They had extracted the last remnant of the Cult's poison from his arm, and explained that, ironically, it had been what saved his life. The toxin had rendered him comatose, reducing his vital functions to a minimum and making his body as limp as a wet blade of grass. Had this not been the case, the shock of his fall would likely have killed him, and if not, the harsh waters most certainly would have. Good fortune had seen the currents carry him east, and he regained consciousness on the shore north of the valley's entrance. By sheer force of will, and the poison still numbing the sensations of his broken body, he had dragged himself across the land, until he was found by the scouting party. While miraculous that he had survived such a tribulation, the healers did warn that he was unlikely to ever fully recover from the extensive trauma.

But Fuster could not have been more elated. His spy mission had been a success, and the information he brought back had foiled the Cult's plan. Though it had cost him dearly, he was being lauded as a hero of the day, and that brought him more satisfaction than he had yet experienced in his life.

"But Andor," he asked, after hearing their story from the Heart of the World, "how did you know you'd need the artifact Enoch brought you? You couldn't have known you'd face Unheil."

"I didn't," Andor said. "I requested the reliquary for use against the Cult. I thought they might attempt some divine intervention from Primzahl, or conjure demons of their own, and I would need it for those threats. Enoch never trusted Webb, and so I was careful never to specifically mention that the artifact was a weapon to be used in the siege. But thank the Narra I had it at the Fields of Ruin."

"I'll say," Kelm said, "things would have played out a lot differently if it weren't for that little parcel."

"Speaking of Webb," Fuster said, "I almost can't believe you beat him, Kelm. But I'm glad that traitorous bastard got what he deserved."

"Well…" Kelm began, scratching his head. The others were fascinated as he told the story of his battle with Webb. Eshwar and Andor were particularly captivated, while Fuster worried that his friend may have taken one too many blows to the head. Kelm wondered if someone else had been there, some guardian that had saved his life, but Eshwar reminded him once again of Hague's prophetic words, and Andor assured him that it was unlikely anyone in the garrison had such an ability. Time manipulation, if that was what it had been, was rare, and poorly understood.

"If it really did come from me," Kelm said, "then I have to try to understand it, and see if I can do it again, of course."

"You must return with me to the Magehold," Eshwar told him. "Telling Hague what happened is your best shot at getting any answers."

"Agreed," Andor said.

"I think you're right," Kelm replied, "and as soon as things settle down here, that's exactly what I'll do."

#

The next day, Kelm prepared a traditional Riisgardian funeral for Hutta, and despite the protests of the healers, Fuster was carried out to witness the ceremony. Hutta was laid upon a pyre, clothed in a clean white robe. His hair and beard were unbraided and washed, then combed straight. His arms were crossed over his chest and his belongings were placed all around him. With teary eyes Kelm ignited the wooden dais which he had built for his friend, and he watched in silence with Fuster as the flames carried Hutta to the Eternal Forest.

Webb's body was given no such honor or respect. It was thrown in a pile with the dead cultists and burned, not ceremoniously, but as one disposes of trash. Fuster spat as the fire ate at the mound of carcasses, then was carried back inside to his bed. Over the successive weeks, the battlefield was cleaned of bodies and debris. A cool rain washed away the red sheen from the grass and restored it to its previous green luster, but scorched earth and pockmarks remained as a reminder of the siege.

Thanks to the potions from the Magehold, Backus soon recovered from his wound, but Fuster remained bedridden and weak. The field hospital was broken down and the great hall once again became a place of refreshment and camaraderie, and Fuster was given a private room in the citadel in which he could continue his healing. It was a lengthy and at times frustrating process, but after a long Amalgam month he was precariously walking, with assistance. After another he could carry his own weight, but he fatigued quickly, and his body ached and screamed in places he had never been aware existed. But eventually he was able to function much the same as he had before his nearly fatal experience, though his body had never felt or looked more scarred.

When he felt ready, he brought Kelm and Eshwar with him to meet with Josalynn. Andor was there as well, in the war room, as was Backus, but the atmosphere was light and casual, far removed from the impending doom that had clouded their previous visits to the map table. None of them were even wearing their trademark armors, and were clothed instead in comfortable cottons and linens, though Andor was still mantled by his black cloak.

"Commandant Willet," Fuster began, "I cannot thank you enough for the care you've provided for me since the siege. I wouldn't have survived but for the men of this garrison. But..." he stopped and lowered his gaze from her face, and fidgeted with his thumbs, "but I have decided to ask your permission to be relieved of duty here at Bastion. I feel I must return to Riisgard. I now know that the stakes of this war are beyond any of us or our worlds, but I want to protect my home. If I can secure the portal on our side, then the tide could turn against the Cult, and Riisgard may find itself free of them."

He raised an eye back to her face, fearing that she might be angry with him, but her eyes were bright and her lips were curled into a smile. She walked around the table and placed her hands on his shoulders, then pulled him into a careful embrace.

"Fuster," she said, pulling away again, "if not for you, every one of us might be dead. Consider yourself relieved. And, I shall have Backus assemble you a squad of trained voidwalkers. You can send them back to me once your portal is secure and you have mustered a force of your own."

"I...I don't know what to say," Fuster stammered, "th-thank you, Josalynn."

"Think nothing of it," she replied, "and know that you will always have a place in this garrison."

Though it was difficult, and his body protested, Fuster managed to bow to her in a final display of gratitude.

"I'm afraid that I must ask to be relieved as well," Andor said after a few moments. "I promised Enoch that I would return to Magna. There has been no sign of retaliation from Unheil, so for now He seems to have forgotten my trespasses, and the Heart is safe from the Cult. But my quarrel with them isn't done, and I will return as soon as I can."

Josalynn nodded at him, then turned to Kelm. "And I suppose you'll be wanting to be relieved too? I've heard about your plan to return to the Magehold."

"Yes ma'am," Kelm replied. "I have to understand what happened on that battlefield."

"I couldn't agree more," she said, "such a power could prove invaluable against the Cult...or any other trouble you might find yourself up against. You of course have my permission to go."

"Thank you, Commandant." Kelm rapped his breast in salute.

#

"Are you sure you don't want to come home with me, Kelm?" Fuster asked as they supped in the great hall.

"You know I'd love to," Kelm replied, "but I need to at least see Chancellor Hague. With his guidance I might become more prepared than ever to fight against the Cult." He smiled at his friend as he took a sip of ale, "Hopefully you don't gut them all before I make it home. I wouldn't want to miss all the fun."

"No promises," Fuster smiled back.

Soon the day came that they would depart. Kelm was in Andor's private room, assisting him with his possessions. They loaded his excess clothing, trinkets, and reliquaries into packs and went to join the others in the yard. As they exited the room, Kelm noticed that the bronze statue still stood on the table.

"Don't you need that?" he asked, nodding toward it.

"No," Andor replied, "when I arrive on Magna, my goddess will be there to greet me when I look upon the sea. But I need to make sure She is here as well, for one day I will return."

"Bastion will need you if the celestials ever decide to move this way."

"Yes. But I'm more concerned about the Cult. We've struck a heavy blow, but their operation is vast, and extends far beyond Amalgam. And you, Kelm, whatever secret is inside you may prove to be as formidable a weapon as any against them."

When they arrived in the yard, a small company was gathered around the stable. Eshwar was assisting Fuster by strapping his pack to a horse, and Backus and Josalynn were there to see them off. Backus had assembled an eclectic squad to escort Fuster back to Riisgard, consisting of some of the more unique members of Bastion's garrison. There was a reptilian male, clothed in dark robes but for his clawed bare feet;

two humans, a blond man in asymmetric plate and a dark-haired woman carrying spear and shield; and a hooded male elf with bronzed skin sporting an intricately carved longbow. Each of them had already saddled and laden a horse from the stable, of which precious few would be left once the company had departed.

"Each member of this squad has been briefed on your mission and has volunteered to accompany you," Backus explained to Fuster. "They are experienced voidwalkers, and have fought against the Cult on their homeworlds and others. If the cave hasn't been cleared, they will make short work of the rubble. And even if the Cult had the foresight to station more men at your portal, I promise each of these warriors is worth twenty of theirs."

"I don't doubt it for a second," Fuster said.

"Once you've rallied men of your own, they will return here," Josalynn said. "But with you in control of the Riisgardian portal, the Cult will be cut off, and you will have a direct supply line to Amalgam and, if necessary, to us. Just remember, Fuster, keep the portal locked down at all times. The Cult can retaliate from any world, but if you stay vigilant and keep them bottlenecked, you'll be able to repel any threat."

"My guard will always be up, Commandant."

"Good," she said, patting him on the shoulders. Then she turned to Kelm, "I hope you keep me informed of your progress. And should you need a break from academia, you know where to find us."

"I appreciate that, Commandant," Kelm replied. "I hope to fight alongside the men of Bastion again some day."

"And Sir Kardos," she said, turning now to Andor, "I will miss you, though I'm sure I'll be cursing you in the coming weeks as I retrain the men of the upper citadel from your…unorthodox command style. '

"Come now, Commandant Willet," he said, "it'll be fun. A little insubordination will liven this place up. It gets so boring when ghouls and demons aren't running amok." He wrapped her in an embrace, "I'll see you again, Josalynn. Backus," he said, releasing her, "any messages I should take along to Enoch?"

The warden's muzzle twisted into a fiendish grin. "Tell him I hope he chokes on his own racist tongue."

"Gladly," Andor laughed.

"It was an honor to fight alongside you, Backus," Kelm said to the warden.

"And you, Kelm," Backus said, reaching out with a large padded hand and grasping Kelm's forearm. "You and Hutta fought fiercely."

"Eshwar," Josalynn said, "your assistance was invaluable. You have my thanks. And pass my regards on to Chancellor Hague. The potions were a boon both in battle and recovery."

"I'm happy I could be of help," Eshwar replied. "And the chancellor will be pleased that the Magehold's contribution was useful."

After their farewells, Kelm mounted Tallow and the others their respective steeds. It was a bittersweet feeling, watching Bastion shrink behind them as they moved westward through the valley, but each of them planned on one day looking upon the fortress again. Josalynn, Backus, and Zurofel watched them turn to specks from the Bulwark, and then finally disappear from sight, and then the three remaining commanders returned to business as usual, falling back into the mundane schedules of running the stronghold as if nothing had interrupted their routines. But Josalynn's heart was heavy. The conflict was on hold, for a time, but she knew it was not over, and she was going to be sure Bastion was prepared for the next phase.

#

They rode south together, the dark paladin, the prodigy, the spy, and the sellsword; Kelm and Eshwar bound for the Magehold, Andor, Fuster, and the host bound for Artesia. It was a casual and lighthearted trip, though more than once the Riisgardians noted Hutta's absence. When they reached the crossroads at Deltaville, they bid a fond farewell, each offering the others the customary blessings of his homeworld, and promising that they would meet again. The bulk of the company then rode north and entered the Wastes, following the clear waters of the Artesian river.

Kelm and Eshwar continued east, and later, after the others had vanished across the multiverse, they once again found themselves mounting the last rise into Taikanìk. They left their horses in the stable and walked up the path to Hague's tower. Bill Tallert was there, casually standing guard just as he had been at their first visit. He didn't say anything, but he looked at them and smiled, and gave Eshwar a nod. Then he opened the tower door and gestured for them to enter. Eshwar entered first and disappeared up the stairs.

Kelm took a deep breath and nodded to the steward, then moved forward across the threshold and stepped into a world of possibility.

Epilogue

"Justiciar Barrett has failed. And Archbishop Marley is missing."

"Then it seems your recommendation against the Inquisition was justified."

The two men stood in a cavernous study. The first had just entered from a dark, arched door. He was wearing the simple purple robe of a Cult clergyman, but trimmed in crimson. The second was dressed more ornately, with a white overtunic covering his gold-trimmed purples, and a tall white headdress emblazoned on all sides with the eye of Primzahl capping his head.

The study was constructed of dark, unwelcoming stone bricks, but large rugs of varying shades of purple and featuring arcing patterns covered portions of the cold floor. For some height the side walls were hidden behind stocked bookshelves of darkly stained wood, and large beams of a similar color stretched across the vaulted ceiling. The rear wall was dominated by an opaque window of violet stained glass that mimicked the arch of the ceiling. A double door in the bottom center of this window stood open, and daylight poured through and reflected off the overly polished desk that sat in the center of the room.

The ornately dressed man stepped over to this desk, unstrapped the headdress from around his jaw, and placed it upon the surface. Underneath was dark gray hair, shot through with streaks of the youthful black it had once been. He wiped his brow, which was smooth but for the first impressions of wrinkles.

"Am I to assume, Castellan, that you recommend mobilizing the Flamekissed?" he asked.

The man in the red trim looked surprised at the suggestion. "I was going to suggest a few battalions of crusaders. It would make for an impressive display of force."

"I am no longer interested in displays," the other sighed. "I want decisive action. I don't care if there are prisoners, I don't care to show mercy, I don't care if anyone survives to recount the tale. I want victory. The Flamekissed will give it to me."

"With all due respect, Your Worship," said the castellan, "I, even you, don't have the authority to authorize such a campaign. Only a vote from the full council can accomplish it, and that will take time."

"Time is something of which we have plenty. Time will eventually bring us victory. The Cult is like a vine, ever growing. As long as our roots are protected no amount of pruning can stop us, we will continue to spread until all of the multiverse is wrapped in our embrace. Come with me."

The man stepped through the double door and out onto a balcony, with the castellan following close behind. The afternoon was bright and clear. To the horizon stretched countless buildings of dark stone. The steeples and spires of churches and cathedrals rose all around above their peers, but none seemed to challenge the high vantage point of the two men. Below them was a terraced cloister. Figures were relaxing in the shade of the arcades all around, observing the training exercises going on in the central yard. Men in dark armor and crimson cloaks were facing off against men in regular suits of plate and mail. Each of the cloaked men was surrounded by at least five opponents, and they were spinning about and parrying wildly as strikes came in from every direction. Their weapons were not uniform, and likely had been chosen by personal preference, but their off-hands were all free, and occasionally one of them would throw up a ward in place of a parry.

One of the men missed parrying a particularly aggressive strike, and his opponent's blade landed across his upper back, slicing his cloak and denting a plate of his armor. The man's eyes filled with rage and he reached out and grasped the offender around the throat. A hot glow enveloped his gauntlet and the other man began to squeal and struggle. He held him there until the life left his eyes. The mail rings of the man's coif still glowed molten around his neck as his body dropped to the ground. The other opponents backed away, their bodies tense and their guard slightly raised. A group of squires appeared from within the arcades and carried the body away, and the cloaked man, his eyes now calm, signaled for his group to resume sparring.

"You see," the white-clothed man said to the castellan, "they are eager for battle. They grow restless with this constant training."

"Indeed. I will draft a formal request for a council meeting. But as I said, assembling the cardinals and archbishops won't be quick."

"It will be worth the wait, when the Flamekissed go forth to spread Primzahl's light. See it done."

"At once, Your Worship." The castellan bowed and took his leave.

The white-clothed man placed a hand upon the balcony railing and turned his attention back to the yard below. The sparring was continuing in routine fashion, with no more casualties, but the cloaked men seemed to move with more fervor all the time, following their parries with ripostes and counter-strikes. A faint smile formed out of the white-clothed man's thin lips, and his fingers glided softly back and forth across the railing as he watched the action in the cloister.

"Soon," he whispered. "Soon."

APPENDIX A

MAPS

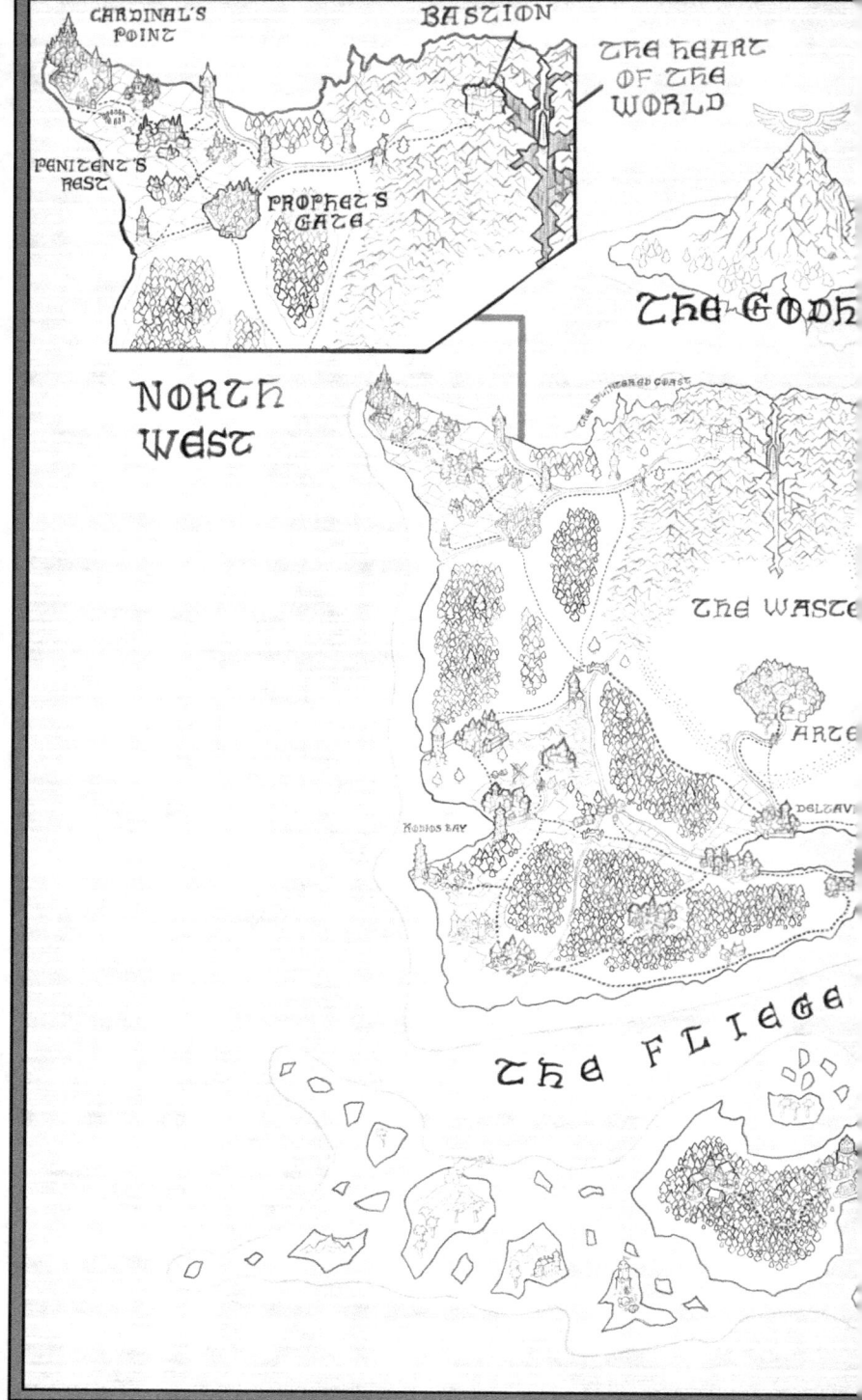

HISTORY OF AMALGAM

Unknown - Creation of Amalgam

Unknown - Heil and Unheil are created and begin their cosmic struggle

1439 BS - First settlers arrive on Amalgam.

1437 BS - Kirjath Reutlinger founds the Kingdom of Leerwandler in the name of King Eichborn Rhand.

1352 BS - Gath Lenel founds the Empyrean Magehold.

1335 BS - The Artesian Republic is founded.

1291 BS - Praxis Elias founds the Foskaran Republic.

1182 BS - The Kingdom of Norstead, a splinter from Leerwandler, is founded

344 BS - The Foskaran Republic is destroyed and its peninsula home shattered in a battle between the celestials. Over time, the Shattered Republic forms in its place.

0 - The Sundering. Artesia is wiped out and its verdant landscape converted into the Wastes. The Kingdom of Norstead is destroyed.

11 AS - Devonna Willet founds Bastion.

282 AS - The Cult of Primzahl arrives on Amalgam.

544 AS - Josalynn born on Amalgam.

545 AS - Enoch born on Magna.

546 AS - Andor born on Magna. Hutta born on Riisgard.

547 AS - Fuster born on Riisgard.

549 AS - Kelm born on Riisgard. Daffer born on Riisgard.

552 AS - Eshwar born on Agrafell.

568 AS - The Siege of Bastion

APPENDIX C

WORLD PRIMERS

AMALGAM

Originally serving as a battleground for the gods Heil and Unheil, Amalgam was first settled by mortals two-thousand-seven Amalgamite years ago, when humans from another world founded the Kingdom of Leerwandler. Since then, Amalgam has been established as the hub for multiversal travel, as well as a home for academic and magical study. The various nations that have established themselves on the world coexist peacefully, and accept visitors and citizens of all races, faiths, and creeds. The world itself is quite small compared to others in the multiverse, with its single continent measuring less than three-hundred-thousand square miles.

Calendar: Lacking measurable celestial bodies, unified faith or culture, or singular government, the structure of Amalgam's calendar became a purely arbitrary decision. For simplicity's sake, it was agreed that a year would be five-hundred days long, consisting of ten fifty-day months, each divided into ten five-day weeks. This system vastly differs from those of other worlds, but it has proven easy to adopt for visitors who wish to make Amalgam their home. The timeline has been divided into two portions, delineated by the Sundering, a catastrophic event in Amalgam's history. Dates now follow a Before Sundering (BS) and After Sundering (AS) convention, and the year that Kelm, Eshwar, and the others arrive on Amalgam is 568 AS.

> Josalynn was born in 544 AS, making her 24 Amalgamite years old. It is important to note, however, that despite being nominally one of the younger characters, Amalgam's long years make her biologically older than all of the recent newcomers.

Agrafell is a world steeped in magic, possibly even more so than Amalgam. Many of the biomes would be overwhelming to visitors from other worlds, such as fungal forests and trees of massive scale. Humans, dwarves, and beast races, including reptiles, canines, and felines, have coexisted peacefully here for generations. Faiths are too many to count, and are separated by both race and region. Eshwar comes from a remote corner of Agrafell's largest continent, from a forest that has been left largely undisturbed by the surrounding nations.

Calendar: Agrafell's calendar is tracked completely by the passage of seasons. The four seasons each last an average of ninety-eight days, which was chosen to calculate a year at three-hundred-ninety-two days. This was then divided into eight months of forty-nine days, each divided into seven seven-day weeks.

Agrafell's history is long and well-documented, and the year Eshwar travels to Amalgam is the year 289 of the Matrellian Era.

 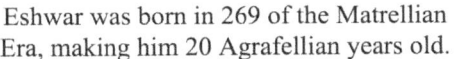 

Eshwar was born in 269 of the Matrellian Era, making him 20 Agrafellian years old.

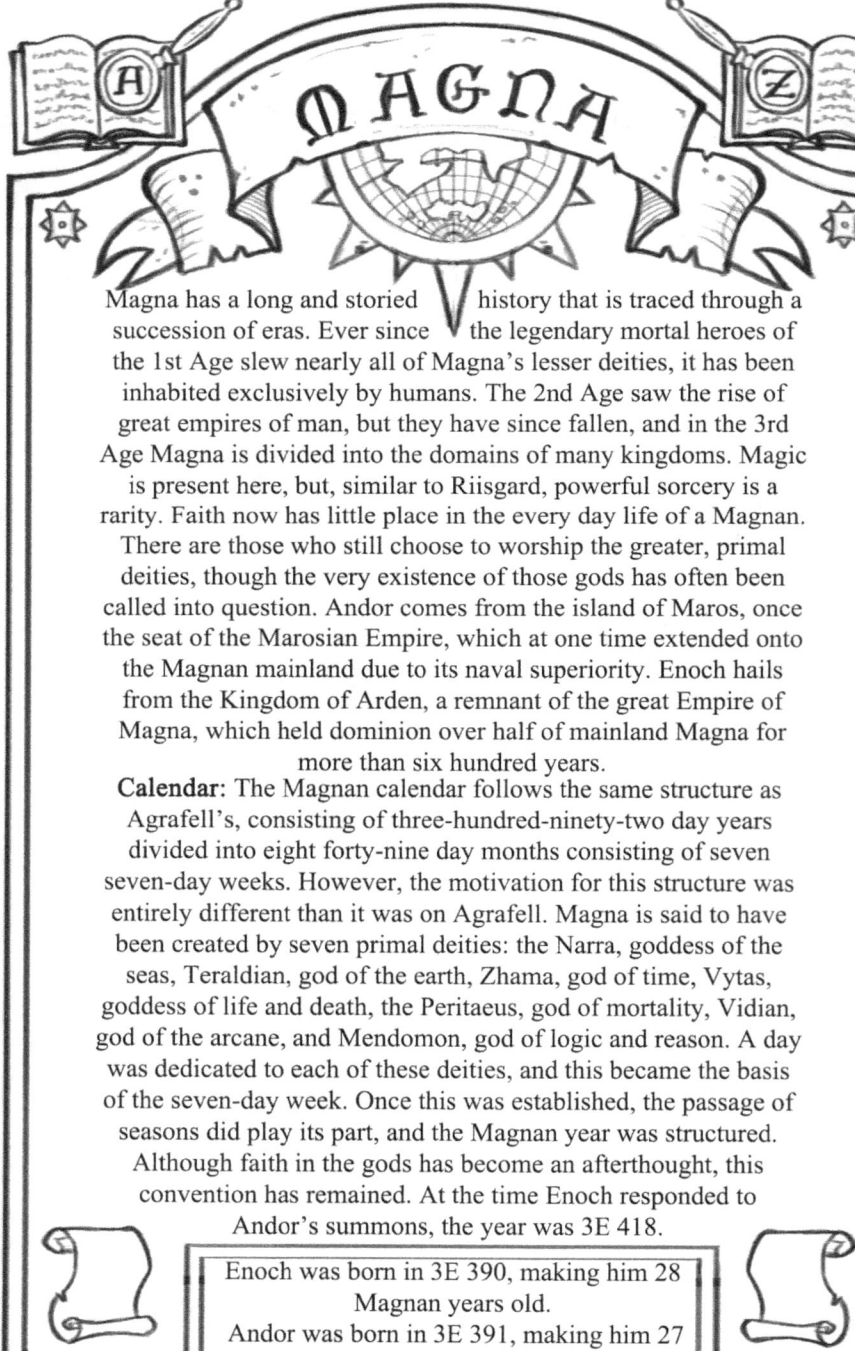

MAGNA

Magna has a long and storied history that is traced through a succession of eras. Ever since the legendary mortal heroes of the 1st Age slew nearly all of Magna's lesser deities, it has been inhabited exclusively by humans. The 2nd Age saw the rise of great empires of man, but they have since fallen, and in the 3rd Age Magna is divided into the domains of many kingdoms. Magic is present here, but, similar to Riisgard, powerful sorcery is a rarity. Faith now has little place in the every day life of a Magnan. There are those who still choose to worship the greater, primal deities, though the very existence of those gods has often been called into question. Andor comes from the island of Maros, once the seat of the Marosian Empire, which at one time extended onto the Magnan mainland due to its naval superiority. Enoch hails from the Kingdom of Arden, a remnant of the great Empire of Magna, which held dominion over half of mainland Magna for more than six hundred years.

Calendar: The Magnan calendar follows the same structure as Agrafell's, consisting of three-hundred-ninety-two day years divided into eight forty-nine day months consisting of seven seven-day weeks. However, the motivation for this structure was entirely different than it was on Agrafell. Magna is said to have been created by seven primal deities: the Narra, goddess of the seas, Teraldian, god of the earth, Zhama, god of time, Vytas, goddess of life and death, the Peritaeus, god of mortality, Vidian, god of the arcane, and Mendomon, god of logic and reason. A day was dedicated to each of these deities, and this became the basis of the seven-day week. Once this was established, the passage of seasons did play its part, and the Magnan year was structured. Although faith in the gods has become an afterthought, this convention has remained. At the time Enoch responded to Andor's summons, the year was 3E 418.

Enoch was born in 3E 390, making him 28 Magnan years old.
Andor was born in 3E 391, making him 27 years old.

Riisgard is a large but sparsely populated world. Temperatures are low on average, though the equatorial region has some warmer climes. Moving toward either pole, however, one will quickly find boreal forests, tundras, and glacier-filled mountains. Lovik, the kingdom that Kelm and his companions call home, is situated at the planet's northernmost limit of human habitation. Only the elves known as the Jokullfar choose to live in the icy wastes closer to the poles. In addition to these elves, humans share the world with typical mountain-dwelling dwarves, as well as tribes of humanoid giants. Magic on Riisgard is limited, but present, and mages are typically found in the form of shaman or basic enchanters, rather than the powerful wizards and sorcerers found on other worlds. Worship of animal spirits is the predominant religion throughout the world, but the dwarves and elves have faiths of their own that are little known to the humans and giants.

Calendar: The Riisgardian calendar follows the phases of the moon and the passage of the seasons. A month consists of twenty-eight days, one full cycle of the moon, divided in four seven-day weeks. A year consists of thirteen months, three-hundred-sixty-four days. The thirteenth month of every year is a Blood Moon, a time when the animal spirits are said to be most present in the physical plane, and is a time of worship and celebration for the faithful. There haven't been any significant events on Riisgard's timeline that have standardized the tracking of years, but it is generally accepted that the year Kelm and the others traveled to Amalgam is the year 3021 of recorded Riisgardian history.

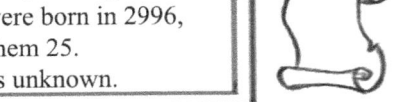

Hutta was born in 2991,
making him 30 Riisgardian years old.
Fuster was born in 2993, making him 28.
Kelm and Daffer were born in 2996,
making them 25.
Webb's age is unknown.

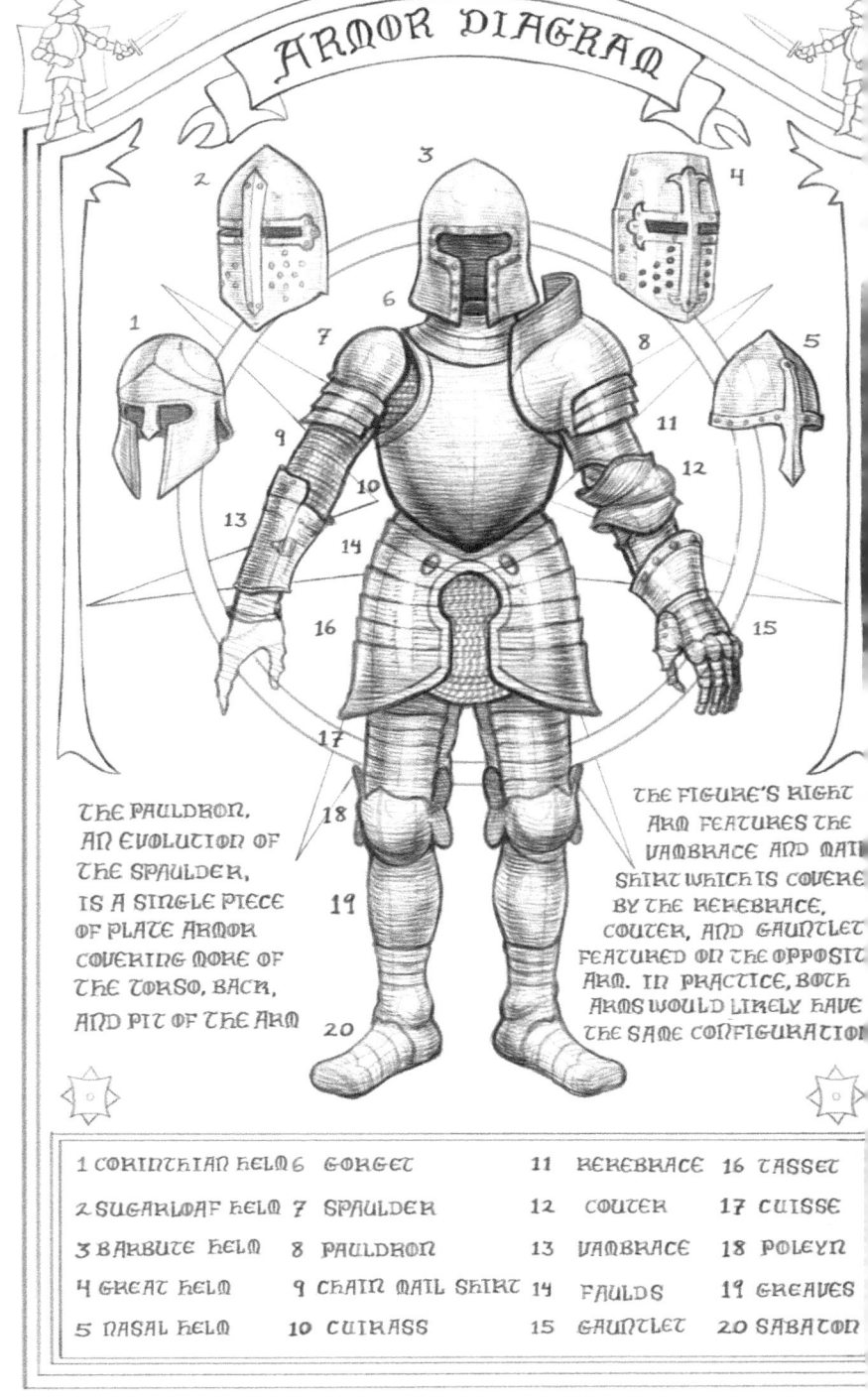

ARMOR DIAGRAM

THE PAULDRON, AN EVOLUTION OF THE SPAULDER, IS A SINGLE PIECE OF PLATE ARMOR COVERING MORE OF THE TORSO, BACK, AND PIT OF THE ARM

THE FIGURE'S RIGHT ARM FEATURES THE VAMBRACE AND MAIL SHIRT WHICH IS COVERED BY THE REREBRACE, COUTER, AND GAUNTLET FEATURED ON THE OPPOSITE ARM. IN PRACTICE, BOTH ARMS WOULD LIKELY HAVE THE SAME CONFIGURATION

1 CORINTHIAN HELM	6 GORGET	11 REREBRACE	16 TASSET
2 SUGARLOAF HELM	7 SPAULDER	12 COUTER	17 CUISSE
3 BARBUTE HELM	8 PAULDRON	13 VAMBRACE	18 POLEYN
4 GREAT HELM	9 CHAIN MAIL SHIRT	14 FAULDS	19 GREAVES
5 NASAL HELM	10 CUIRASS	15 GAUNTLET	20 SABATON

APPENDIX D

ARMOR DIAGRAM

Acknowledgements

Writing your first novel is a daunting process. Along the way, you often doubt yourself, wondering if it's good enough, if people will enjoy reading it as much as you enjoyed creating it. Beyond that, some of it is just plain difficult; from creating a cover to properly formatting. Fortunately, I had a lot of help, and I would like to use this space to thank those who dedicated their time and effort to my dream.

First off I'd like to thank my host of test readers and editors: my mom, Cathy; Hank Piasecki; Shaina O'Brien; Ben Jones; Brad Forsyth; Ben Kohl; Diane McClary; and Alicia Shipley.

Special thanks to my brother, Brad, for allowing me to use his world of Magna and its inhabitants as part of my multiverse.

Special thanks to Mike Foreman for inspiring the chapter *Caught* and the epilogue.

Special thanks to Ben Dize and Chris Knight for turning my map into a work of art. Further thanks to Chris Knight for his beautiful illustration and illumination work on the appendices, and beautiful cover design.

And special thanks to Sam Branham, my first test reader, who read the book chapter by chapter as I wrote it and encouraged me to keep going and helped me format the book into its proper form.

Thank you all so much!

About the Author

 Aaron Bramble grew up on the shores of the Chesapeake Bay in Kent County, Maryland. He credits *The Hobbit* and *The Lord of the Rings* for initially plunging his imagination into the realms of fantasy. He enjoys spending time on the water, gaming, reading, and spending time with his friends.

 Amalgam is his first novel.